## The Hunt for Jack Reacher Series

Don't Know Jack
Jack in the Box
Jack and Kill
Get Back Jack
Jack in the Green
Jack and Joe
Deep Cover Jack
Jack the Reaper
Black Jack
Ten Two Jack
Jack of Spades
Prepper Jack
Full Metal Jack
Jack Frost
Jack of Hearts
Straight Jack
Jack Knife
Lone Star Jack
Bulletproof Jack
Bet On Jack
Jack on a Wire

## The Michael Flint Series

Blood Trails
Trace Evidence
Ground Truth
Hard Money

## The Jess Kimball Thrillers

Fatal Enemy
Fatal Distraction
Fatal Demand
Fatal Error
Fatal Fall
Fatal Edge
Fatal Game
Fatal Bond
Fatal Past
Fatal Heat
Fatal Dawn
Fatal Shot

## The Hunt for Justice Series

Due Justice
Twisted Justice
Secret Justice
Wasted Justice
Raw Justice
Mistaken Justice
Cold Justice
False Justice
Fair Justice
True Justice
Night Justice

# Diane Capri

# Ground Truth

Published by: AugustBooks

http://www.AugustBooks.com

ISBN: 978-1-962769-32-7

Original cover design by: Cory Clubb



Published in the United States of America.

Visit the author website:

http://www.DianeCapri.com

## Cast of Primary Characters

Michael Flint

Kathryn (Katie) Scarlett

Alonzo Drake

Madeline (Maddy) Scarlett

Carlos Gaspar

Sebastian (Baz) Shaw

Ernst Hedinger

Hanna Campbell

Greta Campbell Reed

Phillip Reed (Stephen Brand)

For the readers who have supported me and enjoyed my books and asked for more.

I couldn't do this without you.

Thank you.

# Ground Truth

"Ground truth is the reality we must confront, no matter how inconvenient or uncomfortable it may be."

**—Margaret Atwood**

# Chapter 1

## Switzerland

The modified microlight's electric engine purred in the early-evening darkness. Michael Flint adjusted its direction as the wind gusted, keeping the tiny craft stable and low to the ground. At twelve thousand feet, the Alpine weather was always a problem, tonight more than most. But he had a schedule, and he would stick to it.

The view as he crossed the snow-covered terrain was a vista that inspired millions of advertising dollars. The Alps stretched for hundreds of miles on either side, peak upon peak, with exposed rock where the gradient was steeper than snow could cover.

The machine was perfect for his needs. It was lightweight, even with the small electric motor and batteries. A single spar allowed him to fold the wings. He could slide in and out of the harness with ease and jettison the whole assembly with a single safety release.

Flint eased the craft rightward and up.

Golden light spilled from the Swiss municipality of Naters a few miles to the south, and from myriad clusters of homes across the Nesthorn peak, his destination.

# 3 Ground Truth

Despite the photo-worthy homes, the cherry on the top was the Château Loggerhorn, a mile ahead. Imposing, even from a distance. Built in the 1500s, Loggerhorn had stood empty through much of the twentieth century. The current owner, Ernst Hedinger—one of the wealthiest men in the world—had purchased and updated Loggerhorn.

The modifications were completed a month earlier. Large steel and glass balconies looked down over a one-hundred-foot sheer drop. LED lighting outlined the structure and upward pointing lights highlighted the centuries-old stone.

Fortunately, the architect had been so pleased with his work, he'd described it and published detailed drawings in the European edition of the **Architectural Review**. Flint had memorized every detail.

One of those details was the name of the contractor.

Flint had worked his way down the chain until he'd found carpenters and stonemasons who'd worked on the renovation. For a hefty fee, they'd been willing to share vital and unusual elements of the construction.

A helicopter sat on a pad to the rear of the property, and a private cable car crawled its way up from a small village to the south. In fickle mountain weather, the cable car provided a second option for transport. The roads were impassable in winter.

Tonight, riders in the cable car looked out the windows, admiring the view. Their party clothes looked incongruously flimsy for the mountains. But the billionaire host ensured that they never suffered from exposure to the elements.

Flint adjusted his flightpath, aiming for an outcrop of trees a couple of hundred feet below the château. He wore several layers of clothing to ward off the worst of the wind and subzero temperatures. Concealing all the tools he needed for the evening had also required extra padding. The clothes made certain movements tricky.

The cable car reached the château and disappeared under a canopy. The riders would disembark and climb a series of steps to an entrance into the château. Flint had spent the previous two days examining the château from all angles through high-powered binoculars. He knew those steps would be the only way in tonight.

The now unoccupied car set off downhill to collect another batch of partygoers.

He slowed the microlight as he reached the trees, finally touching the ground and skimming over the snow for a few yards before coming to a halt. He stopped the engine and listened. The faint clank of cables in the distance was the only sound he heard in the crisp evening air.

# 7 Ground Truth

He'd spied a narrow, winding pathway through the trees. The path was likely created by skiers seeking a few extra thrills on the descent.

Nearby, he found a spot he had scoped out the day before. He stowed the microlight there and unclipped a waterproof bag.

He unzipped his snowsuit and tucked the microlight's key into the pocket of his dinner jacket.

Tonight's operation was absolutely necessary because this party was his only chance to breach the château's security short of a full-scale assault by the Marine Corps. Which the Pentagon wasn't likely to authorize. He grinned briefly and then put his head back in the game.

His watch showed 8:43. He had an hour and two minutes. Plenty of time, if all unfolded according to plan.

He started uphill, aiming for a line of trees that led around an outcrop of rock to the side of the building. His white snowsuit blended in with the conditions as well as he could hope for, but anyone with infrared goggles would pick him out instantly. He hoped Hedinger was merely safety conscious and not paranoid.

Flint reached the end of the trees without seeing any movement at the château's windows and balconies. He unzipped his snowsuit and breathed in the cold air. He couldn't gate-crash a billionaire's party sweating like a marathon runner.

# 9 Ground Truth

A few minutes later, the cable car returned. It wasn't the ordinary, lightweight affair used by ski resorts the world over. The windows were double-glazed, and the interior had been created by an ex-Bentley designer. The riders sat in pairs, each pair in their own leather-appointed cocoon. Outside, the whole car was painted in the deepest blue and outlined in gold, all made visible by dramatic lighting.

All of which meant the cable car was obviously visible to even the most casual observer.

Flint moved to the side of the building and waited at the corner. The cable car passed, slowing as it entered the canopy. He peeled off his snowsuit, stepped around the side of the building, and vaulted a chain barrier. He kicked off his snow boots, donned a pair of dress shoes, and discarded his bag.

In front of him, fifty steps led up to the cable car stop. His reconnaissance the day before had taught him the cable car operator wouldn't be able to see far over the car once it was docked at the château. Which meant he was out of the operator's sight line.

Flint took the steps two at a time. Above him, the cable car doors opened, and passengers stepped out. Overhead heaters pushed back the frigid air. He slowed his pace, smiled at the last of the riders, mingled with the group, and followed them up the final couple of dozen steps to the entrance door.

Despite the building's impressive facade, the entryway was a simple double door designed to take the brunt of the Alpine winters. Just inside the exterior doors, two greeters stood to either side, smiling and nodding, and directing the guests to an elevator.

Flint walked in, smiling like the others. He didn't dare speak. The guests sounded German and Italian. His American accent would attract far too much attention. Fortunately, they were only interested in chatting among themselves. No one spoke to him, and he returned the favor.

He followed the group into the elevator, bumping against a woman in a red silk dress and the doors closed.

"**Excusez-moi**," he said, keeping his voice low. He looked away to avoid being drawn into conversation as the elevator ascended.

When the doors opened, he gestured for the group to go ahead of him. One or two nodded their appreciation as they exited, but most simply ignored him.

He followed them into an expansive reception room. The far side consisted of a two-story curved glass wall that probably cost more than Flint earned in a year.

# Chapter 2

Glittering chandeliers hung down around a central, live pine tree that looked to be a permanent fixture, and modern art decorated the walls. On either side of the room, life-size figures depicting Roman gods formed the centerpieces to elaborate fountains.

A string quartet played Vivaldi on a discreet, elevated stage.

Waitstaff in close-fitting black uniforms threaded their way through a crowd, shoes clicking on a marble floor. Flint scooped a champagne flute from a passing tray and ambled his way into the throng, smiling and nodding at people as he passed.

He glanced casually around the ceiling and noted the absence of any obvious security cameras. Which didn't mean there were none.

The half-dozen square-shouldered men that stood to attention around the walls screamed that armed security was ever present.

Flint took a sip of champagne and relaxed. Aside from attending a party to which he hadn't been invited, he wasn't guilty of anything. Even when the evening was over, he wouldn't be guilty. His goal was simply to restore property to its rightful owner.

Just then Ernst Hedinger came into view.

## 15 Ground Truth

Flint turned away and headed for cover behind a fountain. Now that he knew the host was actively engaged at the party, he could move on to the next stage.

He took an exit the **Architectural Review** article said led to a restroom.

A guard heading in the opposite direction eyed him as he walked down the corridor. Flint raised his glass and smiled. The guard grunted. Flint didn’t stop.

He entered an enormous restroom and locked the door. The guard could be a problem, but there was no way to change the plan now.

A second door, painted to blend in with the walls, took him to an empty service corridor. He paced silently toward the corner and glanced around before proceeding.

A window revealed he was at the rear of the property. The upward slope of the ground now put him at ground level.

Three doors down, he found a sign that identified a wet room for skis. He listened a moment before entering and heard no one inside.

The wet room was also enormous. Skis lined one wall and snowboards, the other. A couple of dozen snowsuits hung on a rail in the middle of the room.

## 17 Ground Truth

Two snowmobiles were parked by the far wall. A large door in front of them obviously exited onto ground level. He found the ignition wires on both machines and pulled them out, which would prevent the snowmobiles from starting easily.

Flint swapped his dress shoes for snowboard boots from a rack. He searched until he found a wiring closet in the corner.

To his relief, the closet was an access shaft that ran up four floors. Just as he'd guessed.

The guess had been a gamble. The magazine article's diagram had simply shown the closet as "electrical access," but he'd reasoned that a sixteenth-century building would be limited for modern electrical cables. Which was likely to force routing through one access point. He'd been right.

Flint climbed a ladder to the top floor, where a dusty hallway exited through a door into a laundry room. Flint paused, listening a moment before opening the door wide enough to stick his head through.

Pillows, bedsheets, and towels were stacked on shelves. Two large washing machines stood on pedestals, likely to isolate them from the floor, where vibrations could disturb their pampered owner. Tiny green LEDs on the front of the machines gave the room a faint, eerie glow.

## 19 Ground Truth

Flint grabbed a towel from the stack and kept moving.

He reached another exit, which opened into a corridor to the owner's rooms. He knelt and pushed an endoscope camera under the door. On the other side was an empty and dimly lit corridor. He waited and watched. Nothing moved.

Flint opened the door, counted twenty-five paces to the right, and turned to face the oak door that should have led to Fuchs's study.

Another quick check with the endoscope confirmed Hedinger's study was unoccupied, as expected. But the door was locked and the handle didn't turn.

He took out a set of small, fine tools and began picking the lock. Thirty seconds later, the door clicked open. He swept in and eased the door closed quietly behind him.

More faint LEDs illuminated the room. He covered the gap at the bottom of the door with a towel before turning on brighter lights.

His watch showed 9:10. Thirty-five minutes to go.

Rich colored wallpaper adorned the walls with flowers and birds, a design Flint recognized as historic toile. Bookshelves lined one side of the study. Glossy leather-bound volumes were stacked in perfect order, indicating the books were there for decoration instead of reading. Flint wondered who Hedinger felt the need to impress.

An old stone fireplace occupied another wall, the grate filled with an enormous display of dried flowers. An ornate desk with matching leather chair sat in the middle of the room. Behind the seat, another glass wall offered an astonishing view into the darkness with lighted homes and villages below.

Flint knelt by the fireplace, placed a hand into the grate, and found a small button. When he pushed the button, an audible click came from the wall beside the fireplace. A hidden door popped open. The joint around the door was barely visible due to excellent craftsmanship. He grinned at the hard-to-believe cliché and silently thanked the construction workers who'd clued him in to the room's secret entrance.

Flint stepped into another large room. Small museum-quality lights dotted the ceiling. They gave the room a subtle shine instead of heat or glare. For good reason. The walls were filled with Renoirs, Picassos, and Turners. Busts and figures in marble and gold stood on pedestals. Necklaces and orbs sat on velvet cushions in the middle of the room.

Flint ignored the breathtaking displays and strode directly to a violin on a pedestal.

The instrument had a dark golden hue that twinkled in the soft lighting, a reflection of copper and aluminum traces in its own unique varnish.

A small label stated, ANTONIUS STRADIVARIUS CREMONENSIS FACIEBAT ANNO 1709.

Created by the master himself and one of the greatest violins ever made. The owner, Flint's client, paid twenty million dollars for this one a year ago. It was worth more now.

Flint smiled at the irony of what he was about to do while a string quartet played three floors below.

Working quickly, he took off his jacket and shirt. Two cans of spray foam and two large plastic bags were taped to his midriff under a layer of latex. He pulled them all off.

He found a case for the Stradivarius in an opening behind the pedestal and rested the instrument inside it. He added a half-pound bag of desiccant to keep the violin dry and stable, given the conditions to which the masterpiece was about to be exposed.

He opened one of the large plastic bags. He inserted the case and violin into the bag and compressed it to expel excess air. After that he sealed the bag with a zipper.

He shook one can of foam and filled the second bag halfway. Then he squeezed the first bag into the sticky substance. Holding it in place, he used the rest of the foam to completely enclose the violin in six inches of the sticky material and ziplocked the second bag.

According to his calculations, the foam would insulate the contents so that they would suffer a change of only one degree in temperature for every ten minutes of exposure.

Flint had tested the foam's claim that it would solidify in minutes. It performed perfectly here in the field as well. The entire can hardened within two minutes.

# Chapter 3

He wrapped the latex around his torso and donned his shirt and jacket.

The next part of his plan would be frigid. He'd chosen it after rejecting everything else. Plan A was the least risky option.

He pulled at the belt around his waist, which yielded two long tapes. He wrapped them around himself and the violin, attaching the foam package to his back.

All he had to do now was get out with the Stradivarius without damage to either of them.

## 27 Ground Truth

When Flint returned to the study, he looked out through the enormous glass wall. Even though the glass was triple glazed, he could feel a chill rising from the surface. The exterior temperature was exponentially colder and quickly falling lower.

Each floor of the building had an emergency escape mechanism installed. On this, the downhill side, the escapes had been made of collapsible ladders. Hedinger didn't want ugly metalwork to adorn his château. **Aesthetics above safety** seemed to be his motto throughout the construction.

According to the magazine, the ladders were stored in shelters on each of the balconies. He relied on the escape setup to get him out and down without being discovered.

Flint could see the shelter from his position, but it contained only spindly metalwork designed to roll the ladder easily. The ladder itself had not been installed. The escape mechanism wasn't usable.

Quickly, Flint looked across the study and weighed his options. The only safe route out of the château was to return the way he came, through the wet room.

He used the endoscope to check the corridor. All clear.

Flint stepped out, raced to the laundry room, and down the ladder inside the wiring closet.

No one was in the wet room. They were all at the party.

## 29 Ground Truth

He took a snowboard and strapped his leading boot securely into the binding.

The area to the side of the building was somewhat flat. Which meant he'd need his other foot free to gain speed when he stepped outside.

He checked the package and confirmed that it was still securely attached to his back. He placed a hand on the exit door and breathed hard to oxygenate his body.

He needed to turn left immediately and get to the end of the building. Then he'd angle across the downslope to the trees to reach his microlight. There was little cover on this side of the building. He'd be exposed to view and the risk of discovery was high.

He'd need to be fast. No room for error.

A buzzer sounded. Flint turned toward the sound.

A red light flashed on a white box at head height on the far wall. An alarm.

He couldn't read the labels given the distance, but the outline of the château illuminated on the white box was obvious. The red light blinked on the top floor.

Flint caught his breath. No time to waste. They had discovered the missing Stradivarius.

He ripped the door open. Another alarm sounded. A second light flashed on the white box.

## 31 Ground Truth

They were onto him. Stealth meant nothing now.

Flint threw himself out the door, leading with the snowboard and pedaling his back leg hard and fast. But not fast enough. He gained no speed. Lights from the château revealed the ground at this point was frustratingly flat.

Flint had a hundred feet to cover before he reached the edge of the château. He strained to keep moving, pedaling with his back leg, wobbling too much on the snowboard.

The château's exterior lights were extinguished. Darkness enveloped the entire snowy, frigid mountain.

Flint stumbled and rolled, his sense of balance thrown in the dark. He stood and pushed forward, holding his arms out to improve his balance while protecting the Stradivarius.

He searched the horizon for anything that would provide a reference point in the dark. But he saw only glowing red dots high up around the building.

The red dots outlined the building and indicated where to find the corners, but he knew what they really meant. Hedinger's security team had infrared goggles. They'd be able to see while he was, quite literally, in the dark.

An engine started behind him. The angry buzz of a snowmobile. They'd found the wires he had disconnected and reconnected them.

## 33 Ground Truth

A second engine started. A rumbling noise followed. Which must have been the door to the outside rolling up to open. The engines revved and roared. They'd escaped the wet room.

Flint reached the corner of the building and angled across the slope. The faint moonlight reached downslope. The cluster of trees where he'd left the microlight was protected in a silhouette.

He pushed off, clipped his rear boot into the binding, and gained speed at last.

The board bucked and twisted. Flint kept his knees flexible and arms out fore and aft, absorbing the shocks and steadying his balance.

Speed combined with cold, cold wind and made his eyes water. But he grinned. Even though it was hard to tell in the dark, the wind and the cold confirmed that he was moving fast.

The bad news was the snowmobiles were moving fast, too. Engines screamed as they followed, gaining ground.

Flint heard the engine notes change in a moment as they crested the slope by the corner of the building. They were heading down toward him now.

The trees came up fast. He leaned into a broad turn, raced into a gap, and unclipped his boots. Flint prepared to run the rest of the distance.

## 35 Ground Truth

He'd entered the trees close to where he'd hid the microlight, but he couldn't see it. He had no choice. He flicked the flashlight on, swept the area, and clicked it off as fast as possible.

The tiny craft was twenty feet away to his left. Which was okay.

But the snowmobiles had seen the light. He heard them maneuvering as they rounded the trees. Which was not okay.

Not even remotely.

He collected the microlight and continued downhill. He'd exit on the downslope to help gain speed.

Shots sounded above him along with noises of breaking branches.

The security team had dismounted the snowmobiles. Their determined approach meant they would be taking no prisoners.

A branch to his left cracked. They'd lost his trail. Away from the château's infrared lights, their night-vision equipment wasn't as good as before. He'd caught a break.

Flint exited the trees, pulled back on a spar that spread the microlight's wings, and switched on the electric engine.

Nothing happened.

He staggered while digging in his pocket for the key. He found it and wedged it into the slot.

## 37 Ground Truth

The single-bladed propellor buzzed to life and threatened to pull the craft from his hands.

Flint stumbled forward, slipping his arms through a safety harness, and ran down the slope. He felt the craft gaining lift and pushed off with both feet.

The craft dipped, bringing his feet back to the ground.

He ran a few more paces and finally, he was airborne.

Shots sounded behind him. The microlight's engine was very quiet but not silent. Flint and the microlight were silhouetted against the sky. Pursuers would have a good view of him now.

# Chapter 4

Flint moved his weight forward, keeping the microlight's nose down to make the most of gravity's assistance to gain more speed down the slope. His eyes watered in the icy blast.

He angled right, toward Naters.

The security team stopped shooting. Flint turned back to look but could not see them in the dark.

They'd likely be calling the police, perhaps expecting him to land and take a car. He grinned in the arctic air. They'd be disappointed.

## 39 Ground Truth

The microlight gained altitude and Flint found his goggles. His watch showed 9:33. He had twelve minutes. He was making good time. So far.

The lights below provided a good navigational reference. Moving at sixty miles an hour, he spotted his target just five minutes later. He saw the twin arched entrances at the base of a mountain. The Simplon Tunnel.

In operation for well over a hundred years, the tunnel linked Switzerland to Italy by train in an almost straight line through the Alps.

A train set off from the station in Brig. He saw the light from a long line of slowly moving windows. Flint checked his watch. Right on time.

The SBB, the Swiss rail service, kept its reputation for timeliness intact.

Flint vectored ahead of the train as it gained speed. His plan was foolish and dangerous, but there were no other options. He'd looked.

He had a small window of opportunity. Not three strikes, like baseball. Only one chance.

The train passed out of the town at no more than fifty miles an hour. He was ahead of it, but he knew it would soon pass under him.

Flint steered the microlight down, gaining speed.

As expected, the locomotive passed under him, maybe two hundred feet below. He counted the carriages. There would be twelve.

## 41 Ground Truth

When he counted number six, he steadied his nerve and angled down hard, almost at a collision course.

The carriages continued to pass him, but he was gaining speed all the time.

The last carriage barely crawled past as he descended the final thirty feet.

With one hand steering the microlight and the other reaching out, he grabbed a ladder that ran up the rear of the carriage onto the roof.

The speed difference between the train and his microlight yanked at his arm and slammed him onto the top of the carriage. His head hit the roof. Lights twinkled in his vision and his balance swam.

Everything seemed to go dark.

The microlight's wings gained lift as the train raced forward, trying to lever him up and back.

Flint slid an arm through the ladder rungs as he fought the desire to roll on his back and ease the pain in his head. It took a moment for the word "concussion" to register in his brain.

The microlight bounced up and down, its wings snapping from side to side in the draft. He reached for the emergency release to separate himself from the craft, but it wasn't there.

He ran his hand over the strap around his chest, fumbling, searching for the buckle.

## 43 Ground Truth

He realized he held the wrong strap. This one was holding the Stradivarius on his back.

Flint blinked and refocused his efforts. Breathing hard to oxygenate and clear his head.

The release buckle he needed was under his arm. He found it and jerked it open. With a hard jolt, the microlight ripped itself free.

Flint caught the blurry sight of the microlight tumbling through the air before it disappeared in the darkness. A fraction of a second later, the train entered the tunnel.

The noise was deafening. He could feel the blast of air trapped between the train and the roof a couple of feet above his head.

He crawled backward, squeezing himself as low as possible and moving rung to rung along his belly until he was off the roof and on the rear of the train. He was still dizzy. He clung to the ladder for a minute to regain his balance and slow his breathing.

The ladder wasn't intended to be used while the train was moving. There was nowhere to step at the bottom. The ground was moving beneath him, making him even more dizzy.

He reached for the door to the rear of the train and twisted the stiff handle.

As the door opened, he leapt from the ladder into the rear of the train, stumbled on the floor until he regained his balance, and closed the door behind him.

He'd entered a giant cotton cocoon filled with nothing but shocking silence.

Not just the contrast from the noise on the roof but also the faces of an entire carriage filled with passengers staring at him.

He staggered forward. No point in waiting.

"Inspections up top," he mumbled as he struggled past the curious passengers.

Flint took the door to the next carriage and kept going.

After he passed through a couple of carriages, no one paid attention to him.

He moved through a small café and into the first-class section at the front of the train. Here, passengers were sectioned off in cabins. Most had their window blinds raised.

He peered into the café as he passed until he found the person he was looking for, Maria Blunt. She was sitting alone.

He opened the door and stepped in. The woman rose, an astonished look on her face.

"Mr. Flint. I thought we were meeting at the station?"

## 47 Ground Truth

"Change of plans." He had to grab for a handhold to stay upright. He wasn't sure if his loss of balance was from the impact of his head with the roof or if the train had taken a slight curve.

"Are you all right?" she asked.

"I've had better days." He rubbed the back of his head. "Probably just a minor concussion."

"Did you pass out?"

"No."

"You should sit."

"In a moment." He pulled the foam-encased violin from his back and handed it to her. "Yours, I believe."

Blunt took the bundle, a look of horror on her face. "What's happened to it?"

"What hasn't happened to it?" He sank into a seat. "But seriously, it's sealed in foam for insulation and protection."

She turned it over, examining the rips and scratches. "I…don't know what to say."

"Hedinger isn't the kind of man to forgive and forget. From his point of view, you've stolen what belongs to him. You'll need to double your security for a while."

"I should have doubled it before I allowed that swine into my home," Maria replied with menace. "It's a mistake I won't make again."

## 49 Ground Truth

Flint leaned back and placed his head on the headrest. When he closed his eyes, the dizziness was overwhelming. "You did arrange a car at the station, didn't you?"

"And driver, as agreed."

"And your yacht?"

"Fueled and ready at Marina di Varazze," she said. "We'll be in Italy in thirty minutes."

"Excellent. I'm looking forward to a few days in a deck lounge." Flint closed his eyes, fighting nausea and a killer headache.

# Chapter 5

**Newark, New Jersey**

Hanna Campbell glanced at the clock and dragged herself out of bed after an uneasy night's sleep. She sat on the edge of the bed to practice inhaling oxygen and clearing her lungs without coughing. She'd finally won her battle with dangerously drug-resistant tuberculosis, but the old habits and haunting memories lingered.

Even as she craved the oblivion of sleep, silence and darkness and isolation frightened her beyond all reason these days.

## 51 Ground Truth

Gone was the tenacious, hard-charging, brave young woman she'd been in college. The young Hanna had been so sure, so determined, so self-reliant. Hanna often wondered whether a small seed of that girl might still exist somewhere deep in her bones. A seed from which the stronger, braver Hanna might grow anew.

Humans are a resilient species, her doctors had said many times when Hanna was close to despair. Her hair and strength had begun to return over the long months of treatment and recovery. Perhaps her courage would regenerate somehow, too.

When Hanna was first released from prison weeks ago, she had sent letters and made phone calls to her sister. All of them went unanswered. After a while, Hanna had come to believe Greta must be dead. As stubborn and rigid and angry as Greta had been when they parted, surely her sister would have replied at least once if she was still living, wouldn't she?

Hanna glanced toward the corner of her bedroom where the television offered constant reassurance and provided the soundtrack of her life with around-the-clock programming. Colorful images and silly comedies and cheerful noises soothed her overwhelming anxiety. First during her long hospitalization after she was released from prison. Now as a comforting companion.

## 53 Ground Truth

Hanna sipped from a water glass as she reached for the remote and raised the volume. She flipped through the channels, pausing briefly on the cooking shows, more briefly on the dreadful news, seeking the old movies from an easier, simpler time.

When she landed on yet another replay of last month's royal wedding in London, she let the images mesmerize her. She tuned out the commentary, staring once more at the pageantry of it all. Thirty-two million pounds spent to produce any wedding was a stunning amount of money. Hanna couldn't wrap her head around it.

More than two hundred and fifty members of the British Armed Forces, the reporter said. Many rode as escorts on beautiful horses or lined the streets to corral the crowds as the procession passed. Families of the bride and groom waving toward the crowds from horse-drawn carriages. The whole production was jaw dropping.

Hanna had watched one amusing moment several times.

A young boy waving a shiny silver balloon sat atop his father's shoulders. When one group of mounted soldiers approached riding jet-black horses, the boy became so animated that he lost his grip on the balloon's ribbon.

## 55 Ground Truth

The balloon rose in the breeze, dancing low over the horse's nose. The horse snorted and sent the balloon careening upward. The balloon bounced off the ears of three more annoyed horses before it passed close enough to a soldier's grasp.

The entire display delighted the child. His infectious squeals filled the air. When the soldier managed to grab the ribbon and bring the dancing balloon to heel, onlookers applauded with jovial cheers.

The soldier glanced at the boy and offered a quick smile before he released the balloon into the breeze, where it bobbed a while longer before the cameras returned their focus to the procession.

The whole scene lasted less than a full minute. But it was a lighthearted moment in an otherwise staid performance. For thirty-two million pounds, Hanna would have demanded jugglers and dancers and amusements galore. It was a wedding celebration, after all. Not a funeral.

She pressed the back button on the remote and watched the brief episode again. The boy's joy was contagious. He looked about three years old. He laughed and clapped, and his eyes crinkled with pleasure.

The smilingly proud father held on to his chubby legs while the mother shook her head and grinned. Royal watchers surrounded the young family, joining in the festive mood.

## 57 Ground Truth

Hanna had viewed the scene on various outlets before. But in this version of the video, the camera panned a wider section of the crowd. Spectators stood several rows deep. The briefest of video sweeps passed to the right of the boy when he clapped his plump hands together with unabashed delight.

This time Hanna saw something she hadn't noticed before.

Her breath caught in her chest causing a sharp, deep pain. She willed herself to breathe normally but it didn't happen. She felt herself losing consciousness as blackness closed around the edges of her vision.

"Breathe, Hanna. Breathe," she whispered with as much energy as she could muster.

Through force of will alone, she managed a shallow exhale. Brief inhale. Shallow exhale again. Each effort prolonged her breaths only slightly as she remained still, staring at the screen.

The mother. Could that possibly be her?

The images were not crisp. The distance was more than ideal. The video moved past the woman much too fast.

Even so.

Hanna consciously inhaled, exhaled, and pressed the back button on the remote, playing the sequence again and again. After a dozen repeats, she paused the video to display the mother's face in the center of her screen.

Hanna stared at the blurry image for a good long time, mouth slack, eyes unfocused.

Long enough to convince herself that the woman could be Greta Campbell, Hanna's sister.

While the image held on the television screen, Hanna searched for her cell phone. She snapped photos of the woman's face. Then she hit the play button again and captured the video using the phone's camera.

With every passing minute, every repeat of the footage, Hanna became more convinced. She'd heard it said that everyone has a doppelgänger. Someone else on the planet that looks exactly like you.

Maybe the woman was her sister's doppelgänger.

Or maybe the camera lied.

It often did.

Angles, filters, lighting, editing. All of that and more could be manipulated to distort and deceive.

Something like that had to be the answer to this impossible vision.

How could that woman possibly be her sister? Greta was dead, surely. She must have been dead for years.

## 61 Ground Truth

It simply wasn't possible that this woman was Hanna's sister.

Not even a slim chance in Hell.

Right?

Absolutely.

Likely.

Possibly.

"You won't rest until you find out for sure," she said aloud, shaking her head. "Call the station. Get a better copy of the video. Find that woman and confirm. She's not Greta. Can't be Greta."

Strong words were all she had to work with as she attempted to squelch the hope that rose in her chest. Her efforts failed.

This woman could be Greta Campbell. All things were possible.

Hanna had never expected to be released from the cold, damp prison where she'd spent five long years. Yet here she was.

Was her big sister still alive?

Hanna simply had to know.

She found her phone again and searched through her old contacts list until she found the name and number she needed.

Alonzo Drake. She pressed the button to make the call.

# Chapter 6

**Italy**

Flint was antsy. Maria Blunt was an accomplished hostess, and her yacht was pleasant enough. Excellent chefs. Worthy gambling opponents. Sex with her was fun.

Yet floating around the Mediterranean was not the kind of luxury a man raised in dusty West Texas enjoyed indefinitely.

Under different circumstances, he might have given the relationship a chance. But he already knew Maria was not a woman he wanted to make a life with. She was beautiful and rich, which was okay.

But she was too agreeable and not self-sufficient enough for him. He liked his women more than a little on the feisty side. There was probably some deep psychological reason for that, but he'd never cared to explore it.

He knew it was time to move on. Probably tomorrow.

Which was why, when his colleague Katie Scarlett called with a potential new case, Flint already had one foot out the door.

"How'd things go in Switzerland?" Scarlett asked when Flint picked up the call from his lounge chair on the foredeck.

## 65 Ground Truth

Maria was floating in the pool. Several guests wearing expensive swimwear bought on the Riviera were chatting among themselves behind oversized designer sunglasses.

“Mission accomplished, as they say. Hedinger’s château is filled with impressive collectibles. If the place weren’t so damned cold, I could probably make a fortune retrieving baubles for their rightful owners,” Flint replied with a smile in his voice and a drink in his hand.

“Just what you need. A part-time job,” Scarlett replied dryly. “How’s the sun?”

“I’m worried I might have frostbite.”

"Yeah, well, we can get you warmed up. It's damned hot in Houston," Scarlett said. "Maddy and Whiskers miss you. When are you coming back?"

Maddy was Scarlett's seven-year-old daughter. Whiskers was the schnauzer puppy Flint had given her for her birthday without asking her mother. Which he'd known at the time was extremely risky.

Scarlett was a good marksman and qualified with a variety of weapons.

He grinned and absently rubbed the scar on his chest where she'd accidentally shot him with an arrow when they were children.

## 67 Ground Truth

They'd been playing William Tell in the backyard of the foster home where they'd met and become instantly inseparable. Flint had foolishly offered to wear the apple on his head first.

Scarlett was still annoyed with him about the puppy, but he wasn't worried. Maddy adored Whiskers and Scarlett adored Maddy. Which meant she'd stopped holding this particular grudge already, even if she wouldn't admit it to him.

Flint figured the bristly attitude was just for show. If Scarlett were really angry with him, she'd do more than complain about the dog.

"I'll be home soon. Why? What's up?"

"A couple of things that you'll be interested in," Scarlett said. "You asked me to chase down whatever we could find on Bette Maxwell's death. Looks like she died of old age, honestly."

"You're sure?"

"I mean, I don't have a crystal ball and she's not talking to me from the great beyond or anything," Scarlett said sardonically. "But there's nothing we can find to suggest any kind of foul play."

Flint closed his eyes and leaned back in the lounger.

He was light-years away from Bette Maxwell's foster care home at the moment, in every conceivable way. The orphanage where he and Scarlett grew up might as well have been on a different planet from this floating palace in the Mediterranean Sea.

Both Scarlett and Flint had left Bette Maxwell's place behind long ago. When a case they worked on brought their foster mother back into their lives, Flint viewed it as a gift.

Scarlett preferred to leave the past in the past where, she said, it belonged.

But then Bette died, and the death seemed unexpected to Flint. He'd asked Scarlett to put an investigator on it. Not because he really expected to find anything particularly suspicious.

Bette was as old and dry as the dirt she lived on. She'd told him she didn't expect to live much longer, and she'd been right.

But Flint felt he owed it to Bette to be sure her death actually resulted from natural causes. Her no-account husband and good-for-nothing sons stood to inherit Bette's farm, such as it was, along with the mineral rights that had finally provided a decent income for Bette in her later years.

Flint couldn't let the ne'er-do-wells inherit if they shouldn't have. Bette deserved better than that from him and Scarlett and everyone else she'd helped along the way.

"Okay, well, I guess that's the end of it, then," Flint said because he didn't want to continue this particular conversation now. "Thanks for handling the due diligence."

"There is one thing, though," Scarlett replied. "Bette left a box of stuff with your name on it in one of the bedroom closets. One of my guys went out there and picked it up because her sons are selling the place."

"A box?" Flint asked, puzzled. "What's in it?"

"Bunch of papers, newspaper clippings, stuff like that. Most of it is about you and your exploits. Guess she must have paid more attention to you after you left than she paid to me," Scarlett said, as if she might have been jealous or something.

Which Flint knew was total hogwash. Scarlett didn't have a jealous bone in her body. Nor did she have any reason to be jealous of anyone or anything.

"What about the rest of the contents?"

"An envelope stuffed with materials about Marilyn Baker," Scarlett said quietly.

Flint had investigated Marilyn Baker thoroughly when he'd first learned she'd existed. When Bette Maxwell suggested Marilyn Baker was Flint's biological mother.

After he'd looked into it, Flint agreed. Bette was probably right.

## 73 Ground Truth

But that didn't mean Flint wanted to go any further with the matter. And he'd explained that to Scarlett in no uncertain terms.

Which she seemed to have ignored.

As she often did.

Scarlett said, "I'm calling now only because it looks like Marilyn Baker's grave is being moved. Which means the body will be exhumed."

"What? Exhumed? Why?" Flint said, kneading his forehead.

As far as he knew, Baker had lain in the same grave for more than thirty years. She had no living relatives, unless he counted himself. Who would bother with her after all this time?

"If Marilyn Baker's body is exhumed, you could get a DNA sample, which could be subjected to the right tests and might prove Baker was your mother. Or not," Scarlett explained slowly, as if he were a dimwit.

The option to have the body exhumed had always been there. Flint hadn't decided whether he wanted that or not.

Now the matter was out of his hands.

The decision had been made by someone else.

Which meant he could have the DNA tested easily and without a court order or having any sort of conversation with Baker's living relatives. Assuming she had any. Which seemed unlikely.

## 75 Ground Truth

And Flint was as conflicted about the issue now as he had been before Scarlett's call.

"They're moving the cemetery to put a road through there. It's a pauper's cemetery. They've notified all the families they can find. Bodies will be relocated at county expense if the families have another plot somewhere. Otherwise, the bodies will be cremated." Scarlett paused for a breath. "Meaning, if you want to claim Marilyn Baker's body, you need to do it now."

Flint slid off the lounger and padded around the deck barefoot while Scarlett waited for his answer.

Marilyn Baker had been dead almost as long as Flint had been alive. From what Bette Maxwell said, Baker was probably his mother. But she might not be.

And who was Flint's father?

Flint had lived his entire life without knowing the answers to these questions. Did he want to know now?

When Bette Maxwell died, Flint had buried himself in work.

He'd found Baker's grave and decided to leave her there until a compelling reason to exhume the body and test her DNA arose.

That compelling reason had never materialized.

Until now.

He could take possession of the body. Bury her again. Nothing required him to test her DNA. He could continue to wait.

But why? Was he just a coward?

If Marilyn Baker was his mother, then the obvious question was his father's identity. Who was his father? Did he want to know?

Flint had never cared about his origins.

He lived alone and in the moment. Always had. He liked it that way. He'd also grown accustomed to his independence.

If he dug up a passel of relatives, he'd be connected to others in a way he'd never planned and never wanted.

Katie Scarlett and Maddy had been like family to him. Along with Bette Maxwell, he supposed. They were all the family he needed. All he wanted, too.

So now what?

"Flint? Are you there?" Scarlett was asking across the miles. "What do you want me to do? They're pausing the exhumation until tomorrow so you can weigh in. Should I let it go? Do you even have a plot where they could rebury her? Or a crypt?"

He swiped a palm over his face and inhaled deeply. "Ask them to hold up until I get there. I'll be back tomorrow."

"Okay, I'll ask."

"And Scarlett?"

## 79 Ground Truth

"Yeah?"

"Thanks for this. I don't know what I want to do about it all. But I appreciate your letting me know so I can decide," he said quietly.

"You owe me, Flint. Two weeks of dog sitting coming your way," Scarlett said sternly, but he heard the smile in her voice. "And you can pay up right after you get home. Maddy and I are going to Disney World. So unless you want to come along…"

"Sounds just great," he grumbled before he hung up. He'd never owned a dog in his life. Surely he was too old to start now.

What the hell did a dog sitter do, anyway?

# Chapter 7

## Miami

"What happened to you, man?" Alonzo Drake asked, beer in hand. The two men sat across from each other on the patio in the warm, quiet Miami darkness.

Carlos Gaspar adjusted his position on the hard bench and considered how to answer that question.

His physical condition was a subject he rarely discussed. Talking about it, wallowing in misery? No point. He was what he was. Glory days behind him and nothing to do now but put his head down and move on.

## 81 Ground Truth

But Drake was a good man. A veteran. Gaspar liked him. And he'd asked straight up, which was an approach Gaspar respected. Drake deserved the truth. Or some of it.

Which was that Gaspar had been shot twice. Once in the right side and once in the right leg.

The wound on the right side was worse. It had collapsed the network of muscles there and sitting was painful. The weight of his upper body crushed his organs as if his ribs and his pelvis were the jaws of a vise.

The second shot, a bullet that hit the shinbone and didn't even break it, was dismissed as trivial by his doctors. But day to day, it was far worse to deal with than the wound in his side. The leg ached constantly, like someone was in there with a drill from Home Depot.

To live with both, he swigged the sweet Cuban coffee he loved and gulped Tylenol like a kid eating candy. He couldn't afford to use anything stronger. He needed his wits about him twenty-four seven.

When he had awakened in the ICU his first thought had been: **What the hell do I do now**? Worry for his family attacked his life like a cancer. He had a wife and five kids, and he needed to work at least another twenty years before he could even think about slowing down.

Then his Special Agent in Charge visited and told him he'd always have a job. Modified duty, mostly behind the desk. But his family wouldn't starve. The Bureau took care of its own.

Gaspar had been flooded with gratitude. He'd kept that gratitude top of mind every minute of every day. He never for a single moment forgot that he was a man with much to be grateful for.

His family, all thriving, had stuck with him. His wife. His four daughters. And now a son, too. All five were his responsibility and his alone.

Gaspar knew he was a lucky man. Luckier than most, for damned sure.

But life always moves on.

He no longer carried an active FBI badge. No one had called him Special Agent Gaspar for quite a while.

He wasn't the least bit sorry because his job and his family weren't the only things that had changed.

The Bureau he'd been proud to serve after he left the army had become unrecognizable. The way he saw it, thousands of good men and women were betrayed every day by the bureaucrats who ran the place now. Nothing he could do about any of it.

But the changes at the top had made him insecure, and when an opportunity almost too good to be true came his way, he'd retired from the FBI. No looking back. No what-ifs and if-onlys.

Most days he didn't miss the old job. He did miss his last and best partner.

## 85 Ground Truth

But he still talked to her regularly anyway.

Scarlett Investigations was a better employer in every way that mattered. Scarlett paid a lot better, which made his family more financially secure. He had access to the best equipment and top-notch personnel, which made doing the job possible.

Unlike government service, budget restrictions and miles of paperwork never thwarted. And he had room to move without the restrictions of unqualified hierarchy and rules that strangled government agents.

Hell, Scarlett hadn't even asked him to relocate. His wife and kids were settled here in Miami, the town Gaspar grew up in and still loved.

His old man was still alive and not getting any younger. They wanted to stay inside the Cuban American community. They didn't want to live in Houston. Scarlett was good with that, too.

It was like the Bureau was trying to get rid of him, and he suspected they'd found him a soft landing. They didn't push him out, but he'd had the feeling they would have if he'd refused Scarlett's offer. So he took the leap under his own steam and never worried about the choice.

Drake wanted the truth? Except for Gaspar's damaged body, everything was okay.

He was long past the stage of life where he needed to prove how good he was every day. The work was challenging because Scarlett Investigations handled tough cases for clients who could afford to pay the steep fees. No problem.

As long as they didn't ask him to cross his personal lines, he was fine as wine with the whole setup.

Gaspar told Drake none of that. Gaspar spent no time wallowing in the past. He liked to stay on track.

So he offered the bare minimum. "Hurt on the job. Dirtbag shot me a couple of times before I killed him. A while back, though. Docs fixed me up. It's all good."

Drake nodded, but Gaspar offered no more.

Instead, Gaspar asked the only relevant question. “What do you need?”

“Not sure. That’s the problem,” Drake replied between swigs. “I’d ask Flint, but he’s not back from Italy yet. Give that guy a yacht on the Med and he’s glued to a lounge chair.”

Gaspar smiled. “Yeah, well, can’t blame him for that.”

Drake lifted the beer in Gaspar’s direction. “He’s got a lot of respect for you. Scarlett does, too. Thought you might have some good suggestions.”

“Okay.” Gaspar said. “Hit me with it.”

# Chapter 8

## Atabei

The sunny, warm winter weather was perfect for a walk. Hands loosely draped in the pockets of his linen trousers, Dr. Stephen Brand sauntered the few short blocks to the Atabei Country Club. Behind his Cartier aviators, his gaze scanned the neighborhood and found nothing lacking.

Pristine sidewalks were washed regularly. No trash of any sort littered the streets. He was free to enjoy the island's bright colors and the wafting scent of gardenias in bloom without experiencing even the slightest irritation.

Atabei was the best of what Caribbean Island countries had to offer, Brand confirmed once again. Atabei natives numbered fewer than one thousand now and continued to dwindle. The country's population was otherwise composed of carefully chosen residents. About two thousand total.

Atabei's founders had adopted their successes and learned well from their mistakes.

As a result, unlike the other islands, Atabei's poverty level was nonexistent. Security stellar. Health care the best money could buy. Nutritional needs were abundantly satisfied and consistent with residents' preferences. Some ate well. Others did not. By choice.

Atabei Island was privately owned, structured similarly to an extravagantly luxurious condominium community with a benevolent dictator as the chairman of the board.

Every potential resident had been professionally vetted by the ex–Mossad security experts who kept order here. The security staff was small but well trained and extravagantly supported with the best technology money could buy as well.

Approved visitors were few, strictly limited in number, and subject to unrestricted surveillance as deemed necessary.

In all the years since Brand established his business here, crime rates had been near zero. Infrequent violators were swiftly identified, arrested, punished, and dealt with. All property of established criminals was confiscated and added to Atabei's portfolio.

Thus, the justice system, like all the other systems on Atabei, worked exceptionally well.

"Welcome, Dr. Brand," the white-gloved doorman greeted him, hand on the oversize brass handle at the front of the Atabei Country Club. He opened the big white door and stood aside.

"Good afternoon, Tito," Brand replied with a nod and a wide smile as he crossed the threshold.

## 93 Ground Truth

Brand ambled into the enormous, air-conditioned lobby where he stood for a moment on the cool mahogany floor. He removed his sunglasses and allowed his eyes to adjust to the dim interior. He straightened his sport coat, used both hands to swipe his brown wavy hair back from his face, and strolled to the dining room.

Brand spied his client seated at a table overlooking the golf course and waved the hostess aside. He meandered through the room, avoiding full tables of diners engaged in suitably muted conversation, until he reached Jordan Rush.

Rush was seated with his back to Brand, gazing out the open window across the lush, verdant fairway. This was the fifth hole. Had the clubhouse been situated at the seventh hole, Rush would have had an unobstructed view of the clear turquoise Caribbean Sea.

Brand cleared his throat to avoid startling the man who seemed nervous enough already.

Rush looked up and stood for a formal handshake. He was that kind of traditionalist. “Hello, Stephen.”

“Jordan,” Brand replied with the same level of informality, seeking to put the man at ease.

Nothing about the surgery Rush needed was routine and men like him were always more comfortable with familiarity. In the absence of routine,

## 95 Ground Truth

Rush craved control. When he controlled the situation, he controlled his fears.

Brand understood the anxiety. He'd dealt with similar anxiety in his patients many times before.

"Please, have a seat," Rush said, waving to the chair beside him.

"Thanks." Brand followed Rush's invitation because, seated close together, they could talk quietly without being overheard and still enjoy the view.

Brand understood the psychology of Rush's situation. His patients were invariably wealthy people whose entire worlds revolved around their own preferences.

Because patients were so wrapped up in their own worlds, they spent very little time quizzing him about his life. Which suited Brand perfectly. He had no desire to share his background. The less everyone knew, the better.

Rush gestured toward the beach. “What are those workers doing out there on the beach?”

Brand sighed. “Our beaches are pristine, but it doesn’t happen by magic. We have crews who work hard to keep the beaches open and inviting year-round.”

Rush shrugged. “I guess I thought the gentle surf out there would take care of things.”

## 97 Ground Truth

“The waves do a good job. But right now we’re suffering through sargassum. It’s a type of seaweed that washes ashore. It needs to be removed and dealt with before it rots.” Brand shook his head. “Mother Nature needs a hand now and then, you know.”

“Are these people the same crews that handle the landscaping and gardening? Every plant I’ve seen so far on Atabei is lush and thriving.” Rush shrugged. “I wish my gardeners were as good as yours.”

“I’ll pass along your compliments to our groundskeeper,” Brand said with a smile.

The two spent a few minutes engaged in more polite small talk while a smartly clad waiter collected their orders and delivered lobster salads and sparkling water. Neither man ordered alcohol.

"Thanks for speeding down here, Jordan. Time is always of the essence in these situations," Brand said, broaching the subject they'd come to discuss.

Rush could buy anything his weak heart desired and always did precisely that. This time was different, and it was obvious that he didn't like the situation at all. "I've had my bag packed for weeks. I assume you have acquired a donor."

Rush had been on the official organ donor lists for only ten months. He was no stranger to heart disease.

## 99 Ground Truth

He'd had his first heart attack at the age of thirty-five. He'd had five more since then. He'd had bypass surgeries and angioplasties, too. Each heart event left him weaker than the last.

He'd found his condition increasingly exhausting and time consuming. The procedures interfered with his lifestyle and his businesses.

Neither Rush's wife nor his mistress was happy with his unavailability. His kids were all adults now, but they had no room in their lives for an invalid.

That truth infuriated Rush even as he understood it. He felt impotent about his circumstances, which made him furious, too. Waiting for an organ donor required patience and acceptance of likely failure, neither of which Jordan Rush or his family had ever needed or possessed.

“Schedules.” Brand gave him a level stare. “We’ve talked about this. What you need is a fairly common heart transplant. Any competent transplant surgeon can do the surgery for you. You didn’t need to wait for my particular skills.”

“We both know that’s not true.” Rush leveled a cold-eyed glare.

Brand offered a polite shrug in return.

He did understand the problem. Brand’s entire successful billion-dollar empire rested precisely on scratching this particular itch for patients like Jordan Rush.

Even in the world Rush inhabited, the world of polo and Alpine skiing and months-long jaunts on the world's largest private yachts, healthy human hearts were one of a very few things not available to buy at the snap of his fingers.

The need for a heart transplant and his inability to satisfy that desire instantly by payment of a reasonable portion of his fortune fell a long, long way outside Rush's usual experience.

Fortunately, the situation landed perfectly in Dr. Stephen Brand's wheelhouse. Thanks to his wealthy amoral benefactor, he had access to a plentiful pool of donors more than willing to sell their organs.

For the right price, Brand could procure and transplant whatever the patient desired.

Brand, one of the top transplant surgeons in the United States at one time, was more than willing to profiteer. As it turned out, selling human organs for outrageous fees came easily and naturally to him as well as Hedinger.

Everybody wins, Brand had said to more than one prospective organ recipient.

He reached into his breast pocket. He retrieved a thick cream envelope embossed with his private hospital logo that contained the invoice and payment instructions. His fee was stiff. When Hedinger's surcharge was added, only men with significant fortunes could afford the cost.

What price would such men pay? As it turned out, a much higher price than Brand had assumed.

Brand placed the envelope on the crisp white linen tablecloth between them. If Rush wanted the transplant, he'd first be required to pick up the envelope.

The simple act was a test of sorts. How badly did Rush want his new heart?

# Chapter 9

The envelope symbolized Rush's willingness to kill another human for his own selfish purposes. Some men would never do such a thing.

Rush wasn't one of those men.

He snatched the envelope like it might magically disappear if he waited one full second.

"We've scheduled your surgery for tomorrow morning. Details are included along with your preoperative instructions," Brand said, hiding a smile as he finished the last bite of his lobster. "We'll confirm your wire transfers tonight at eight o'clock local time. Assuming all financial requirements have been satisfied, our limo will pick you up tomorrow morning at five a.m."

Rush opened the envelope and skimmed its contents quickly before sliding it into his pocket. "This is all satisfactory to me."

"Do you want to know more about your heart?" Brand asked. "The donor's health history? Age? Sex? Race? Substance abuse? Prior heart issues? Anything like that?"

Rush's eyes widened. "Why would I?"

Brand shrugged. "Surgery carries risks."

"When the donor dies, you've confirmed that her family will not come back on me," Rush said, revealing the only issue he actually cared about. Himself. And the assets he believed were his alone.

Brand wasn't impressed with the patient's worry. Rush lusted after this heart like an addict craves his next fix. He was too close now to back out, even if he wanted to. Which he surely did not.

"Her family will be well compensated," Brand replied.

"How?"

The donor's life wasn't worth much. She'd made the choice to sacrifice herself for her family. Brand was a man of his word. The donor's family would receive the promised fee.

This was the one thing that made Brand's services more desirable to the poor donors than others offering the same service. Brand always paid the full fee. Other doctors were not so scrupulous.

Brand had perfected the process over the years, and it always ran smoothly. Everybody wins, as he'd said many times.

"That's what life insurance is for." Brand shrugged again. "Any other questions?"

"I've checked you out. People I trust have used you before," Rush replied with a look that could only mean he'd put retaliatory measures in place should Brand fail to deliver as expected. "How long will I need to stay here afterward?"

"You're not a prisoner, Jordan. You may leave anytime you wish. But we recommend that you stay at least a few days under our supervision before we transfer you to your own private physician's care. And longer is better," Brand replied. "There's always the risk of rejection. We can't guarantee your body will adapt as we hope it will."

"That's what the extra ten million is for. In case there's a problem and we need to find another heart fast," Rush said, nodding, repeating what Brand had told him in previous conversations. "I'm paying for two hearts, even though I should only need one."

Brand narrowed his eyes. "To be clear. No refunds. Regardless of the outcome or results."

"I understand." Rush replied. "How long will the new heart last?"

"We talked about this. It varies, of course. About half of known transplant patients are still living after twelve years. Some live longer. At least one woman has lived more than forty years after a heart transplant," Brand said. "The statistics are improving all the time."

"And if my heart needs to be replaced in the future? You'll be able to do another one, I assume," Rush said, his anxiety popping through his control once again.

Brand smiled. “Let’s not borrow trouble, shall we? We’ll get your new heart installed and functioning tomorrow. After that, we’ll see.”

Rush looked a little green, but he nodded.

Brand pushed his chair back. “We’ll look for your payment tonight, and then we’ll see you in the hospital in the morning.”

Rush stood and the two men shook hands. Neither expressed any qualms about their bargain. Each was getting precisely what he wanted.

Brand sauntered toward the exit. When he reached the entrance to the club's private lounge, a big cheer from a group of men watching football on the television over the bar erupted into the foyer. He turned his head to glance at another TV hoping to catch the replay.

Instead, on the second television an entertainment news show was on. They were rehashing the most recent royal wedding, laughing about a young boy and his balloon in the crowd.

When the cameras panned the spectators, a woman's face magnetized Brand's gaze. The satisfaction he'd felt when he confirmed Rush's procedure a moment ago vanished like a magician's rabbit.

He stood as if glued to the spot, staring at a woman who looked too much like her. He couldn't turn his head away from her image.

She was dead. Long dead.

And then the image was gone.

The show moved on to a different film clip.

Brand shook off his slack-jawed trance and continued mindlessly toward the exit.

He waited half a moment for Tito to open the door and ambled outside. Unaware of his surroundings, he somehow moved along the sidewalk toward his office.

## 113 Ground Truth

Preoccupied, he walked into an intersection that seemed to be busier than usual. Two vehicles swerved to miss him, laying on their horns and shouting obscenities.

The angry cacophony jolted him back to the present.

He shook the woman's image from his mind and hurried away from the intersection. Like a metronome, he used each forced step to manage his mounting anger.

He was in control.

She was dead.

He'd survived.

One last rich transplant recipient to handle today.

One more fortune to claim.

He shrugged off his uneasy feeling, reassuring himself.

That woman in the crowd couldn't possibly be his long-dead wife.

He'd only caught the briefest glimpse.

He hadn't seen her clearly.

He'd been working long hours lately.

That woman was not her.

By the time he reached his office, he'd regained confidence and control.

No reason to notify his mistress or Hedinger about the woman in the crowd.

At least not yet.

# Chapter 10

## Miami

Drake ran his own one-man shop. Gaspar wasn't sure exactly what his business was. But he supplied muscle, and from time to time Drake served as Flint's wingman. They'd known each other going back to their military days.

Neither Drake nor Flint worked at Scarlett Investigations, but the organizational lines between the three were blurry.

The focus was always on getting results for the clients. No one was overly picky about how those results were accomplished. Which was just fine with Gaspar. Debating the ethics of means and ends was fun for philosophers and students but a total waste of time for those who fought in the trenches every day.

Gaspar recalled the words one of his army drill instructors screamed two inches from his face during basic training.

“Soldier! Don’t EVER confuse effort with results!”

It was a lesson Gaspar never ignored.

Based on what he’d seen at Scarlett Investigations, Drake and Flint, and even Scarlett herself, lived by the same creed. Which was one of the reasons Gaspar felt at home now in a way he had no longer felt at the FBI.

"What's the case about?" Gaspar asked.

"Missing woman. Maybe."

"Maybe she's a woman? Maybe she's missing?" Gaspar teased with a smile.

"Nah." Drake flashed a big grin in return. "I'm sure she's a woman and sure she's missing. But maybe she's dead."

Gaspar frowned. "Start with that."

"The client is her sister. I dated Hanna Campbell in college. She's had a rough time lately," Drake said quietly. He cleared the emotion from his throat before he continued. “Because of her circumstances, Hanna hasn’t seen her sister in years. Not since their mother died. Makes it hard to know where to start looking for Greta.”

“Hanna and Greta? Seriously?” Gaspar joked. “Were their parents gingerbread bakers or something?”

“Dunno.” Drake shrugged. “People name their kids some crazy stuff.”

Gaspar’s five children all had normal names, but he agreed. He’d seen his share of fans naming their kids Elvis and Prince and Madonna and crazier names over the years. Thing was, crazy names could mess kids up. He’d seen that happen, too.

“What’s Hanna done so far to locate Greta?”

“The sisters were, I guess you’d say, estranged. Hanna tried to contact Greta for several weeks and got no response. She called me, but I was on a case. While she waited for a call back, she went to Greta’s last-known residence in Orlando, but someone else bought the place a couple of years ago. No forwarding address.”

“What about work? Did Greta have a job?”

“She was an on-air reporter for a local television station in Orlando. Hanna went there. Talked to the HR department. They said Greta died four years ago. Some kind of boating accident,” Drake replied. “They gave

Hanna the name of one of Greta's friends, but the woman is on vacation or something."

"Sounds like the answer, doesn't it?" Gaspar asked. "They're saying she died. Doesn't get much more final than that."

Drake shrugged. "Except in this case, it's not so final."

"What do you mean?"

"Greta and her husband were on a smallish sailboat of some sort. The boat sank in a storm," Drake explained. "They found pieces of the boat. But they never found the bodies."

"Makes things a little less complicated, though, doesn't it?

If she's been declared dead, she probably is."

"Except Hanna thinks Greta didn't die. And either way, she wants to be sure. I told her I'd help, but the investigation side of things is outta my wheelhouse." Drake shook his head and swigged the last of his beer. "I can't really ask Scarlett to take this on. Hanna doesn't have the money to pay."

"Scarlett might do it anyway," Gaspar pointed out. "She's got a softer heart than some people think."

"She does. And I know she would do this. That's why I can't ask her," Drake replied. "She's got too much on her plate already."

"Ah." Gaspar paused a few moments to let Drake's unspoken request linger. "So you think Hanna's engaged in wishful thinking?"

"Possibly."

"There's another possibility. A more hopeful one. Even if Greta's not dead, could be she isn't missing at all. I mean, she's an adult. She can come and go as she pleases," Gaspar said. "Nothing says she has to be involved with her sister or anyone else, for that matter. People drift apart for all sorts of reasons."

"Yeah, that's what I told Hanna. But she's convinced there's more to it."

"Why?"

"Long story," Drake said. "When Hanna called me, I thought I'd just make a few phone calls, locate the sister or get a date of death, and that would be the end of it."

"But it didn't work out that way."

"Not even close. We can't find Greta and can't find any actual hard evidence that she's dead, either," Drake said. "Right now I don't even have a death certificate."

"What's the friend's name? The one Greta worked with."

"Margo Brady. She works at an independent station. Channel 32 in Orlando. She's a producer, I guess." Drake wiped a palm across his face. "Hanna has never heard of her and has no idea what she might know about Greta."

"If they were close friends, Margo Brady may be your best resource. Women tell each other all kinds of stuff. When's she due back in town?"

"Today." Drake glanced at his watch. "Arriving at the station a few hours from now. I'm going up to Orlando. Talk to her in person. Might get more that way."

"Okay. Leave me the information you have on Greta, and I'll check a few databases, see what we can learn before you interview Margo Brady," Gaspar said, slurping the last of his now cold, sweet coffee the consistency of pudding. "Might even find Greta quickly and save you the trip. How's that?"

"Thanks, man. I'd owe you." Drake pulled his cell phone out of his pocket and forwarded texts to Gaspar's phone. "Here's Greta's last-known address, birth date, social. Work address. She had a car, but the plates are expired and so's the insurance. I'm hoping maybe Margo Brady knows where the car is now."

"Did Greta or someone else drive it out of the state of Florida? Retitle the car in another state? If they did, there'd be no record of that in Florida databases," Gaspar said. "One reason car theft rings get away with stealing cars."

"Well that sucks. What a stupid system." Drake shrugged, standing. "Okay. Guess I'll hear from you when you have a chance."

But the missing sister had captured Gaspar's interest. "What about the husband?"

"Hanna never met the guy, but yeah. They were on the boat together when it went down."

"So he died in the same accident?" Gaspar's skepticism crawled up his spine. "Let me guess. His body was never found, either."

Drake shrugged. "Spouses die together in tragic accidents all the time, don't they? I remember Flint telling me that. There's a whole bunch of law out there about who inherits in those situations."

"I've got a bit of time today. Let me get a quick shower," Gaspar replied, making up his mind in the moment. "I'll ride up to Orlando with you."

He didn't have any active cases hot right now and he'd feel good to get out into the field for a while again. Give him a chance to size Drake up, too. In case he needed to use Drake in the future.

Flint said Drake was a good guy, and Flint would know. But now Gaspar wondered what Drake's skills were, exactly.

"I really appreciate this, man. Pick you up in an hour." Drake headed toward his rental. "I'll fill you in on the way and we can figure out what to do next."

# Chapter 11

## Orlando

The address for Orlando's Independent Television Channel 32 located it south and west of downtown in a mixed-use commercial district. Traffic along Florida's Atlantic coast roads was, as always, heavy.

Drake had followed the navigation system directions north from Miami on the Florida Turnpike and then across on the Bee Line Expressway to another state highway running north. The route wound around a bit before reaching the right street.

# 129 Ground Truth

The long drive allowed plenty of time to discuss the few facts Drake knew. Most of which he'd told Gaspar during their initial chat on the patio in the dark.

Gaspar used his laptop and secure hot spot to research Greta's disappearance during the trip. They'd tossed around several theories and Gaspar researched the issues. He listed the relevant facts.

"Looks like Greta Campbell's married name is Reed. She and her husband, Phillip Reed, left from Sarasota, Florida, for a two-day cruise in a twenty-nine-foot sailboat. Not technically a yacht, but big enough. When Greta didn't show up for work as scheduled, coworkers reported her missing. The boat was never located, but searchers found a debris field in the area. They recovered items consistent with what would have been carried on the boat. After a lengthy search, both Dr. and Mrs. Reed were declared lost at sea, presumed dead."

"Dr. Reed? First time I'd heard she was married to a doctor. Guess Hanna didn't know that, either." Drake paused to digest the report and then said, "That actually sounds kind of promising, doesn't it?"

Gaspar arched one eyebrow and said nothing. He continued his internet search, digging up public records mostly, and not many of them. Greta's life seemed less interesting than her death and the reports of that were few.

When Drake pulled up into the visitors' parking lot at Channel 32, he said, "You're a whiz with the tech, aren't you? I'd never have found that stuff about Greta on my own."

"Grow or die, as they say. I'm not much good in the field anymore. I had to learn new skills." Gaspar closed the laptop and slid it under his seat. "I've spent a lot of time behind a desk. There's plenty of intel out there if you have the right clearances and know where to look for it."

Drake parked the big Navigator across two parking spaces and squelched the engine. "Maybe you're not good at fieldwork, but I'm no trained investigator. Why don't you take the lead with Margo Brady? I'll chime in when it seems appropriate."

Gaspar opened the door and paused as the electric running boards deployed. “Yeah, that’s fine.”

He waited for Drake to get out. Long rides in a restricted space had become a significant struggle since he left the FBI and rarely spent time cooped up.

Gaspar put his aching right leg onto the running board and rested it there until he slid his left foot onto the pavement for strength and balance. He put all his weight on his left leg as he moved his right foot to the ground and steadied his body. He finished the maneuver before Drake made his way around the front of the big SUV, which meant Drake might not have noticed Gaspar’s struggle.

He reached into his pocket for four Tylenol and swallowed them dry. He focused on ignoring the pain and refused to limp as he joined Drake for the long walk to the front entrance.

An armed security guard stood to one side with his hands resting on his utility belt. He carried himself like an off-duty cop or maybe retired military. Square, sturdy, no-nonsense.

Drake pulled the handle on the big glass entry door and stepped inside. Gaspar followed. The guard didn't try to stop them.

The lobby was clean and stark. There were a couple of benches on either side of the entrance and a big desk fifteen feet inside. Another armed security guard stood behind the desk.

Drake took the lead. He stepped up to the desk and said, “We’d like to see Ms. Margo Brady, please.”

“Is she expecting you?”

“Probably not. Tell her we’re here at the request of Greta Campbell’s sister,” Drake said.

“Will she know who Greta Campbell is?” the guard asked.

Drake gave Gaspar a quick look. Gaspar stepped up. “Greta Campbell Reed was one of your employees until she died four years ago. We’d like to talk to Ms. Brady about her.”

"I see," the guard replied. "Can I see your ID please?"

Gaspar handed over his Scarlett Investigations business card. Drake didn't have a card. But the guard seemed okay with just the one.

"Have a seat over there. I'll call Ms. Brady," the guard said.

"Think she'll see us?" Drake asked as they moved away from the desk.

"Why not? There's two armed guards standing here. What does she have to worry about? Besides, she works in a news station. She's gotta be used to talking to people she doesn't know," Gaspar replied.

The desk guard clacked a keyboard. Probably sending a message up to

Margo Brady. Or maybe to her boss. Five minutes later, a door beside the reception desk clicked open. A sturdy woman about forty-five years old strode into the lobby.

She was dressed in jeans and a blue chambray shirt that enhanced her deep blue eyes. She had a splash of freckles across her pale face and a mop of red hair the same color as her eyebrows.

She stuffed her hands in her back pockets so her elbows splayed. "I'm Margo Brady," she said as she approached. "How can I help you?"

Gaspar stepped forward and extended his hand. She shook hands with him and then with Drake as he said, "I'm Carlos Gaspar. This is Alonzo Drake. We're here at the request of Hanna Campbell. We'd like to talk to you about her sister, Greta Reed."

She shook her head. "I didn't even know Greta had a sister. I'm not likely to be much help to you."

"Is there a place we can have some privacy?" Gaspar asked.

Margo scanned them up and down like a robot with x-ray vision. Whatever she'd been worried about must have been something she didn't find.

She tilted her head toward the door. "There's a table outside. It's a nice day."

"Lead the way," Drake said.

Gaspar followed slowly behind.

Margo led them to an outdoor smoking section. Four chairs were arranged in a semicircle with an outdoor ashtray next to each. A few cigarette butts poked up from the sand.

Margo fished her cigarettes out of her pocket before she sat. Gaspar and Drake took the chairs opposite.

She offered smokes from the open pack. Gaspar and Drake declined. She extracted a long brown skinny cigarillo and lit it with a disposable butane. After a long drag, she held the smoke in her lungs, then finally exhaled.

Before the next drag, she asked again, “How can I help you?”

# Chapter 12

## Houston

Flint's flight landed in Houston more than two hours late. He collected his carry-on and hustled through the passenger ramp into the terminal. He trotted along the corridors, weaving between groups of slower travelers.

Scarlett had delayed the exhumation of Marilyn Baker's body as long as possible, but the work had been completed in Mount Warren yesterday. The state had sent the body to Houston for cremation. The last message he'd received from Scarlett said the cremation was scheduled in about an hour. No time to waste.

He hoofed it to the escalators and then hopped down the moving steps to the bottom, where he jumped off and rushed toward the exit. When he emerged from the terminal, he hit the humid Houston weather like a brick wall.

Flint was already perspiring when he exited the building and the humidity soaked his shirt, plastering it to his chest like wet cotton.

He twisted his neck to scan the row of waiting vehicles looking for Drake's big SUV. For the first time ever in their relationship, Drake had dropped the ball.

Traffic was heavy. Maybe Drake was running late. Flint had texted from the plane with updated arrival intel.

Flint checked his phone to be sure the text was sent and received. Affirmative on both counts.

He ran a frustrated palm over his clammy face and across his shaggy dark hair. He needed a haircut. And a shave. And clean clothes. But first he had to find a ride.

The line of traffic was moving slowly through the pickup lanes in front of the arrival lines at baggage claim. The taxi queue was longer than the line to enter a rock concert. He could call a car service, but it would take more time to get someone out here than he had to spare.

He heard an impatient driver mashing the horn. Which led to more drivers joining the chorus. Two dozen horns honking repeatedly and out of any reasonable rhythm was beyond deafening.

Flint scanned the mob pushing toward him from all sides. Which was when he heard his name being called from the far lane across six lanes of bumper-to-bumper traffic.

"Flint! Over here!"

A tall, slender woman with tumbling dark hair stood on the running board, driver's door open, waving her arm. The top half of her torso was visible above the SUV's roof.

"Flint! Over here!" she yelled again.

Horns were honking behind her SUV encouraging her to get back in the vehicle and move, although she couldn't go more than a few inches due to the vehicle ahead. Angry shouts added to the cacophony.

One guy a few vehicles back climbed out of his pickup and marched toward her as if he might physically relocate her if she didn't get moving. The visual made Flint grin.

"I'd like to see you try that, buddy," he murmured under his breath as he waved his arm toward the woman and hustled between the barely moving vehicles to reach Scarlett.

Once she realized he'd seen her, she slid behind the wheel and settled in with one foot on the accelerator and the other on the brake. The pickup dude was still coming.

Flint tossed his bag in the backseat and jumped into the front, with barely enough time to close the door again before Scarlett auto-locked all the doors, lifted her foot off the brake, and let the big SUV roll forward.

Flint glanced at the pickup dude in the side mirror. He shook his fist and blew out a stream of curses before he gave up, turned on his heel, and stomped back to his truck.

"That guy isn't going to be bringing you roses anytime soon," Flint teased.

"You're welcome. Sorry I'm late. Had to drop Maddy off. Happy to be your personal car service. Anytime,"

Scarlett replied sarcastically as she flashed a scowl toward him.

Flint laughed. “Aw, you missed me. And you’re just as sweet as ever.”

“I don’t know how Drake puts up with you,” Scarlett said, shaking her head with a grin.

“Yeah, me neither,” Flint replied. “Where is he anyway?”

“Helping a friend out with something or other.” Scarlett shrugged as she inched the SUV closer to the airport exit. “Gaspar went with him up to Orlando as a favor. It’s not a case on our books.”

Flint cocked his head. “Nice of Gaspar to help out. I thought he wasn’t doing fieldwork these days.”

"He's not. Not on a regular basis, anyway. He's got special skills. We need him in front of a computer screen. We've already got plenty of muscle on the payroll," Scarlett said. "Before you ask, I didn't approve the excursion because Gaspar didn't ask me."

Flint grinned. "Guess he's got a mind of his own, eh?"

"Wouldn't be any good to me if he didn't." Scarlett had finally reached the end of the traffic bottleneck and goosing the big SUV's engine to enter the expressway.

When she got up to speed and merged into traffic, Flint said, "Where are we going?"

"A place called Frazier's. They've got a contract with the state to handle cremations for certain classes of decedents," Scarlett explained from behind her oversize sunglasses. She drove expertly and Flint was perfectly comfortable with her behind the wheel.

"I gather indigents who are being exhumed whose families have no money for burial is one of the classes Frazier's has a contract to handle," Flint said.

"Precisely."

"So Marilyn Baker has no living relatives, then?"

Scarlett gave him a look that he couldn't read from behind her dark glasses. "Aside from you, you mean?"

"I guess. Yeah. If we're related. We don't know that yet," Flint replied.

"Easy enough to find out. Wouldn't take that long either," Scarlett said reasonably.

"Right. Are they holding the body?"

"I called in a couple of favors. So they'll hold it a little longer. At least until we get there and tell them what to do," Scarlett said, slowing as they approached the exit.

"Did you get a court order?"

"Didn't need to." She shook her head. "As long as we don't tell Baz Shaw, we shouldn't have to worry about permission here."

By tacit agreement, they rarely discussed Sebastian Shaw. Mostly because he was one of Scarlett's biggest clients and Flint was not Shaw's biggest fan. Shaw had zero control over what Flint did or didn't do. There were no circumstances under which Flint would ask Shaw's permission for anything.

Flint frowned and said nothing. He was a belt and suspenders guy. He'd have felt better with a court order requiring Frazier's to hold the body until he figured out what he wanted to do with it.

"Look, this is totally your call. But why did you come back here if you have zero interest in Marilyn Baker?" Scarlett asked. "Don't you want to know? The woman is dead. She has no family. No one is going to interfere with your precious independence. There's no downside here, Flint. Not that I can see."

"That's where you're wrong," Flint replied. "If I know she's my mother, I'll want to know other things."

"Like what? Like who murdered her? Why they did it?"

Flint inhaled deeply and added, "Like who was my father, and did he kill her?"

# Chapter 13

**Orlando**

Uncomfortably warm in the Orlando sunlight, Gaspar rested his forearms on his thighs and leaned forward. "This is a delicate situation, Ms. Brady."

"Call me Margo. Everyone does." She tilted her head, rounded her lips, and popped out three quick smoke rings. The gentle breeze pushed the rings out of shape as it lifted them toward the afternoon sun.

"Margo, Greta Reed's sister is Hanna Campbell. She was unable to reach out to her sister until recently. She didn't know Greta had died. As you can imagine, she's bewildered and distraught and looking for answers," Gaspar said. "We're hoping you can help us give her some closure."

Gaspar hated asking witnesses and family members to help with closure. In his experience, and he'd had way more than most, closure was a myth.

Survivors moved on, sure. Life kept going whether they wanted it to or not. But he'd learned long ago that people get through grief, not over it. The years make grief bearable as the loss is pushed deeper into history. But closure was just a word people used. What did that even mean?

Margo narrowed her eyes against the rising cigarette smoke. “Not sure how I can help. Like I said, I didn’t know Greta had a sister.”

“You two weren’t close, then?” Drake asked.

“We were. I mean, Greta was relatively new here. She moved to Orlando after her first husband died in a car crash. She wanted to get away from the things that reminded her of him, she said.”

“She’d been married before?”

“Yeah, about a year or so. She moved to Orlando for a fresh start and a new job. Then a few months later, she married Phillip Reed.” Margo’s eyes narrowed against the irritating smoke. She already had more wrinkles than a woman her age should have. “He was a transplant surgeon from Atlanta. A great one, by all accounts. The only thing bigger than his reputation was his ego. He was overwhelming. Greta was overwhelmed by him, I think.”

“Why do you say that?” Gaspar asked.

“Greta was fragile. She’d had a lot of tragedy in her life. Her mother was killed by a drunk driver. Then her husband died in another car crash. She was spooked. Nervous about everything,” Margo said. “She felt more comfortable being with Phillip than looking for another man, I guess.”

“Why?”

“He was familiar. They’d dated in high school or something,” Margo explained, talking around the cigarette she still held between her lips.

Gaspar nodded. “Where did they live?”

“A gated community north of town. On a golf course. They both liked to play golf. Phillip traveled a lot and Greta liked the security. We run into some scary people in this job, and she was still a little terrified of everything and everyone,” Margo said, stubbing out the butt in the ashtray. “I can give you the address. But the house went into foreclosure when Greta and Phillip died. It’s been sold. Someone else lives there now.”

"Tell us about the boating accident. What happened there?" Gaspar asked, sensing that she was about to bolt.

"It was all over the local news. We did a segment on it, too. You can find the video online, I'm sure." Margo shrugged. "Supposed to be some sort of romantic getaway. Phillip rented the boat. Neither one of them knew how to sail, but they thought it would be fun to try. Didn't work out that way, though."

"What happened?" Gaspar asked again. He'd read the news accounts online. But there was always more to every story.

Margo cocked her head as if she were thinking about what to say.

She reached into her pocket for the cigarettes, drew another into her mouth, and used the butane to light up.

When she had the smoke going again, she said, "Like I mentioned, the boat was rented. Later, we learned that it wasn't in great shape."

"In what way?"

"Just old and not well maintained. It was a sailboat, but it had an old motor, too. It was way under powered. When the surprise squall popped up, the winds blew the boat too far out. When it capsized, they simply couldn't get back to shore, I guess."

"Was the boat equipped with life vests?"

"According to the boat's owner, there were life vests aboard. Nobody can say whether Greta and Phillip were wearing vests when the boat went down," Margo said, finishing the cigarette and stubbing the butt into the ashtray again, joining a dozen others exactly like it.

"So a tragic accident, then," Gaspar said. "No foul play suspected."

Margo shook her head. "None as far as I know. I suppose if the bodies ever turn up, they may find something to suggest otherwise. But after all this time, that's not likely."

"Where did they find the boat?"

"South of Sarasota. And quite a long way out into the Gulf, too. You can ask the FWC. They'll have reports and you can talk to the agents who handled the case."

"FWC?" Drake asked.

"Florida Fish and Wildlife Conservation Commission," Gaspar explained. "Do you know the officer's name?"

Margo shook her head. "Sorry. I didn't talk to him, and I don't remember. If we didn't include his name in the original report, I'd start with the PIO. Public Information Officer."

"You said the Reeds' house was sold. I presume that means there was a probate proceeding," Gaspar said. "Did Greta leave a will?"

"I'm not sure. Probably." She shrugged. "I mean, both her mother and her first husband died and she inherited. So she'd know how important it is to have a will. Is that what this is about? Someone wants Greta's money?"

"Did Greta have any other friends around here we can talk to?" Drake asked.

A few moments passed. Margo stood up. "You could try the homeowners association at Turtle Creek. She lived there awhile, and I think she might have been on the board. One of the other board members might know more. Anyway, I need to get back to work."

"Can we follow up with you if we need to?" Gaspar asked, handing her a business card.

She gave him a quizzical look, but she took the card and shoved it into the back pocket of her jeans. "Sure. I guess. But I don't know any more than what I've already told you."

"One more thing. If Hanna was your friend, what would you want us to tell her about Greta?" Drake asked.

Margo seemed to think about the question for a bit before she said, "I'd tell her to move on with her life. Greta's never coming back."

Gaspar replied, "But what if she's not dead? Anybody in Greta's life who might be unhappy about that?"

"Not dead? They don't declare people lost at sea if there's any chance they might still be alive." Margo stared at him and cocked her head. "You sound like a bad movie. Are you asking if she had any enemies who might want her dead? That's more than a little crazy."

"So the answer would be no, then?" Gaspar pushed. "No one who might benefit from Greta's death? Nobody waiting in the wings to collect her estate?"

Margo gave him a hard glare. "Other than some woman I've never heard of claiming to be Greta's long-lost sister, you mean?"

# Chapter 14

Gaspar and Drake watched Margo as she strode toward the entrance, went inside, and disappeared. Then they headed back along the sidewalk to the parking lot and the SUV.

"That's a valid point," Gaspar said when Drake didn't bring it up.

"About Hanna, you mean?"

"Yeah." Gaspar climbed into the front seat.

"Except I know more of the story than Margo does," Drake replied. "Hanna's not that kind of girl. She wouldn't pounce on Greta's estate for money."

"Why not? If she's the only heir, she'd be entitled to it. If someone doesn't claim the estate, the money goes to the State of Florida," Gaspar explained. "What would be the point of that?"

Drake shrugged. "I guess."

"Beyond that, if there's an estate, Hanna could pay Scarlett to investigate Greta's death. Maybe she'd want to do that. Put some resources into the search. Find out for sure what happened to her sister," Gaspar suggested.

Drake nodded, thinking about the idea. "Maybe."

Gaspar glanced at the clock. "Let's detour to Turtle Creek Reserve. The gated community where Greta lived. We've got time to take a look at the place before we head back."

"You think if it's a nice place, there's likely to be some money somewhere." Drake nodded. "Makes sense."

"Transplant surgeons make a nice living. Even if the house was foreclosed for nonpayment of the mortgage, Florida real estate prices have been booming for several years. The bank could have sold the house for a profit above the mortgage debt. In which case, there could be some money left," Gaspar explained. "There was probably a probate proceeding, too. The court file would contain a list of assets. It's worth looking into, at the very least."

"Okay," Drake replied. "Find Turtle Creek Reserve in the nav system and let's see where it is. No harm in checking it out. Since we're here. Maybe we can learn something to help Hanna."

Gaspar found the address and hit the go button. "Fifteen miles from here. Keep north on the state road and then we'll wind around a bit. Looks like it's a golf course community with a special conservation classification of some sort. Probably means they get special tax advantages."

"What do you know about that Florida commission Margo mentioned? The one that investigated the boating accident. They should know more about what happened," Drake said.

“Possibly. But boating accidents are not rare in Florida. I grew up here. We’ve had about sixty boating fatalities every year for as long as I can remember. Some years, more.”

Drake gave Gaspar a quick glance. “What’s up with that? Are people just bad boaters or what?”

“Mostly. Accidents on the water happen fast. Usual cause of death is drowning. People don’t wear their life jackets, and a surprising number of them can’t swim,” Gaspar said. “Could Greta and her husband swim?”

Drake shook his head. “I don’t know. We can ask Hanna.”

The navigation had been leading them northwest through a series of turns for the past ten miles. Up ahead on the right was a large, landscaped area surrounding a guardhouse dividing two lanes of traffic.

The elaborate sign out front and the navigation's computerized voice announced their arrival at Turtle Creek Reserve's entrance gate.

A swing arm blocked the entrance and another blocked the exit on the other side of the guardhouse. Drake pulled up behind a car stopped at the entrance where the driver and the gate agent were arguing.

The gate agent gestured that the driver should reverse away from the gate. The driver shook his fist in response.

"Wonder what this is about," Gaspar mused.

Drake lowered his window and the angry voices carried. The driver demanded entry. When the agent told him to go away, the driver refused.

The guard pulled out his phone and made a call, shouting a voice command. "Turtle Creek Reserve Security."

"This is Security. How can we help?" the dispatcher asked through the phone's speaker.

"Front gate security here. A belligerent male is threatening to break through the gate and into the Reserve. He refuses to stand down. Requesting assistance."

"On the way," the dispatcher replied. "Two minutes out."

The guard lifted the phone and snapped a picture of the driver, although CCTV cameras mounted on the corner of the gatehouse were aimed directly toward arriving vehicles and should have captured reliable video of the incident.

After the guard made the call, the driver of the car screamed obscenities, flipped him off, and mashed the accelerator.

The car jumped forward and slammed through the gate arm, breaking it off near the post.

The driver sped into the residential neighborhood and careened around the first corner.

“What the hell?” Drake said, moving the SUV up to the guard shack. “Need help?”

The guard was a man about sixty with a paunch and a red face and a name badge identifying him as Harris.

Harris said, “Hell yes! Stop that little prick. I’m calling the police right now.”

“We’ll see if we can find him,” Drake said, moving the SUV forward as Harris raised his phone and yelled into the microphone, “Call 911!”

Gaspar fastened his seat belt and Drake pursued. He sped toward the car, which was about twenty yards ahead, narrowing the gap.

The driver took the curves fast and the straightaways faster. Drake, in hot pursuit, downshifted the SUV for more traction.

The driver swerved to miss two couples in golf carts up ahead. The golf cart drivers laid on their tinny horns, but the speeding car kept going.

When the driver reached the turn leading to the golf course, he went in the opposite direction. He headed toward the pickleball courts across the road.

In the parking lot near the courts, he jammed the brakes. The car stopped hard, just short of a high curb that would have taken out his front bumper and maybe his front axle.

He killed the engine, opened the door, and jumped out of the vehicle, running fast toward the pickleball courts.

Drake parked and gave chase.

The car's driver was a wiry little man. Maybe five six. Thin and agile. Drake was a bigger guy. Longer legs. And he was in good shape. His stride covered twice the distance and he soon made up the lost ground.

Gaspar slid out of the SUV and waited for Drake to overtake the jerk.

The car's driver had reached the pickleball courts when Drake caught up to him. He'd been a football player in high school, and he remembered how to tackle. He jumped forward and landed on the driver, taking him down, while the guy kicked and yelled and tried to bite his way out.

Drake put a big palm on the side of the guy's head and mashed him to the grass, pinning his arms to the ground. The guy's legs were kicking at Drake's knees, but he couldn't reach them or do any real damage.

Gaspar walked up behind them, pulled his weapon, and showed it to the wiry dude on the ground. "Keep it up and I'll be justified," he growled.

"Get off me! Let me up!" the guy yelled between Drake's splayed fingers, still trying to get away.

"Just calm down. Cops are coming. Nobody needs to get hurt here," Drake said forcefully. "What's your problem?"

"What the hell do you care? Get off me!"

Gaspar replied lazily, "Let him up. Maybe he'll run again. I can hit a moving target nine times out of ten."

"I've seen you shoot. You're more like ten out of ten." Drake grunted and shoved the guy's head farther into the sod. "That what you want, buddy? To test my friend's aim?"

The front gate guard, Harris, pulled up in a golf cart and stomped over. He set his feet apart and rested his hands on his utility belt.

"Police will be here any minute, Jeffers. Stay put," he growled toward the guy on the ground. He turned to Drake and Gaspar. "Thanks for the assist with this little twerp."

Drake released his hold on Jeffers's head. He had Jeffers pinned to the ground with his knee. "Should I let him get up?"

Harris shook his head. "Not yet. No point in chasing him again. This is the third time this week he's busted in here looking for his girlfriend. She's got a restraining order against him, but he don't care."

Harris tapped Jeffers lightly with the side of his boot. "Ain't that right, Jeffers?"

"Let me up, Harris. This is none of your business," Jeffers growled.

"Stalking's a crime, Jeffers. As you well know," Harris replied.

Drake kept his knee on Jeffers's back with just enough pressure to hold him.

The police arrived. Two officers joined the tableau in full view of the pickleball players and other local residents.

Harris gave one officer the details while Drake moved aside and the second officer escorted Jeffers to the squad and put him in the backseat.

The second officer came back. He asked Drake and Gaspar for brief statements and contact information.

Gaspar handed over his business card. Drake supplied his full name and phone number.

About twenty minutes later, the police car left, the pickleball players went back to their game, and the gawkers returned to whatever they'd been doing before.

Harris came over to thank them again and asked, "What were you guys coming into the community for, anyway?"

Gaspar gave Harris their names, handed him a card and replied, "We're private investigators working for the sister of a woman who lived here a few years ago. Thought maybe we could talk to the neighbors. Try to figure out where the sister and her husband moved to."

"We have a stable community here, on the whole. Not many transients. I've been working security at the front gate for about ten years. Who are you looking for? I probably knew them," Harris volunteered.

"Greta Campbell Reed is the woman we're trying to find. We're working for her sister, Hanna," Drake replied.

Harris nodded solemnly. "I knew Greta. Her husband, too. Phillip Reed. He was a doctor. Good people. The whole community was upset when they died in that boating accident. Couldn't believe it, really."

Drake and Gaspar said nothing.

"I didn't know Greta had a sister, though. The house was sold. New couple lives there now. But they're on vacation," Harris said thoughtfully, as if he were dredging it up from memory. "I don't think they'd be much help to you. They moved here from California. Couple of lawyers, I think. Greta probably never met the Kings."

"What about the other neighbors?" Gaspar asked. "Any of them particularly close to Greta or Phillip?"

Harris cocked his head as if he were thinking deeply about the question. "Maybe. Phillip traveled a lot. But Greta was pretty active here. Maybe check with the president of the HOA. Let me give you her contact information."

He reached into his pocket for his phone and pulled it up. He handed the phone to Drake, who texted the information to himself.

"I gotta get back to the front gate," Harris said, jerking his thumb over his shoulder in that general direction. "You guys want me to get you added to the visitors' log so you can look around and talk to people while you're here?"

Gaspar replied, "We've run out of time for today."

"Yeah, long drive back to Miami," Drake said. "We'll just take a quick pass by the former Reed house now. We'll call ahead next time."

"Okay. You'll let me know if we can help," Harris said before he returned to his golf cart.

Drake and Gaspar watched him drive toward the front gate as they climbed into the SUV. The nav system talked them through the winding streets to the house on Hummingbird Lane where Dr. and Mrs. Reed had last lived.

"Nice place," Drake said, slowing as they passed a large stucco home with a terra-cotta tile roof.

"There must be thousands of homes just like this all over Florida," Gaspar replied. "Relatively new construction. About four thousand square feet. Large lot. Manicured lawn. Pool and lanai in the back."

Drake grinned. “Everything’s bigger in Texas.”

“So I’ve heard,” Gaspar replied.

The garage doors were closed and there were no lights on inside. Similar houses on all sides and across the street were occupied, so there could be plenty of good intel behind those suburban doors. Neighbors always knew more than they should.

“Sorry, Drake. But I’ve got to get back,” Gaspar said, hitting the reverse route button on the nav system. “There’s nothing more for us to do here anyway.”

“Yeah, I guess Flint’s back from Italy, too. He’s texted me several times already," Drake replied, as he headed for the southbound turnpike.

"But would you work your magic on Greta's digital life and see if you can find anything else I can try to track down?" Drake glanced across the console toward Gaspar. "Hanna's a good kid. I'd like to know I did everything I could to help her before I give up, you know?"

"Probably makes sense to investigate Greta's husband, too," Gaspar replied, nodding. "Transplant surgeons shouldn't be hard to track. We can get some background on him, anyway. Give you a place to start."

# Chapter 15

### Houston

Flint stared straight through the windshield without really watching the road ahead. He was a little surprised to feel a tightness in his chest as he thought about Scarlett's question. What the hell was he doing here, anyway?

Until a few months ago, he'd have said he had zero interest in finding his birth parents. Even now he wasn't sure he cared.

Flint had no idea who his father was. Not really. He had his suspicions. Nothing more.

But his suspicions alone were more than enough. There were advantages to being an orphan. As an adult, anyway. The freedom from family drama was a definite asset.

He could choose and create his own family if he ever felt the need for one. Which, quite honestly, he hadn't. Not yet anyway. Maybe if he met the right woman, he'd feel differently someday.

Scarlett slowed the big SUV and made a right turn onto a well-traveled street in an older industrial area. Probably first constructed in the 1950s, he guessed, given the lack of style and the exterior conditions. Cracked pavement, rusty fences, flat roofs.

Several of the buildings along this street had big smokestacks probably grandfathered into current environmental laws, given the amount of smoke they spewed into the air.

Scarlett followed the navigation system's directions to an old concrete block building surrounded by an eight-foot rusty chain-link fence.

A faded sign posted at the gate said FRAZIER'S. Nothing else. Not even a phone number. Flint guessed mostly service trucks of one kind or another passed through this way. Deliveries and removals probably.

There was nothing remotely comforting about the place. Flint guessed that grieving relatives never came here. This was where the business of cremation occurred when families couldn't bear to watch, and the dead were long past caring.

Scarlett pulled into the drive and waited at the gate.

Someone inside must have pressed a button, or maybe there was an electronic trigger. Either way, the gate slowly slid open all the way across the driveway and clanged to a stop.

When the opening was wide enough, Scarlett rolled through.

Flint waited until she'd pulled into one of the half-dozen empty spaces out front. She slid the transmission into park.

“Want me to come in with you?” she asked. “Or I can wait here. Whatever you want.”

“You can come in. This is not some big emotional journey. We won’t be taking a coffin with us now,” Flint replied as he opened the door and stepped out onto the pulsing hot tarmac.

Scarlett shut the engine down and followed. At the front entrance, he opened the door and they stepped into weakly cooled air. He imagined the heat from the ovens in the back made cooling the place impossible during Houston’s oppressively muggy summers.

Flint scanned the lobby quickly. There was money to be made in the funeral business, but Frazier's didn't seem to be anywhere near the top of the revenue chain.

The small room was ten-by-ten and matched the age and practical design of the building's exterior. The cheap tile on the floor was cracked and yellowed. Faded paneling halfway up the walls. The top half was cement block painted gray which had probably been white when it was applied sometime last century.

An abandoned metal desk and a metal chair with cracked green vinyl padding on the seat occupied one corner of the room. Both were probably bought cheaply from government surplus at least two dozen years ago. Maybe longer.

"This place looks cheerful," Scarlett deadpanned, pushing her sunglasses onto her head. "Good thing their customers can't complain."

Flint grinned at the gallows humor but said nothing.

The doorway to the back of the building opened. A stout man with a fringe of red hair running around his head from ear to ear and a full red beard came through, wiping first his head and then his hands with a brown paper towel.

"How can I help you folks?" he asked with a Louisiana accent. Houston wasn't far from New Orleans, so the accent wasn't uncommon around here.

Scarlett said, "We understand you're holding a body for us. The decedent's name is Marilyn Baker. Her remains were exhumed as part of the Mount Warren Interstate bypass project."

"Yeah, that's right." The man stuffed the soggy paper towel ball into his pocket and pulled a clipboard out of the top desk drawer.

He ran his finger down the page, flipped to the next page, and then the next, and finally stopped about halfway down.

"Marilyn Baker. Found it." He looked up, still holding his place on the page. "Are you wanting to have the remains interred somewhere? We don't do that work here. You'll need to get yourselves a mortician to arrange everything for you with the cemetery."

"We'd like to see her," Flint said before Scarlett could reply.

The man looked uncomfortable and stammered slightly when he said, "If I'm honest, there's not really anything you'd want to see. The body had been down there a long time. More than thirty years, according to the plot map. Mostly, she's just bones now."

"We understand but we'd like to see her," Flint said again, nodding. "What's your name?"

"Nick. And we can't take you in the back. State law," he said, looking down, beads of sweat popping out on his bald head.

“Bring her out here, then, Nick,” Flint replied. “We’ll wait.”

“Look, I’ll be honest. What we have is a cardboard box with some bones and a bit of dirt. The coffin was just a pine box and it deteriorated to nothing, so we left it out there,” Nick said apologetically, refusing to meet Flint’s gaze.

“Yeah, that’s about what we expected. Can you just give me the box? I’ll sign for it,” Flint replied.

Nick looked up, eyes wide. “No. I mean, we can’t do that. We’d lose our license.”

"Look, Nick"—Scarlett moved closer and lowered her voice—"we promise we'd never tell."

"No. I'm sorry. Can't do it." He shook his head. "But I can put a hold on her cremation for you while you get a court order. Would that help?"

"Not much. But if that's the best you can do." Flint shrugged when Nick shook his head vigorously. "I'd still like to see the remains before we leave."

"Okay, you wait here—"

"Nope," Flint said, shaking his head. "I want to see how you've complied with chain of custody. I'm only interested in Marilyn Baker's remains. I need to be sure that what you have is really her."

"All I can say is that the remains were delivered here in a box with a metal ID tag saying it's Marilyn Baker. I can't vouch for what happened before the remains reached our receiving dock," Nick said, aggrieved. "These days, families can have DNA testing done on the deceased before and after cremation to be sure we've returned the correct body. But that's a relatively new thing. You could do it now, though. On Ms. Baker's bones and teeth."

"Right. That's the plan," Flint said. "Show me."

"Okay. But don't touch anything. Follow me," he said, opening the door and slipping through to the main part of the building where it was hotter and louder than the small lobby.

The bulk of the open space was occupied by three large industrial furnaces currently in operation. There were shelves on either side of each furnace.

On one side, shelves were stocked with coffins in various states of decomposition. On the other side, the shelves stocked uniformly sized, white cardboard boxes, about nine inches by six inches by four inches.

Flint imagined that the small boxes held about three to nine pounds of mostly bone fragments swept from the chamber after the cremation was completed.

The ashes would be put into an urn and returned to the families.

“How long does the cremation take?” Scarlett asked.

“Usually about three hours, give or take,” he replied. “Depends on the size of the body and how hot the chamber is. We usually run at eighteen hundred degrees, which is a couple hundred less than the max recommended.”

“What’s the rest of the process?” Scarlett asked.

“We wait until the body cools afterward. Then we remove any metal from the ashes and put them into those boxes.” Nick nodded toward the shelves. “Then we return them to the funeral home where they're put into the urn the family selected."

"What will you do with Marilyn Baker's ashes since she has no family to return them to?" Scarlett asked.

"We bury the ashes in a mass grave if no one claims them," Nick explained solemnly.

He'd reached the shelves on the left side of one of the big furnaces. Checking his clipboard, he put his dusty finger on the case number. Then he moved to one of the bottom shelves and squatted down to run his hand across the square boxes until he found the one he wanted.

Nick checked the number on the clipboard and compared it to the label again. Then he looked up at Flint. “This box is the remains of Marilyn Baker.”

Flint knelt down and grabbed the box. He lifted it and paced to a nearby table, where he set the box carefully. Then he pulled out his phone and snapped photos of all sides, taking special care with shots of the seals and labels.

Flint glanced toward Scarlett.

She moved closer to Nick and lowered her voice, putting an arm around his shoulders and turning him away from Flint. “Nick, we think Marilyn Baker may be my friend’s mother.”

“Really?”

Scarlett lowered her voice further and Nick leaned his head down to hear. “To know for sure, we plan to test the DNA, like you said.”

“That would be best.”

“But we really need to take this box.”

Nick nodded. “I’d love to give it to you. I just can’t.”

“Are you sure there’s nothing you can do to help us out?” Her husky voice was seductive and intentionally flirty.

“I’m really sorry,” Nick replied sincerely.

Scarlett looked toward Flint. He moved the box back to its place on the shelves.

She shrugged. "Okay, Nick. We'll get a court order and come back."

"Courts are kinda slow." Nick offered Flint an apologetic nod again. "I'll hold the remains for a couple of days. Give you a little time. That's the best I can do."

"That's good of you." Flint extended his hand and shook on the deal.

"I appreciate your understanding, Mr. Flint," Nick said, leading the way back to the lobby, where he stood until his phone rang just before they left the building.

When he picked up, he said, "Frazier's."

He listened for a moment and then replied, "Yes, Mr. Flint's here now.

Did you want to speak with him?" He looked puzzled as he shifted the phone away from his ear.

"Who was on the phone?" Flint asked.

Nick shook his head.

"What did he want?"

"He didn't say." Nick shrugged as he replaced the receiver with a frown. "He said he was calling about Marilyn Baker. When I said you were here, he hung up."

Flint handed Nick a business card. "If he calls back, please give him my number."

"Sure." Nick slipped the card into his shirt pocket. He flipped a switch to open the big gate. “If he comes in with a court order before you do, I’ll be required to release the remains to him.”

Flint replied, “I understand. No problem. Thanks again for your help.”

Outside, Flint turned to Scarlett. “Did you tell anyone we were coming here or why?”

“Nope.” She shook her head.

“What the hell was that about, then?” Flint asked.

“I thought you didn’t care about Marilyn Baker’s remains.” Scarlett shrugged and punched the key fob. “Change your mind?”

“Not at all,” Flint replied. “But I’d like to know who’s taking an interest in Marilyn Baker after all these years besides me.”

“I’ll check the phone records. Find out who made that call.”

“Thanks.”

The SUV gave a chirp as the doors unlocked. They climbed aboard and she started the engine and headed toward the exit.

“Did you get what you wanted back there?” she asked as she turned from the driveway onto the road.

“A couple of small bones. The label was easy to peel and replace. He won’t even notice they’re missing,” Flint replied. “Forget the court order.”

"You're sure?"

"One thousand percent." Flint kneaded his forehead. "Last thing I want is a searchable public record."

Scarlett gave him a side-eye. "Headache?"

"I banged my head when I was leaving Hedinger's château. Probably a slight concussion. Nothing serious," Flint replied.

"How's your vision?"

"Good enough."

"We need every one of the gray cells you have left in your big head." Her tone brooked no argument. "Call Drake. He'll drive you around for a few days."

Flint scowled. "I tried, remember? He didn't show up. That's how you got the job today."

Scarlett maneuvered the SUV expertly through the streets of Houston and pulled up into Flint's driveway. "You planning to go anywhere else right now?"

"Not until I get some sleep," he replied as he opened the SUV's passenger door and stepped out. He retrieved his bag from the back.

"I'll send Drake over," Scarlett said before he escaped. "Who's gonna dog sit for us if you pass out behind the wheel and crash before we leave for Disney? Maddy would never forgive you."

"Yeah, yeah." Flint flashed a mock scowl in her direction, and she flashed a grin in return.

He gave up the fight. Years of familiarity with Scarlett's bullheaded behavior informed his choice.

The only way to deal with her was to nod and smile and then do whatever the hell he wanted once she drove away.

Which, of course, she was absolutely expecting.

He smiled as he let himself into the house, dragging his weary ass to bed. Where he hoped to sleep for twelve hours straight.

# Chapter 16

Flint felt worse than he'd let on. He'd been experiencing several of the classic concussion symptoms for the past few days. He'd had concussions before. The situation would correct itself in a week or two.

He'd expected to wait out the concussion symptoms while sunbathing on the yacht. Now that he'd returned to Houston, where Scarlett watched him like a hawk, his head injury would be more difficult to conceal.

He took a handful of painkillers and flopped down on his bed fully clothed.

Next thing he heard, sometime the next day, was Drake's fist pounding on his bedroom door like an amateur drummer practicing a military tattoo. The cadence matched the pounding inside his head.

Flint rolled over and opened one eye. "What do you want?"

Drake's fit body filled the open doorway. He leaned against the doorjamb. "Thought you might be hungry."

Flint was hungry, but the mere thought of food made him nauseous. Which reminded him that somewhere over Appalachia on the plane, he'd vomited his breakfast hours ago.

Not something he wanted Drake or Scarlett to know, so he said, “Sure. Can I get a shower first?”

Drake hung around while Flint showered and dressed. They met up in the kitchen, where Drake had plopped a couple of sodas in paper cups and takeout bags from the local barbecue place they both loved.

Flint leaned his back against the kitchen counter across from the table, watching Drake dig into the big bag of sandwiches and fries. The smell of pork fat and spicy sweet sauce roiled his stomach even from a distance.

He reached for the soda and took a couple of sips. “Aside from this half-assed apology, what’s up with you?”

Drake grinned, showing a mouthful of sandwich. “Ain’t nothin’ half-assed about it. This is the best barbecue in Houston right here.”

Flint nodded. “True. But tell me why you ghosted me at the airport and forced me to deal with Scarlett along with the jet lag.”

A troubled look settled itself on Drake’s face. He swallowed the bite of his sandwich and washed it down with soda, then cleared his throat like he was trying to decide what to say and how. Which he probably was.

“Okay, so, while you were gone, I got a call from Hanna Campbell,” Drake began.

“Hanna Campbell? The smokin’-hot wild child you had that massive crush on in college?" Flint teased. "The one who left the country just to avoid you after you graduated? Didn't fancy herself dating a Marine. That Hanna Campbell?"

"I'm not sure that's quite fair, but yeah. The very same." Drake blushed and ducked his head to hide the grin.

"What's not fair about it?" Flint asked, sipping the soda to calm his queasy stomach before he tried the french fries.

"Her mother died. Killed by a drunk driver. Kinda threw her sideways," Drake replied, returning to his half-eaten sandwich. "Then she had a big fight with her older sister about the mother's estate. Lots of family drama. Remember that?"

"I didn't remember that, actually." Flint shook his head as he pulled the chair out and sat across from Drake. "It's been a minute. Lots of water over the dam since then for both of us."

"You got that right. For Hanna, too." Drake balled up the waxed paper and traded it for another sandwich from the bag. "She got herself into one of those really bad situations that no kid ever thinks is going to happen. Until it does. And then it's a thousand times worse than they imagined it could be."

Drake's eyes were filled with genuine concern for the girl. Maybe she'd been the one that got away for him.

But that was light-years ago.

There had been a parade of women through Drake's life since then. Flint's, too, for that matter. Hell, the only woman Flint could remember from back then was Scarlett.

Sensing Drake's story might bog down way too long, Flint asked, "Is the whole sordid backstory relevant to whatever Hanna's problem is now?"

Drake had polished off another sandwich, which made Flint turn a bit green. "I don't think so. I mean, there's no reason to believe that Hanna had anything to do with her sister's death."

"Hang on." Flint held up his hand. His headache hadn't subsided, and he was having trouble following. "Sorry.

Hanna's sister died, too? Another drunk driver?"

"No. Boating accident, they say," Drake replied, shaking his head. "She and her husband were sailing off the coast of Florida when a squall came up and the boat capsized, I guess. The bodies were never found."

"Okay. Well, it happens," Flint said. "We've dealt with our share of people lost at sea over the years. I gather Hanna inherits?"

"Maybe." Drake shrugged. "We never got that far in the conversation. Hanna doesn't know if her sister had kids or a will or anything like that. She's trying to find all of that out now."

Flint frowned and tried one of the cold fries. He forced it down with the soda and didn't pick up another. "You're no kind of estate expert."

"Right. I'm not even an investigator, obviously," Drake said. "You are, though. The best investigator I know. The situation is confounding. And you're between clients at the moment. Thought we could help Hanna."

"Help Hanna with what, exactly?" Flint's foggy brain struggled to pay attention.

He swallowed a hard gulp of soda to keep the bile in his belly where it belonged. He was losing the fight.

He stood abruptly, turned, and vomited into the sink. Not much in his stomach, so the spasm didn't last long. He rinsed his mouth with water and slumped back into his chair.

Drake had cocked his head, watching the situation unfold. "What is it? Flu? Worse?"

"Concussion. Not too serious. I'm improving daily. Just have to wait it out, the doc said," Flint replied. "But for the love of God, don't tell Scarlett. Please. She'll have me whisked to the ICU at Houston Methodist by helo and tied to the bed."

"I'll keep your secret from Scarlett only if you agree to help Hanna." Drake grinned and palmed his phone off the tabletop. “Otherwise, I’m calling the dragon lady right now.”

Flint glared. “Don’t touch that phone.”

Drake hit the number on his screen assigned to Scarlett. Her photo came up on the screen as the phone began to dial. Drake put the sound on speaker.

In Flint’s head, the ringtones came through too loud and fuzzy and combined with the ringing in his ears. He reached over and missed three times before he punched the disconnect button.

Drake raised his eyebrows and poised his finger above the redial button.

"Not sure I'll be much help to you for the next few days," Flint said.

"Which means you can't take on any other clients right now, anyway. I like our chances even with a brain-damaged Flint." Drake took a big chomp of his third sandwich. "Even at twenty-five percent capacity, you're better than all the rest of us."

"Flattery will get you everywhere." Flint scowled as he teased. "But for your own well-being, don't let Scarlett hear you say that."

Drake laughed. "Hell, she'll be glad to have you out of her way for a while."

"Okay. I'm in for whatever this is, I guess. Under protest." Flint sighed and ran his palm over his face. Wearily, he said, “Gaspar was helping you out, right? He’s the best Scarlett’s got on her payroll at what he does. Didn’t he find out anything we can use to help Hanna with whatever this is?”

“Yeah. Actually, he did.” Drake glanced at the clock. He swallowed and sipped before he said, “Hanna will be here in a minute. Then we’re all set up to talk to Gaspar in the den. We can keep the lights dimmed for your eyes. Come on.”

# Chapter 17

In the den, Flint fell hard into his recliner, put his feet up and his head back, and closed his eyes. Drake moved around finishing his setup for the videoconference with Gaspar.

When the doorbell rang, he said, "That's Hanna now. She's staying at a local hotel. I told her to take a taxi."

Flint could hear the hum of quiet conversation moving closer as Drake entered the dimly lit room. He must have been giving Hanna the unvarnished truth about Flint's physical condition because she entered quietly and didn't try to approach him.

"Hanna, this is Michael Flint," Drake said with his hands shoved into the pockets of his jeans.

"Hi, Michael. I'm Hanna Campbell. Thank you for agreeing to help me." Her voice was quiet but strong and firm at the same time.

Flint glanced toward the young woman, who looked nothing like he'd expected. She was petite. Short wavy brown hair. Enormous brown eyes.

She was a few years younger than Drake, so maybe thirty, give or take a couple of years either way. Wearing a sleeveless blue dress that landed just above her knees and canvas flats.

In the dim lighting he couldn't see her complexion well, but she looked pale even from across the room. Her gait was unsteady, and she clasped her hands together as if they might wander away when she released her grip.

"Have a seat, Hanna. I'm not antisocial, but I've got a wicked headache. Drake's videoconference will start here in a minute. He'll get you a drink if you'd like," Flint said, closing his eyes against the pulsing glare of the oversize television mounted on the wall.

"Just water, please," she said. "And I can get it myself."

Drake pointed her toward the kitchen. She returned a few minutes later with three water bottles and passed them out. Flint's was room temperature.

"Cold water bothers me when I have a headache," she said as she handed the bottle to him.

He took the bottle and thanked her. "Drake tells me you've had a hard time since you left college. Everything okay now?"

"Pretty much, I guess. I had TB, but they say it's cured. Then they say it could come back, too. I don't know." She shrugged and picked at the label on her water bottle until she peeled it off in one piece.

"TB? We've pretty much conquered that one in the US. But Drake said you'd been traveling. You must have seen some exotic places to catch TB," Flint said, making an effort to put her at ease even though he felt like he was staring straight into a strobe light every time he opened his eyes.

"Not so exotic, I'm afraid." Hanna lowered her gaze and spoke softly. "I was in prison in North Korea for five years. I got TB right away. They treated it with drugs, but I became drug-resistant after a while. So they finally released me because they were worried that I'd die and they'd be blamed for killing me."

"Yeah," Flint said. "It's happened before. Not that they need much of a reason, but why did they arrest you?"

“She defaced government property. Ripped a poster off a wall,” Drake said angrily.

“Stupid kid does stupid thing and gets caught. Pretty common story,” Hanna replied with a shrug and no excuses.

“Sounds rough.” Flint appreciated people who stood up and owned their behavior.

“In my case, the punishment was way worse than the crime. But at least I didn’t die there,” Hanna said, opening her water bottle and sipping. “One of my friends did die. Many times I thought I would.”

The videoconference startup image came on the screen. Flint’s setup was exceptionally secure, but the security level on Gaspar's end was better than the Pentagon or the development division at any major business in the country.

Gaspar behaved as if he were being watched twenty-four seven. Maybe he was. He'd been involved in black ops at the FBI. Flint never heard the particulars.

After a moment, Gaspar's weary image filled the screen.

"Flint, you look like hell," Gaspar teased, as if his own appearance were a lot better. "Weren't you lying around on a yacht in the Med a couple of days ago? Where's your tan?"

"Yeah, well, you know how these things go. Duty calls," Flint replied.

"Nice of you to agree to help Hanna find her sister. Don't let it get around that you're doing pro bono work," Gaspar jabbed him again.

"Find her sister? You mean find her body?" Flint missed the humor because he'd lost his focus. "She was lost at sea, right? How exactly do you plan to find her body after all this time?"

Gaspar glanced at Drake and Hanna. "You didn't tell him that you believe Greta is alive? That's the whole point of this exercise, isn't it?"

Drake grimaced. "We didn't get that far yet. You've been looking into the situation. Why don't you bring us all up to speed."

"Right. Okay. Let's start with the players." Gaspar moved his image off the screen and displayed a few photos of Greta Campbell Reed and her husband, Dr. Phillip Stephen Reed. "This is Hanna's sister and her second husband on the day they married. Here's a few headshots we dug up from the databases. Passport photos, driver's licenses, work ID images. Even a few articles published in newspapers, magazines. Next are candid shots from online websites and social media."

The images of her sister revealed a slightly older version of Hanna. Greta was blond instead of brunette. But the same big brown eyes. Same waifish build. Flint guessed Greta's age at about five years older than Hanna.

Gaspar moved on. "This is Sarah Campbell, the mother. Forty-five when she was hit in a crosswalk in the middle of a bright, sunny day by a drunk driver. Here's the scene of the accident. She died at the scene."

"Where were you when this happened, Hanna?" Flint asked, eyes closed for a break from the throbbing glare.

Hanna winced and cleared her throat, but her voice was husky when she replied. "I was, uh, at a frat party. It was a weekend thing. I didn't find out about the accident for several days."

Gaspar said, “That’s why you and your sister stopped talking? Because you weren’t there when your mother died?”

Hanna sighed and inhaled deeply, as if she were summoning the courage to talk about things she’d avoided for years.

“Mom wasn’t one of those nurturing helicopter moms you hear about these days. After Greta left home, she made it clear that she couldn’t wait to have me gone, too.” Hanna paused, sipped, cleared her throat again. “I obliged her when I turned eighteen. I didn’t see her much after that. I moved in with my boyfriend for the last year of high school. Then I went off to college. Then I left to travel the world.”

Flint understood her point, although Gaspar probably didn't. Gaspar was a family man through and through. He'd never allow one of his daughters to leave home like that.

But Flint had lived on his own from the same age and so had Scarlett. Hanna's choice didn't seem so odd to him.

"When did you last see Greta?" Flint asked.

Hanna dipped her head and looked at her shoes. "When I left Mom, I left Greta behind, too. She tried to call me several times and I ignored her calls. I thought she could have helped me after she left home and I was a kid, and I guess I just didn't have the maturity to deal with everything."

"So you haven't seen any member of your family since you were eighteen?" Gaspar's incredulous tone suggested something close to horror.

Hanna sighed. "Right. Dad died when I was ten. Greta left home when she was eighteen and I was thirteen. I saw Greta a few times after that because she'd come back to visit. She helped Mom as much as she could. But we were never close, and I guess we just drifted apart until Mom died."

"And then what happened when your mother died?" Gaspar asked. "Surely you attended the funeral and worked things out with Greta then."

Hanna shook her head again. “No. I had answered one of Greta’s phone calls. She was furious with me. She said I shouldn’t have left Mom alone. She said lots of other things. And so did I, to be fair. After we hung up that call, we never connected again.”

“Greta didn’t reach out to Hanna while she was in prison. Hanna thought it was because Greta was still angry. But when Hanna was released, after a long period in the hospital to recover from TB, Hanna tried to reconnect with Greta.” Drake explained to Flint what Gaspar already knew. “And that’s when Hanna was told Greta had died.”

Flint scowled. “Guys, I’m sorry. My head is just not on straight here. Is Greta Reed dead or not?”

"Based on what we've found so far, we don't know," Gaspar responded. "Could go either way."

Gaspar pulled up the video of the crowd at the royal wedding that Hanna had seen from her room. "Here's the first video Hanna saw. We're interested in this woman in the crowd."

He stopped the image and circled the visible portion of the woman's body. Next was a still image, enlarged and enhanced, of the same woman.

"I ran the image through our specialized face recognition software. No matches were found, even though I checked the passport files and the driver's license files," Gaspar said.

“Did you feed those images into the software and try to match them?” Flint asked.

“I heard you’ve got brain damage,” Gaspar replied dryly. “Of course I did. We have several issues with the available images that make the software twitchy. So the results are not conclusive, but they’re close enough to warrant a harder look. Point is, Greta Reed could very well be alive.”

Hanna heard the news and began to weep silently, head bowed. Drake put a big arm around her shoulders.

“What else do you have?” Flint asked. “Like is there somewhere on the globe to actually start looking?”

“My suggestion is to start with the husband,” Gaspar replied.

“The husband? Why?”

“He was older. Established professional. More places to look,” Gaspar said. “You can start in Atlanta. He was a hotshot transplant surgeon there for several years before Greta.”

Flint sat up in his chair, ignoring the nausea and the headache. “Sounds promising.”

“Yeah, I thought so, too.” Gaspar smirked.

“Guys, I’m gonna run Hanna back to the hotel. She can’t help with any of this. I’ll be back in a couple of hours,”

Drake said. “Feel free to keep going without me.”

When Drake and Hanna walked out, she was still weeping. Whether she was happy or sad or just exhausted and sick, Flint couldn’t tell.

“There’s something else.” Gaspar had waited until the front door closed behind them to speak again. “I called in a couple of favors and reached out to the Florida Fish and Wildlife Conservation Commission. He said the official final disposition on both deaths, Greta and her husband, was accidental drowning, lost at sea. But privately, the guys were not so sure.”

“Why not?” Flint asked, patting his pockets for more Tylenol.

"There were life vests in the boat. It was a rental, so the owner kept records," Gaspar said.

"Lots of idiots go out in boats without life vests on. You know that."

"Right. And the boat was never found. The owner said the life vests were accessible. He went over the safety protocols with Greta and Phillip before they set out," Gaspar said.

"So the suggestion is that they could have had life vests on and could have survived."

"It's possible. That's all he's saying."

"Did they find anything from the boat that might support his theory?"

"They did find some debris about a week later and about fifty miles south from where the boat is presumed to have run into trouble, yeah," Gaspar replied. "And my source says that with life jackets on, they could have floated quite a ways from where they started."

Flint shrugged, clasped the back of his neck in his palm and tried to knead the ache from his shoulders. "Let's check all the financial records on this couple. If they staged this whole thing, might be easier to start with why they did it."

"Already started," Gaspar said. "And I'm running traces worldwide on the husband, too. He's a doctor. If he's resurfaced somewhere and is practicing medicine, we might find him in official licensing databases or something. With luck."

"Good work, Gaspar. Like you said, makes sense to go up to Atlanta and check this guy out," Flint said. "Keep in touch."

He used the remote to turn off the pulsing television screen, rested his head back against the recliner, and closed his eyes to catch a few winks before Drake returned.

# Chapter 18

## Atabei

Dr. Stephen Brand had observed his hands shaking during the morning's heart transplant. Sweat popped out on his forehead, soaking his surgical cap during the early stages of the procedure, too.

He'd glanced at the team to be sure no one noticed. They seemed focused on the patient, not on the surgeon's unusual bio-responses. As they should have been.

Brand could perform transplant surgery better than most other surgeons even on the worst of days.

Of course, the procedure had been a success and the patient was doing well in recovery. He'd never lost a patient and he didn't lose this one.

He exercised iron control at all times. But these vexatious symptoms suggested his control was slipping.

Physiologic tremors were temporary and harmless in most situations. In his case, the triggers were stress, fatigue, and anxiety.

Too much caffeine and missing his breakfast were contributing factors.

Brand diagnosed all these contributing factors as consequences of only one thing.

Greta.

When he saw Greta's strange image on television, his first instinct was to ignore the situation.

Greta was dead. He'd watched her drown. Even though he couldn't check her body to confirm, he was sure she'd died out there in the Gulf, as planned.

He'd left his old life behind in every way. And he'd slept well enough every night for the past four years, secure in the knowledge that his ex was no longer a threat to him or anyone else.

Until the woman he'd seen in that damned royal wedding video began to intrude on his sleep. And then interfered with his daily activities. And now she was causing tremors during surgery.

This had to stop.

He'd tried other remedies and now realized the only way he could get back to his idyllic life was to confirm Greta's death.

Which was impossible.

He'd watched her flailing in the water until she sank. He'd waited a good long time for her body to bob up. It had not.

Days later, she was officially declared lost at sea.

Of course, so was he.

And he was right here, right now, still living.

But Brand had cheated death only with Hedinger's intervention. Greta absolutely could not have done the same. She couldn't possibly have pulled it off.

So what the hell?

Her body could have been washed hundreds of miles from where she went down. She would have been gnawed by sea creatures of all sorts. Finding identifiable remains of her after all these years was simply not possible.

Which had been the beauty of his solution to the Greta problem in the first place. The plan had worked flawlessly.

Greta could not possibly be alive.

Of course she couldn't.

Which was what he'd planned to tell Hedinger early this morning.

"We have a new client. Brace yourself," Hedinger had said when Brand answered. "He's insane."

"Aren't they all?" Brand replied, wiping his sweaty face with the damp bedsheets.

"Well, yes. I suppose they are. Fortunately. Or do you grow weary of your luxurious lifestyle, **Doctor**?" Hedinger laced the title with disdain, as he always did. "You can return to working at the university hospital anytime. Endless red tape while you hold the wringing hands of pitiful supplicants who have great needs but no cash. You can wipe the tears of their families when your patient dies because no matching donor can be found. Would you prefer that, **Dr.** Brand?"

Brand sat on the edge of the bed, head in his hands, listening to the cruel but true words Hedinger had uttered many times. Brand had never been altruistic in any way, and he was way too old to change, even if he wanted to.

Which he definitely had no desire to do.

He'd become a doctor to get rich and he'd finally discovered a decent payoff. He would never revoke his membership in the billionaire's club. Not for Greta Campbell or anyone else. No chance.

When Hedinger reached the end of his litany of horrors, Brand replied truthfully as he always did. “I’m perfectly satisfied with my life the way it is. How can I be of service to you?”

“As I said, we have a new client. An extremely powerful man. You will recognize him instantly when you see him.” Hedinger paused. “He demands anonymity. I’ve agreed.”

“It’s not an easy request, but we’ve done it before. We’ll do what’s necessary to prevent disclosure while he’s here,” Brand replied.

The client’s identity made no difference to the quality of the health care Brand’s hospital delivered.

But securing the anonymity of a recognizable face meant extra security and private nursing and longer hospitalization, all of which raised costs exponentially.

More challenges brought more money. Why would Brand object?

"He'll arrive later today. Our courier will deliver the documents and the donor to you personally. Surgery is tomorrow. Be prepared," Hedinger demanded curtly.

In light of this new client and his complications, Brand lacked the courage to mention Greta.

"Yes, of course. No problem at all." Brand held his finger poised to close the call a moment after Hedinger disconnected.

Instead, the old bastard continued loudly breathing a few moments longer.

"I assume you know I have traps on private and government databases around the world," Hedinger said, softly ominous. "We scan for all sorts of triggers. Such as names or search types or the identity of individuals making certain inquiries."

Brand's internal threat meter jumped up all the way into the red zone. The needle held there as if it were glued in place.

His sweaty face heated another couple of degrees and his heart pounded wildly in his chest.

He said nothing.

Experience had taught him to wait for trouble instead of running toward it.

"Every day we receive and repel potential threats to our operations around the globe," Hedinger continued, as if he were revealing closely held secrets. Which he probably was. "One of the entities we monitor is searching for your dead wife."

Brand felt his heart stop abruptly. His breath stopped, too.

He felt dizzy, cold, and clammy pain in the center of his chest.

Darkness gathered around him like a total eclipse of the sun.

He muted the phone and forced himself to take deep breaths to stave off a fit of hyperventilating.

Hedinger demanded curtly, “What’s going on, Doctor?”

Brand took another deep breath and unmuted the phone. He forced his voice to reply as evenly as possible. “This is the first I’m hearing about it.”

“Someone is investigating your wife and you didn’t know,” Hedinger said, slightly incredulous, as if this answer was worse than Brand’s full awareness of the situation could have been.

“I can’t imagine why anyone would do that,” Brand said, continuing to focus on getting air into his lungs and out again. His reply walked the fine line between candor and deadly consequences. “What do they hope to find?”

“You tell me,” Hedinger said. He paused as if he were expecting a solid answer.

Brand replied, “I would if I could.”

A longer pause followed.

“I have many enemies, Brand. Your association with me could well be the cause. Perhaps these people are fishing for something to use against me instead of you.”

Brand waited, hoping for a lifeline.

“We’ll investigate further.”

“Good.”

“Meanwhile, the new client and his donor will arrive separately within the hour. We can discuss this further when I see you.” Hedinger paused and then continued, "Until we resolve this business with your wife, carry a weapon at all times. Be ever vigilant."

A moment later, Hedinger hung up.

Brand closed the connection on his end and tossed the phone onto the bed.

**Be ever vigilant**. What the hell kind of advice was that?

# Chapter 19

## Atlanta

Flint had never been the wallowing type. His concussion was improving, although slower than he'd prefer. Every day he felt slightly less nausea.

Dizziness and headaches were the worst of it, but he put some of that down to the blurred vision. When the vision issues improved, he expected the others to improve, too.

Drake's Hanna Campbell matter was helping. The case gave Flint a not-too-taxing problem to focus on until he could get back to his own work. It also gave him a reasonable excuse for not following up on Marilyn Baker's DNA.

The Campbell case was straightforward. Either Greta Reed was dead or alive. If she was alive, then finding her shouldn't be too difficult. Flint made his living locating people after others had failed.

He boasted that he could find anyone, anytime, anywhere, dead or alive. Which was true. He'd never failed. It might take him a while, but he would not allow the Greta Campbell Reed case to be his first.

When the commercial jet landed in Atlanta, Drake handled the luggage and the rental car, and they were on the road. Traffic around Hartsfield Airport was at least as congested as any major airport in the country. Which meant it took a while to reach Dr. Phillip Reed's old stomping grounds.

"Do you have any idea where we're going?" Flint asked.

"Sure. I know this place like the back of my hand. Every last Peachtree Lane and Peachtree Avenue of it. I was a taxi driver while I was at Emory. You knew that, right?" Drake claimed with a grin.

He avoided the bottlenecks and took the winding roads around high-traffic areas like a pro, so Flint wasn't surprised.

"Hell, I didn't even know you went to Emory. Why did I think you went to college in Texas somewhere?" Flint asked, his eyes concealed behind very dark sunglasses, which made the sunlight almost bearable.

He'd never seen Drake's résumé. Never needed to. He'd learned all he needed to know when they served in the Marines together. Since then Drake had saved Flint's bacon more times than he cared to remember.

"Because I did. But that was later," Drake said with a grin. "I was at Emory for my first year before my mom said she wasn't paying tuition for me to party and snatched me back home. I took a couple of years off and then, having grown up a little, got a job. I helped my folks pay tuition. After a while I finished out at the University of Houston before I joined the Marines."

"Guess that helps explain why you're a few years older than Hanna Campbell, too," Flint said.

"Yeah. We were freshmen together. She was younger than usual, and I was older than usual." Drake paused and gave Flint a side-eye. "Look, don't think Hanna and I had some great romance. It wasn't like that. I mean, she was the kind of girl I liked back then. Wild and crazy and fun and unserious with zero patience for books and learning. The best thing she had going was the ability to drink me under the table."

"And you want me to believe you've matured," Flint deadpanned.

"Yeah, well. You know. Leopards don't change their spots." Drake laughed. "Point is, Hanna was a girl I dated. That's all. I dated a lot of other girls after her. She moved on, too. There's hundreds of people I knew in college that I've never seen again and probably never will. Same as you and every other kid in college, I'd bet."

"So why are you so interested in helping Hanna find her sister now?" Flint asked.

"It's a challenge I guess." Drake shrugged and wagged his head. "And, okay, I feel sorry for her. Sure, she was a wild kid back then. Truth be told, whatever happened between her and her sister was probably eighty percent Hanna's fault."

"At least," Flint said straight-faced.

Drake grinned. "I did some dumb things when I was young and stupid, too. They didn't land me in a North Korean prison or leave me debilitated with a chronic disease for the rest of my life. I just feel like Hanna deserves a break, you know?"

Flint understood. Mistakes were made. Bills were paid. Could be the six-word story of a lot of young lives, including his own.

Hanna was still young, and she should have a good life ahead of her. Maybe if they solved the puzzle of her missing sister, she could move forward.

Hell, if Greta was still alive, then even better. They could move forward together.

Flint knew too well that not many people got second chances like that.

Drake wanted to give Hanna what she had no right to hope for and Flint owed Drake debts he could never repay.

So here they were.

Simple as that. 'Nuff said.

Drake made one more turn onto yet another Peachtree Street. He drove halfway down the block and stopped in front of the house where Dr. Phillip Reed and his wife once lived.

It was an old neighborhood. The house itself was probably a hundred years old, at least. But it had been restored at some point within the past twenty years. Paint was fresh, lawn lush, flowers plentiful, porches inviting.

“Are we going in?” Drake asked, glancing toward Flint.

“We didn’t come here for a drive-by.”

“Why did we come here again?” Drake asked.

“Gotta start somewhere.”

“Yep.” Drake parallel parked near the house. He ambled across the street and up the paved walkway. He hopped two steps at a time up to the front porch.

Flint trailed a couple of paces, placing one deliberate foot in front of the other. He wobbled slightly. The sensation of missing pavement beneath his feet slowed his progress. When he finally reached the entrance, Drake had already rung the bell.

Flint heard footsteps approaching on the other side of the old-fashioned screen door. An attractive woman appeared behind the screen.

“Good afternoon, Mrs. Hudgins,” Drake said, using the approach they’d planned. “We’re looking for Mrs. Reed. Is she home?”

The woman was already shaking her head. “I’m sorry. Dr. and Mrs. Reed haven't lived here for a long time. We bought this place almost seven years ago."

"Would you have a forwarding address? We're trying to reach her on behalf of her sister."

"Her sister? I didn't know Ella Belle had a sister," the woman said. She opened the screen and stepped outside, probably thinking it was rude to gossip otherwise.

She was dressed plainly. A white apron was tied around her waist. No makeup. Her hair was held captive in a tight bun at the back of her head. She wore a thin gold wedding band and a gold cross on a chain around her neck.

Gaspar had searched thoroughly, under the circumstances. Ella Belle Reed, Phillip's first wife, had had two brothers but no sisters. So far, the neighborhood, the house, the bare facts, and the woman on the porch were all exactly as reported.

"Sorry for the confusion, ma'am." Drake dipped his head in a respectful nod. "We're talking about Phillip Reed's second wife, Greta. It's her sister we're trying to help here."

The woman's eyes widened, and her mouth formed a little O, as if the second Mrs. Reed was a surprise to her. "I see. Well, we didn't know Dr. Reed well, I'm afraid. We didn't even meet him when we bought the house after Ella Belle died. I didn't realize Dr. Reed had remarried."

"So you knew Mrs. Ella Belle Reed, then?" Drake asked, barely keeping the hope from his tone.

"We knew her before she married Dr. Reed." The woman nodded. "Ella Belle went to our hall for worship. Joined us when they first moved to Atlanta. Dr. Reed wasn't much of a churchgoer. But Ella Belle was very devout. She came to our hall two or three times a week, at least."

Flint wondered why they'd buy a house where a friend was murdered, but it wasn't relevant so he let it go. "But Dr. Reed didn't come to services with her?"

"Never." She shook her head sorrowfully. "Not once. Even though we invited him many times. Ella Belle said he traveled so much, and he treasured what little time he was able to spend at home. He was gone for months on end. I feel like Ella Belle came to the hall so often because she didn't have anything else to do. And after Ella Belle's funeral, Dr. Reed didn't come back to Atlanta much."

"Where was Mrs. Reed buried?" Flint asked.

"The funeral was held at Kingdom Hall Peachtree Park. And her body was cremated. I don't know what her husband did with her ashes."

She lowered her gaze. Flint waited, but she didn't fill the silence. He cleared his throat to bring her attention back to the conversation.

"I'm sorry for your loss, Mrs. Hudgins. Ella Belle sounds like an amazing person. And didn't she donate her organs to several of Dr. Reed's patients when she died?" Flint asked as respectfully as possible. "He did the heart and lung surgeries himself, didn't he? It must be comforting to you all to know that even though her life was tragically cut short, Ella Belle was able to give the gift of life to others."

"Actually, we were more than a little shocked about that," Mrs. Hudgins said stiffly while raising her eyes and staring directly into Flint's face.

"Why is that?" Drake asked.

"Ella Belle was devout, like I told you. We're Jehovah's Witnesses. We discussed this matter many times at worship, and I know her desires caused friction between her and Dr. Reed," Mrs. Hudgins replied, crossing her arms over her chest as if she were unconsciously protecting her own organs.

"I'm sorry, but I don't understand what you mean," Flint said, softening his tone to encourage her. "Your faith doesn't prohibit the gift of organs after death, does it?"

"Our faith allows it, yes. But the practice is discouraged. Whether to gift or receive is a matter of individual preference," Mrs. Hudgins replied softly. "And Ella Belle's preference was not to donate. She said so at worship. More than once."

"But Dr. Reed, as her husband, must have given permission. The hospital wouldn't have allowed the organ harvesting otherwise."

"His wife, his hospital, his patients. As I said, I didn't know the man." Mrs. Hudgins lifted her chin defiantly. "But I knew Ella Belle. And I'm telling you donating her organs was most definitely **not** what she wanted."

Her telephone rang loudly inside the house. Mrs. Hudgins glanced over her shoulder, as if she expected someone to answer the call. But the phone rang again.

"That will be my mother. She's elderly and lives alone. I need to go. I've told you everything I know anyway. I'm sorry I couldn't be more helpful," Mrs. Hudgins said as she returned through the screen door toward the ringing phone. The door banged closed behind her.

"Now what?" Drake asked as they walked back to the SUV.

"This whole thing doesn't pass the smell test. One guy and two dead wives?" Flint chewed his lower lip as he thought about Ella Belle's situation. "Gaspar accessed the police file on Ella Belle's murder. Let's go talk to the detectives. See what they're willing to tell us."

# Chapter 20

Flint found the address for the local police station in the nav system and pushed the start button.

"I'm on it," Drake said and applied his expertise to driving the short trip.

As they moved through the residential streets, Flint thumbed through more of the data Gaspar had sent. He located the reports completed by the detectives investigating Ella Belle Reed's murder and scanned the pages, reading aloud for Drake's benefit.

"Home invasion. Both Ella Belle and Phillip were home. He'd fallen asleep on the sofa in the den watching football. She was in the kitchen cleaning up after dinner."

"How convenient." Drake frowned. "This guy led a charmed life, didn't he? When's the last time anybody made you dinner and then cleaned up alone while you took a nap?"

"Maybe they alternated the kitchen duty. Who knows?" Flint shook his head and kept scanning, repeating the points of interest aloud. "An unidentified perpetrator broke in the front door while they were in the back of the house. Climbed the stairs to the bedroom where they kept a safe in the closet. The safe was open. He grabbed jewelry and cash and fled. Happened to be bounding down the stairs just as Ella Belle was coming up."

“So just a lucky guess that there was a safe and it had jewelry and cash in it and it would be open and waiting? How does that happen?” Drake asked.

“Intruder shot her twice. Because of the angle, her on the stairs and him trying to get down, one bullet hit her in the groin.”

“That’s not an easy shot. Does sound like a fluke.”

“He shoved her aside and kept running.” Flint continued reading a bit and then said, “By the time Phillip realized the invasion was happening and came to his wife’s aid, the intruder was gone and she was bleeding profusely.”

Solemnly, Drake said, "I'll bet. Hit the femoral artery, she bleeds out quick."

"Right. He called 911 and commenced first aid." Flint kept scanning. "She was still alive when the ambulance arrived. He hopped into the ambulance with her."

"He's a doctor. He should have been able to help," Drake said. "She's lucky he was there."

"Possibly. But she died before the ambulance reached the hospital," Flint said, still scanning and pulling out the most relevant facts.

"Meaning her organs were fresh enough for harvesting and could be immediately donated." Drake's lip curled and he took a quick left at the next corner. “Man, this guy’s a piece of work.”

“Looks like heart, lungs, liver, two kidneys, two corneas. Maybe more,” Flint said, scrolling down the list.

“Wonder how much money the good doctor made selling those seven organs,” Drake mused.

“Technically, he didn’t sell the organs. He donated them,” Flint reminded him.

“Yeah, but he got paid to do the transplant surgeries, I’ll bet. Even grieving doctors don’t work for free,” Drake replied.

“Not to mention the expense of hospital and staff involved in seven transplants,” Flint said. “Had to be well over five million dollars. Probably paid by insurance or the government."

Drake's jaw dropped. "You're kidding."

"Last time I checked this out for a client, a heart transplant was more than $1.6 million. Probably costs more now," Flint replied. "Double lungs, another million. Kidneys are about half a million each. Liver's probably cheaper. Maybe a hundred grand. Corneas about thirty grand each. So yeah, around five million. Just ballparking."

"But close to that much, you're saying." Drake turned the SUV into the parking lot.

The three-story building that housed the local police station looked old but solid. Probably the majority of operations had been moved to a newer facility at some point. This one would be used for special purposes, Flint figured.

The parking lot wasn't large enough and Drake had to wait for another vehicle to leave. He backed into the space and turned off the ignition.

"Lucky break for Dr. Reed, wouldn't you say?" Drake asked. "He lost his wife, but he made a pile of money."

"Yeah, and doing one or more of the transplants himself, right after his wife was murdered like that? Wonder how heartbroken he actually was," Flint mused aloud, scanning the bustling activity around the station. "Are they giving out money here today or something?"

Drake shook his head. "Looks like this place serves a mixed economic neighborhood now. I tried to stay out of trouble when I was a student, but I hear more crime has moved in since then."

"Let's go talk to the detectives at the closest station to the crime. Even if they handed the case off, they'd have been first on the scene. See what we can find out," Flint said.

"You know, Phillip Reed wouldn't be the first man to fake a home invasion to kill his wife. People in that financial league usually have high life insurance policies that pay out the max death benefit for a murder like that, too," Drake said. "But selling her organs? That's not something I've heard of before. You?"

"First time for everything," Flint replied as he climbed out of the cabin. "But yeah, life insurance is easier all around. I'm sure there's a lot more to selling organs than an unsophisticated spouse killer would know. Most of the time, the organs are probably useless. Too much elapsed time between the death and a potential transplant surgery for one thing."

"Yeah, but I'll bet there's more issues than timing. Tissue matching and size of the organs and things like that," Drake replied as if he were thinking about the odds of any sort of murder-for-organs scheme. "Which would mean premeditated murder for sure."

They walked together toward the station's entrance. Flint guessed it must be a satellite services operation. Civilians were coming and going through the double doors and a short line had formed on the sidewalk.

"What's the holdup?" Drake asked the man at the end of the line.

"Same as always. Security check just inside the door before you can get inside," the man replied, turning his back to make it clear he wasn't interested in a longer conversation.

Flint shrugged and shoved his hands into the pockets of his jeans to wait.

He’d done his share of waiting in government lines of one kind or another. Seeking service from any government office was an endless waiting game. Policing services were stretched just like all the others.

Drake stood behind him and they inched forward as the line moved steadily toward the double doors. After fifteen minutes, they made it inside.

Ten feet ahead was a double set of metal detectors and x-ray screening devices similar to TSA airport security. Each screening line was manned by two officers.

Visitors were required to empty their pockets and place their belongings in a bin to be scanned by x-ray. The visitor then walked through the security scanner and was reunited with his belongings on the other side.

A few people were randomly selected for wanding.

Everybody in the line seemed to know the process and follow the drill.

When Flint and Drake made it through, Drake said quietly with a wink, “That’s the full government employment plan in action right there. Six guys each shift, three shifts a day. Maybe another crew on standby for breaks. Yep, our tax dollars at work.”

"Looks like they've got their hands full to me." Flint gave him a side-eye and scanned the large, overflowing lobby until he located the front desk.

A line had formed, and a lone sergeant was manning the desk.

They joined the end of the line to wait their turn like everyone else.

"The American Way." Drake grinned. "See a line. Get in it."

# Chapter 21

After five minutes, Drake mused, "I wonder why there are so many people in here today."

The small lobby was full to bursting. The crowd was hot and noisy.

Old, young, males, females. Tough-looking teenagers and frail seniors.

Molded plastic seats were fully occupied. Two dozen more people were standing, alone or in groups, waiting to be called.

Several of them seemed to know each other. Which wasn't surprising, since this was a community police station.

Flint had been inside police stations before. Some were newer and brighter and not nearly as busy. This one had a compressed, desperate vibe. He sensed barely suppressed anger beneath the defeated torpor.

Two clusters of angry young men were loosely hanging together on opposite sides of the room.

Rivals, probably. Maybe even local gang members. Hard to tell.

Every few seconds a member of one group would shoot a quick stare across to the other group, eliciting menacing stares and trash talk in return.

“Seems like those hoodlums are looking for an excuse to rumble,” Drake said quietly.

"You been watching old movies again?" Flint replied as they shuffled forward with the line. "You think they're the Jets and the Sharks?"

"I'm not wrong," Drake insisted. "Be wary."

"Let's get in and get out before the trouble erupts," Flint replied. "I'm not up for a fight with a bunch of bangers half my age."

"Well, maybe not half." Drake grinned.

After twenty minutes of waiting their turn, Flint and Drake reached the front of the line. Where was a customer satisfaction survey when you needed one?

The desk sergeant was a tired-looking man of about fifty, working toward his pension. He didn't even glance up from his keyboard when he asked, "Can I help you?"

Flint took the lead. "We're looking for Detective Dean Myer. Is he around?"

"Detective Myer is a woman," the desk sergeant said, looking at his computer screen. "I'll check. Who shall I say is asking?"

Flint offered his business card.

The sergeant glanced at him, took the card, scrutinized it. "She'll wanna know what this is about."

"A home invasion she handled seven years ago. Case is still open. Woman was killed," Flint replied, friendly, recognizing he was entitled to nothing and angling for a favor. "I know it's been a minute, but we've got a similar case. We might be able to help each other. We solve ours, might solve hers, too."

"What's the name of the case?" The sergeant poised to type.

"Ella Belle Reed," Flint replied.

He typed Ella Belle's name into the system, which must have confirmed the case existed. "You should work up a better approach when you pitch it to her. We've heard that one a million times."

"Copy that," Flint replied.

The sergeant picked up the desk phone and punched an extension.

"Detective Myer, Seltz at the front desk. I've got a couple of private investigators up here asking about the Ella Belle Reed home invasion. Open case from a few years ago. They say they've got new information."

Seltz listened and then replaced the handset on the cradle. "Must be a slow day in Robbery Homicide. She says have a seat. She'll be right out."

Flint moved away from the desk and through the milling crowd, seeking an unoccupied place to wait.

Drake followed. "Man, a guy could get claustrophobic in here."

A child was arguing with his mother nearby. The boy wanted to leave, and the mother explained that they needed to wait.

The argument escalated, getting louder and more intense. The boy began crying, which graduated to wailing and then screaming. He sounded like a wicked seagull at feeding time.

Flint's headache threatened to take the top of his head off as it was. Added to the existing cacophony, the mother-and-child screaming match definitely didn't help.

Dark edges surrounded his vision, making him feel as though he might faint again. Flint struggled to stay conscious and upright.

The boy's screaming seemed to raise the tension in the station to the boiling point. The two rival gangs, if that's what they were, no longer resisted the pull of a fight.

One of them reached down and pulled a sharp plastic shiv from his unlaced high-tops. He brandished it toward a rival gang member.

"Step back," he demanded with quiet menace.

The second guy opened his arms and moved forward into striking range.

"What the hell's wrong with you boys?" An older man pushed through the crowd, approaching quickly. He slipped between the second teen and the shiv. "You wanna spend the rest of the week locked up back there?"

"No, sir," the glaring young males said in unison.

The second teen smirked insolently as he raised his palms and backed off with a little spring in his step.

The brawl had been about to boil over, but the old man's intervention lowered the heat level for the moment.

The glares the two bangers exchanged made it clear that the underlying disagreement, whatever it was, was simply postponed and not resolved.

The old man had given them an excuse to back off. For now.

Flint had engaged in similar scenarios when he was a rebellious teen spoiling for a fight. Most of the time, the thing they really wanted was not to fight. When an adult breaks up the argument before the fight starts, everybody wins.

Until the next time.

“Get yourselves out of here before you get arrested, then. Go on.” The man glared them into shrugs of submission, and they moved like two separate herds toward the exit.

“Minerva,” the older man said, turning his attention to the mother. “Take your boy home. Bring him to my house tomorrow. I’ll babysit for you so you can get your business done in peace.”

“Don’t you tell me what to do,” the mother said, lifting her pride.

But she walked her son outside, head held high all the way through the doors and down the sidewalk.

Now that the troublemakers had been dealt with, the crowd returned to its noisy, overheated but mostly peaceful waiting.

“What were all those cops doing?” Drake said quietly. “Not one of them came over here to break things up.”

“Probably didn’t see. They’re busy here. Good thing we didn’t need to intervene, too,” Flint replied.

Drake said, “Could have been a serious situation.”

Flint shrugged. “Those young thugs might be all bark and no bite.”

“At least one was smart enough to get the plastic shiv past the metal detectors,” Drake pointed out reasonably. “Trouble’s brewing, for sure.”

“Let’s hope we’re long gone before it does.” Flint’s head was still pounding. “Got any Tylenol?”

“Not on me,” Drake said. “Maybe Sergeant Seltz has some. Want me to get it?”

Just then a dark-haired woman pushed through a set of double doors behind Seltz. She was attractive as all get-out, even dressed in a cheap black pantsuit, yellow shirt, and clunky shoes.

For a brief moment, he imagined her all decked out for an evening in the city. She'd be hot as hell.

He grinned at the image, and it reminded him just how long it had been since he'd had a proper date. Way too long, for damned sure. Something else he'd fix as soon as he had the chance.

She stopped to scan the room and made a quick beeline directly toward them, all business.

At the moment, best not to forget that she wore a badge and carried a gun. No doubt she knew how to use it, too.

"That's gotta be Detective Myer." Drake pointed his chin in her direction. “How’d she know we were the ones asking about Ella Belle?”

“With any luck, she likes cowboys. Gives us the advantage.” Flint grinned appreciatively, standing up straight. “You see anybody else in here looking like they just climbed down off a horse?”

Drake glanced at their jeans and boots and smiled. “Fair point.”

# Chapter 22

Detective Dean Myer strode through the crowded lobby as if she expected the crowds to part for her and yield the right of way. Which they did.

When she approached, Drake introduced himself and glanced toward her path, which had filled in behind her. “Impressive.”

“Michael Flint,” he said as he shook her extended hand and offered a smile. “Please excuse him. He doesn’t get out much.”

“Let’s step outside where we can hear ourselves think,” Detective Myer suggested with a smile, leading the way.

Once again, the crowd opened in front of her and this time closed behind Drake at the back of their train. Outside, the air was fresher as well as quieter and way less tense.

Flint followed Myer to a picnic table off to one side under a shade tree and out of earshot of those still waiting in line to get into the station.

“Are you folks giving away ice cream in there or something?” Drake asked with a grin. “I’ve never seen citizens line up to file into a police station like that before.”

“Kind of. Not ice cream but one-on-ones to listen to their concerns, promising to help where we can. It’s a community policing initiative,” she explained. “Trying to build trust with the citizens in our precinct is an ongoing battle. You two aren't law enforcement, so you probably don't know how it is."

"Guess not," Flint replied and, sensing their time together would be cut short, changed the subject. "We're interested in the Ella Belle Reed murder. Until today, we didn't know she'd been murdered. We knew she'd died."

"What's your interest?" Detective Myer asked.

"We think her murder could be related to a case we're working on," Drake said. "Maybe we can share intel. Three heads are better than two, and all that."

"If you've seen the news reports on Ella Belle Reed, you know everything we know. We didn't hold anything back. We would have, of course. But we didn't find anything worth holding on to," Myer replied in the weary way of all overworked detectives everywhere.

Even tired and dispirited, she was the kind of woman who always appealed to Flint. Competent, self-reliant, strong. He was liking her more with every passing sentence.

"Our case is not quite so obvious. At the moment we're approaching it as a missing person," Flint said.

She raised her eyebrows. "At the moment? You thought it was something else?"

"Initially, the death was declared accidental. But new evidence has come to light and we're no longer sure," Flint said, sensing he was already losing her attention.

"Tell me why you think your case is related."

"We know the cases are related in a broad sense. Because both Ella Belle Reed and our victim, Greta Reed, were married to the same man," Flint replied easily.

Detective Myer's eyes opened wider. "I'd say that's related. I don't believe in coincidences. I do believe in bad luck, though. Maybe Dr. Reed is just unlucky."

"Kind of interesting you say that." Flint ignored the Timpani solo going on in his head. "We were thinking Phillip Reed was exceptionally lucky that night. It's not every day a doctor can donate seven organs from his dead wife and spend the next two days implanting them in other patients."

Myer gnawed her lower lip as if she were considering what to leave in, what to leave out. She clasped her hands together.

Flint paused to give her time to volunteer, but when she didn't, he said, "Nobody local here thought the organ transplanting thing was the least bit odd?"

Myer frowned. “Of course we did. It was beyond odd all the way to flat-out weird. But that alone doesn’t prove Phillip Reed murdered his wife.”

“Or hired it done,” Drake suggested. “The whole home invasion thing was staged. Had to be. Which means Phillip Reed was expecting the guy and probably paid him to kill Ella Belle.”

“And the motive was to give him not only her life insurance but also her organs so he could be both wealthy and a hero of some kind?” Myer’s frown deepened. “You think we’re just local yokels who don’t know what we’re doing, is that it?”

Drake grinned and shook his head. "Hey, to me, y'all are all geniuses. I don't know nothing about policing or investigating either. Just sayin'."

"Just sayin' what, cowboy?" Myer cocked her head and narrowed her eyes, but she smiled. The kind of smile that lit up her whole face.

"We're not saying anything," Flint interjected before she stopped smiling. "We're asking. We assume Atlanta PD ran down all the possibilities and didn't solve the murder. That's why the case is still open."

"Exactly. We were all hands on deck for the Ella Belle Reed case when it happened," Myer replied. "I'm working out of this local Podunk station today as a favor for a friend. But Atlanta's got one of the best police departments in the country. You boys should come on board and try it for a while."

"We're thinking we can help you. We aren't tied to Atlanta. We can travel. We're well funded. We've got resources," Flint explained. "You interested?"

"Of course I am. I want to solve every case on my desk. This one's no different."

"So what trace evidence did you find of the intruder?" Flint asked, moving on to specifics, showing he really had no desire to argue with her. Quite the opposite.

Myer shook her head. “Not one thing. His body was covered from head to foot. He didn’t touch anything except the contents of the safe, which he took with him. No fingerprints, no DNA, no blood, no sweat, and the only tears we saw were the ones Ella Belle’s friends and family shed at her funeral.”

Flint acknowledged each of her list of negatives. “So the guy was a pro. Not an amateur. Hired killer.”

“That was our take on it. And by the time we got there, he was long gone.” Myer nodded. “We checked the airlines and car rentals but didn’t find him. ’Course, we had no clue what we were looking for, either. Atlanta gets thousands of people through here every day. Like looking for a grain of salt on a margarita.”

"What about Phillip Reed? You interviewed him. Did he give anything up? I just need one thing I can run with here. Someplace to start looking," Flint said.

Myer eyed him, looked him up and down like an MRI scanner. "This was seven years ago. The case is colder than Siberia in January. You won't find anything we didn't already check out. But I'll share the interview tapes and the rest of the file with you."

"Great. That would really help," Drake said, nodding.

"On one condition."

"Sure, I'd love to take you to dinner. Anytime," Flint replied with a smile.

She didn't say no.

"You nail that son of a bitch. Ella Belle was one of the nicest women you'd ever want to meet. Everybody loved her. She was way too young to die. And if that bastard killed her, then he's going down, too. I'll see to it." Myer finished talking, spun on her heel, and stomped into a side door at the station.

"Where's she going?" Drake asked.

"I suspect she'll be back in a minute with a copy of the file," Flint replied, kneading his forehead between his eyes as though he could rub away the pain. His body was quivering with tension like he might actually fall flat on the asphalt.

Flint walked over to the picnic table and leaned against it to steady himself. He'd had concussions before. Like the others, this one would heal itself. All he needed to do was get through it.

He repeated those words to himself several times a day. So far he couldn't say anything he'd tried was actually helping. His headache was still there. He felt dizzy, nauseous, and weak too often.

Flint had been banged up and sometimes mangled over the years. Scarlett cussed him out about it pretty regularly. But the human body was a miraculous thing. Everything would level out, for better or worse, and when it did, he'd adapt to the new normal.

Question was, how long would it take?

Less than five minutes later, Myer returned and passed a thumb drive to Flint. “I downloaded our entire murder book on here. It’s all we’ve got. Maybe something in there will help you.”

“Thanks.” Flint touched her hand as he collected the warm thumb drive and shoved it into his pocket.

“I’ve got to get back,” Myer said. She gave him a genuine smile as she turned to leave. “Keep in touch.”

“Just one more question,” Flint said before she moved out of range. “Who was the recipient of Ella Belle’s heart?”

Myer stopped and turned her full attention to Flint. “Curious question. Why do you ask?”

“Some of her other organs could have been harvested without killing her in the process. But the heart…” His voice trailed off.

Myer cleared her throat. “If Ella Belle was killed for her heart, then she got the last laugh.”

“What do you mean?” Drake asked.

“Guy who received her heart died anyway. About six months later.”

“So who was he?” Flint asked.

“Those records are confidential. The press tried to dig up the recipients’ names back then and couldn’t. It’s all in the murder book I downloaded for you, but you didn't get it from me," Myer said.

"Understood," Flint promised. "Who got the heart?"

Myer paused another couple of seconds, thinking, and then she made her decision. "There were seven recipients. All of them had been on the transplant lists for many months."

"Except the one who got Ella Belle's heart," Flint guessed.

Myer glanced down and scuffed the dirt with the toe of her boot. "A minor member of the royal family of some Middle Eastern country we'd never heard of. He was very, very rich, I'm told."

"I see," Flint replied, shaking his head.

Life was cheap in many parts of the world. But he preferred to believe his country was not one of those places. Even as Ella Belle Reed's case proved otherwise.

"Watch your backs." Myer gave him a steady gaze and he thought maybe she'd actually started to care about him a little bit. "The sort of man who sells something money should never be able to buy? The heart of a good and kind woman? That's not the kind of man you want to mess with."

"We'll let you know how we make out," Flint replied. "Can I reach you at the number on your card?"

Myer kept her gaze steady for another moment and gave him an encouraging smile. Then she turned, and hustled toward the station.

“What the hell…?” Drake said quietly as they watched her leave. “We’re investigating a killer and you’re trying to hustle up a date?”

“Come on,” Flint said as he walked. “We won’t find anything here that Myer hasn’t already given us.”

“Where are we going?” Drake said, falling into step beside Flint.

“Sarasota. I want to take a look at the area where Reed’s boat went down.”

“We won’t see anything but lots of water out there. What’s the point?”

"This story doesn't hang together. Phillip Reed is either the unluckiest man who ever lived. Or he's killed two wives."

"Well, yeah. But he's dead now, so what more can we do?" Drake pressed the key fob to unlock the SUV.

"Is he dead though?" Flint said, climbing into the cabin on the passenger side. "I'm not so sure."

Drake's eyes widened as he started the SUV and pulled out of the parking lot headed toward the airport. "So you think both Phillip and Greta survived that boating disaster? What are the odds?"

"Stranger things have happened," Flint said flatly. He pulled out his cell phone to call Gaspar.

Hanna Campbell's sister wasn't a case on Gaspar's books, and he wasn't getting paid.

But Gaspar had volunteered. As ex-military, too. He should have known better.

The first rule of survival was always and forever: never volunteer.

# Chapter 23

**Switzerland**

Ernst Hedinger received a full set of materials every morning before breakfast. The documents were loaded onto a tablet placed beside his chair.

One ongoing investigation he'd been following was the identity of the thief who recently breached his sophisticated security to steal one of his most prized possessions.

Any man who stole from Ernst Hedinger would live only long enough to regret his thievery. Not one moment more.

Finding this particular thief had proven more difficult than Hedinger expected. Which was fine. He appreciated a worthy adversary, knowing that the adversary wouldn't live long enough to enjoy what he'd stolen.

The Stradivarius was his. He'd acquired it from a dictator before the man and most of his family were murdered in a military coup. Of course, he hadn't actually paid the purchase price, since he'd known the dictator had been marked for death.

Hedinger shrugged.

Perhaps the dictator hadn't been the instrument's rightful owner, but his young daughter had played the Stradivarius so beautifully.

Only a barbarian would have sold the instrument to finance a war. What did grubby army generals know of fine music?

Hedinger would not rest until the thief returned the magnificent Stradivarius to occupy its rightful place in his salon.

Alas, that would not happen today.

But soon.

Very soon.

He put the matter aside for now and moved on to another festering problem.

This morning, as usual, Hedinger ate alone in his large personal dining room. He was seated at the head of a priceless antique table offering a breathtaking view of the Alps. His personal chef prepared food fit for kings.

All was as it should be. Hedinger lived like a king because he was now and forever the king of all he surveyed.

This morning his meal was an exquisite omelet, pastries, and potato latkes with applesauce. Finely pressed French coffee, paled by heavy cream and sweetened with syrupy manuka honey, satisfied his need for caffeine and sweets.

Hedinger ate leisurely and with great satisfaction as he perused dozens of reports from his worldwide operations.

His executives in charge of each operational office were more than competent and reports were rarely alarming. Issues arose, as in every business, and were expeditiously resolved on-site. Hedinger paid little attention to the body count.

Which was why he hadn't expected the recent alert from his US Chief of Operations. The Phillip Reed matter, one Hedinger had settled long ago, had reappeared. Not at all what he'd wanted to hear.

The first alert came from a trap on the Atlanta PD cold case database. Monitoring public agency databases was routine practice for Hedinger's enterprises.

He'd learned over the years to respect the data big governments seemed to magnetize like honey attracts ants.

When the old Reed murder file was located by an unidentifiable hacker, Hedinger's alert was triggered. Walter Cade, his COO in the US, had simply watched the situation at first, assuming nothing more would come of it.

He'd been wrong.

Later, the file was opened and copied by Detective D. Myer.

A more urgent alert fired.

When she copied the entire file including all data and saved it to an external device, her actions triggered Hedinger's full scale alarm.

Cade was tasked with terminating the attack. He'd put his best men on it, he'd said.

Despite Hedinger's orders to eliminate all who touched that file by extreme measures, the contents had not been retrieved.

Had he been less than clear? Not likely. Yet he had not received proof that the task had been accomplished.

Hedinger finished his meal and refreshed his coffee before he placed the call on an encrypted satellite signal. Cade answered instantly in Washington, DC.

"What is the status of the Reed matter?" Hedinger demanded without preamble as he sipped the sweet, creamy coffee.

“The detective who shared the police files on the Reed murder died last night in a shootout with local gang members. She can do no further harm,” Cade said.

“I see.” Hedinger smiled. “And the copied file?”

Cade cleared his throat. “She didn’t have it on her. Looks like she passed the thumb drive to the two investigators we previously identified.”

Hedinger’s patience, already thin, strained to the breaking point. “Where are these civilian investigators?”

“They left Atlanta. Bound for Sarasota. They plan to fly over the area where the Reed sailboat sank.”

"That's absurd," Hedinger said, his tone as hard as granite. "What do they hope to find?"

"They'll find nothing. Because there's nothing there. We removed all evidence when we collected Reed from the water," Cade said.

"Surely they know they're foolishly wasting resources."

"As long as they're engaged in distractions, they're of no concern to us," Cade replied.

Hedinger tapped his index finger on the highly polished mahogany table like a metronome. "How do they plan to conduct this flyover?"

"Helicopter. They're both trained pilots. Already organized the flight.

Picking up the rental in Sarasota. Returning the bird after they complete their tour."

Hedinger smiled. "Helicopters go down all the time."

"Yes," Cade agreed. "And when they do, all passengers are often lost."

"True. True." Hedinger **tsk-tsk**ed a few times. "Let me know when it's done."

"Copy that," Cade said before Hedinger hung up.

He was pleased with the plan. The Atlanta PD detective was dead. These two private investigators would be dispatched. The matter would lie forgotten once more.

Of course, Hedinger could simply eliminate Dr. Brand and put an end to the matter.

But the organ-selling operation had become very lucrative.

It was also a perfect source of business opportunities.

Hedinger was somewhat surprised how many of his rich and powerful contacts were willing and able to pay for Dr. Brand's organs.

Since the buying and selling of human organs was illegal in most countries, not to mention how many people found it morally reprehensible, Brand's patients were also easy to blackmail.

The blackmail possibilities were a secondary benefit that Hedinger had exploited several times and planned to exploit more in the future.

Yes, he could close down the organ business. But he simply preferred not to.

# Chapter 24

**Sarasota**

Aside from the usual annoyances of commercial air travel, the trip from Atlanta to Sarasota Gaspar had booked was uneventful.

Flint and Drake had dropped off their handguns to a Scarlett Investigations storage locker designed for exactly this purpose, as instructed. Traveling with guns was nothing but an exercise in frustration. Flint refused to get bogged down in government red tape and Gaspar agreed.

They'd chosen first-class tickets, seats 1A and 1B, for easy on and off, to avoid the inevitable boarding and deplaning bottlenecks. As soon as the door was opened, Flint made a beeline for the exit and Drake followed close behind.

Gaspar had arranged a car service. They didn't need a personal vehicle here.

Neither Flint nor Drake felt comfortable without a sidearm. After a short ride from the main terminal, they made a brief stop to pick up two handguns and other equipment Gaspar had provided.

Less than an hour after landing in Sarasota, Drake and Flint reached the hangar where the helicopter Gaspar reserved was waiting. The weather felt like Houston. Hot and humid. But Flint didn't take off his jacket. Concealed weapons were a normal thing to Flint, but not everybody felt good about having them around. The last thing he needed was some apoplectic tourist calling 911. Easier just to keep his jacket on and avoid the conversation when dealing with civilians.

The hangar floor was polished concrete, the sunlight so bright it seemed blindingly white, even behind his dark glasses. He supposed the sun seemed painfully brilliant due to his concussion. But whatever the cause, the piercing light didn't help his headache at all.

The rental manager, a man named Tony, had a face that seemed larger than his body. He waved toward the helo. “There’s your bird. All ready to go, as promised.”

Flint stared at the old beast. It was a Robinson R44. He’d agreed to pay a small fortune to use it, but now that he’d seen it, he was willing to pay more for something better.

“Is this the best helo you have?”

Tony shrugged. “We got better if you want to wait until tomorrow. This is what we have available today.”

Flint looked around the hangar. Apart from a Piper Super Cub in the far corner, Tony was right. The Piper had the range and would have been faster and more comfortable, but the helicopter offered more options for improvised landings.

On balance, fast and comfortable were important but landings won out.

“It’ll do three hundred miles,” Tony said. “Long as you don’t gas it all the way there.”

“Is it full?”

“To the brim. We fuel up on return. Don’t charge no add-ons either.” Tony confirmed, as if these were fine bargaining points indeed.

“Okay,” Flint said after exchanging glances with Drake. “We’ll take it.”

“Where you headed?” Tony asked.

“Naples.”

“Over water?”

Flint nodded, “Yeah.”

"Two flare guns under the passenger seat," Tony said. "And a life raft under the pilot's. Pull the handle and it'll inflate."

"Sounds good." Drake grinned. "This is just a sightseeing trip. We're not expecting to need the raft."

Tony gave him a hard look. "Might want to check it out. Best to be prepared. If you get my drift."

"Yeah," Flint replied quickly. He always traveled prepared. In this case, with a Glock pistol in a shoulder holster under his jacket and a Ka-Bar knife strapped to his ankle.

"I need a destination for the log," Tony said. "We do get audited from time to time."

"Wing South Airpark," said Drake, pulling his license from his wallet. "I'll be flying."

Tony delivered another hard stare. "Just the two of you, right?"

Drake nodded.

Tony tilted his head toward Flint. "No offense, just you don't seem in the best of health."

"No offense taken," Flint said, but he didn't argue.

Tony was more astute than he looked. Which meant Flint and Drake had been appropriately circumspect around him.

They followed Tony into the rental office. Drake filled out a mass of paperwork. Twenty minutes later the Robinson was out on the apron. Drake checked over the controls and ran the engine to warm everything up.

Flint was impatient. They were burning daylight. They had a lot of surface to cover and he didn't want to be doing this again tomorrow.

Finally, Drake was ready. "Okay. Get in."

The Robinson had simple seat belts, not much different from the type in any road vehicle. They weren't the more specialized four- or five-point harnesses. But for a hundred-mile sightseeing jaunt they'd be just fine.

Flint donned his headset, a reasonably new-looking Bose with great noise reduction. Conversation between the pair of them would be easy.

Twisting his head, he could see around. Almost the entire front was transparent, from above his head all the way to his feet. There were two doors on either side with big windows.

The whole arrangement offered a great scenic view. Unfortunately, there were no vertical reference windows low down, the windows many helicopters had in the floor to help with landing or maneuvering over ground objects. A pity, since straight down was where Flint wanted to look, but they'd manage.

Drake wound up the revs and smoothly lifted the Robinson a few feet before nosing forward, gaining speed and altitude.

Tony watched from the hangar as they headed out. He gave an approving nod and disappeared back inside.

They kept about a mile offshore. Following the coast road and the long stretches of sand when the road disappeared. The coast twisted and turned, inlets and bays, some small, some large.

Flint spied boats of all sizes. Day-trip fishermen and pleasure craft. Powerboats that gave the Robinson a run for its money for a few moments. Farther out, a mega yacht cruised north, a handful of people around its swimming pool. The women scurried to cover up when the Robinson passed overhead.

They passed the Charlotte Harbor Preserve State Park, green and peaceful. A reminder of what the state must have looked like long before the land booms started.

Fort Myers appeared ahead on the horizon. The rigid geometry of its streets a stark contrast to the unspoiled abandon of the park.

“Twenty miles south and ten miles west to go before we reach the point where Reed’s boat went down,” Flint said. He pointed out to sea. “Turn thirty degrees.”

Drake eased the helicopter around, taking the turn gently.

“Thanks,” Flint said.

“For what?”

“Taking it easy on my balance. My head is still swimming if I move too quickly.”

Drake grunted. “Just trying to keep our speed up.”

Flint laughed. Drake would never admit to giving him an easy time. He’d view it as a loss of pride or something.

At only four thousand feet up, they lost sight of land. Drake zoomed out the tiny GPS navigation display. “Good to keep the shore in view. Stay oriented.”

"My visual orientation skills are not that great at the moment," said Flint.

"Want to circle in toward the spot where we think the boat sank?"

Flint held up his thumb.

Drake turned medium hard. Not the Robinson's full performance capability, but enough for the additional half G to mess with Flint's balance and make him woozy.

# Chapter 25

## Miami

Once the Robinson was airborne, Gaspar manipulated his keyboard until he located a satellite with a view of the Gulf of Mexico along the west coast of Florida and set his system to record.

He had his own work to do. The Hanna Campbell case wasn't his problem to solve, and Maria had a late lunch on the table.

Gaspar followed the amazing aromas and made his way to the outdoor dining room, where his family gathered for the Cuban food his kids loved in celebration of his father's birthday.

Ropa vieja, the national dish of Cuba, was his father's favorite. It was a hearty stew made with shredded beef, tomato sauce, onions, and peppers. Served with yellow rice and Cuban bread, the meal was both delicious and filling.

For dessert, Gaspar's mother had made tres leches cake, served as always with sweetened Cuban coffee.

"A meal fit for a king," his father said, toasting Maria with his coffee cup.

Maria blushed and smiled. "Papa, it's always a pleasure to cook for you."

Gaspar's five children adored their grandparents. After the meal, the family cleared the dishes and resettled on the patio for gifts. The celebration promised to last through the afternoon and well into the evening.

"Maria, I'll do the dishes and join you in a bit. I need to check a few things first."

Maria gave him a quick squeeze and a brief kiss. "Don't wait too long."

"Promise. I'll be there soon." After he placed the dishes into the dishwasher, he returned to his home office.

He sat at the desk and pressed a button to wake up the monitor with the satellite feed from the Gulf. He zoomed in for a closer look at the area ten miles off the Florida coast near Ft. Myers.

Even though there was nothing left of Greta Reed's yacht, Flint said he wanted to get a feel for the circumstances. Flint always wanted to see things firsthand. Which explained why the Robinson was miles from shore.

"What's there to see?" Drake had said. "There's nothing but water that far from shore. The sailboat was swamped and they drowned, according to the official accounts. And it's been four years. Whatever was left of the boat and everything on it wouldn't be in the same location anyway."

“Yeah, I know. But it helps me to be surrounded by the conditions. Or at least, as much as we can re-create them. I need to understand exactly what she was faced with. The question we need to answer is, how could Greta be alive?” Flint pointed out. “Unless we believe in miracles, it seems to me there’s only one answer.”

Gaspar agreed. “Somebody picked her up. A recreational boater, perhaps. Because if somebody official rescued her, like the Coast Guard, we’d have an official record of the fact.”

“Don’t bother trying to convince me that we weren’t doing around the clock surveillance of the Gulf in that area four years ago," Flint said. "Can you get satellite footage back that far?"

"Finding video from four years ago isn't a walk in the park," Gaspar replied flatly. "It's not like I'm still FBI and I can just call up Homeland or the Pentagon or even NASA and ask for it."

"Four years back wasn't the Ice Age. There's thousands of satellites up there watching every minute of every day," Flint replied. "Somebody's got that footage. Let's find out who has it first. Then we'll figure out how to persuade them to give it to us."

Gaspar had laughed. "So this is the royal 'we'?"

Flint grinned on the other end of the call. “Okay, you then.”

“And what about Scarlett? I’m fairly sure she’s got a list of paying clients I’m supposed to be working for, right this very minute,” Gaspar replied.

“You let me handle Scarlett. She says anything to you, just send her my way,” Flint said, as if the prospect didn’t terrify him. Which Gaspar knew it probably did.

The relationship between Flint and Katie Scarlett was complicated. Gaspar didn’t know enough about the history there. All he knew was that Scarlett ruled the cases Gaspar worked on, and like him, Flint was a hired hand.

Gaspar wasn't sure where the Campbell case fit into all of this.

Technically, Hanna Campbell wasn't a paying client at all. Gaspar didn't know whether any of the work he'd been doing so far had been approved by Scarlett.

Nor did he plan to ask. No point.

He would do the work anyway. Why give Scarlett a chance to issue an order he had no intention of following?

This was a circumstance where it was better to ask for forgiveness than permission.

He reached into his desk drawer for the Tylenol bottle and swallowed a couple of the tablets as he hit the fast forward button on the satellite video feed, running the footage from the time he'd left for dinner through the present.

Gaspar searched until he saw the Robinson moving toward the boat's last known location and then increased the viewing speed. The Robinson moved along easily until a speedboat approached.

The boat was plowing through the water at a high rate of speed. The captain cut the engine and the boat floated to a stop.

Which was when Gaspar zoomed in on the boat and realized Flint's helo was in serious trouble.

# Chapter 26

## Gulf of Mexico

Flint glanced through the side window and focused on the horizon. The dizzy feeling still spun his head and his belly, but purposeful focus was helping keep him upright.

He'd had vertigo once while he was still in the Marines. Miserable experience. For at least two weeks, he'd had the sensation that everything around him was spinning. He could barely walk until the episode passed.

The dizziness he felt now was similar. He could only hope it would correct itself shortly.

Drake punched a few buttons on the GPS and a circle appeared, their position marked on its edge. “We can fly loops inside the circle, and we’ll home in to center. We might see something on the floor that could lead us to the wreckage.”

“Yeah, but keep in mind that they did a lot of search and rescue in the area at the time. It’s not likely we’ll find anything. I just want to get a feel for the place. Try to understand what happened that day,” Flint said.

“Copy that,” Drake said.

They leveled out, tracing the curve on the screen. The heading indicator showed them rotating around the circle’s center.

A boat passed under them, the curve of the Robinson's flight path making them seem to move sideways.

The Gulf looked mostly blue with mottled green areas floating and drifting. "Algae," Flint said.

They completed a circuit. Drake moved in for another loop closer to the target point.

"Lower," said Flint, pointing down. "Thousand feet."

Flint watched the instruments as Drake brought the helicopter down, feathering their descent to level out smoothly at exactly one thousand feet. The tiny helicopter shook, buffeted by the wind.

The Gulf looked rougher at lower altitude, too. A few feet of swell and some whitecaps were visible close by. A small boat pushed slowly toward shore, rocking as the waves passed under it.

In the distance, a speedboat hammered over the wave crests, leaving clouds of spray in its wake. The driver seemed determined to make the most of his toy even if it meant pounding hard against the water. Or maybe he liked the torture.

The helicopter continued on its curved path and the speedboat rotated out of Flint's field of view. Occasionally, he saw various items bobbing on the waves. Trash. Some from the shore, some thrown overboard, some washed off decks along the shoreline.

They completed another revolution. Drake moved the helicopter toward the center of the circle on the screen.

"Last lap," he said.

The speedboat had closed the gap between them, its captain still pushing the boat's throttle to the max. Now the boat was only a few hundred yards away. The captain stood at the controls and another man stood at the rear. The passenger seemed to be struggling with a harpoon gun.

The boat slowed instantly. Almost like an emergency stop. Its big engine must have been cut from full power to nothing. No longer hammering over the crests, the boat rolled in the waves.

The driver went to help the passenger. Flint scanned the water. “What could those guys be fishing for this far out into the Gulf with a harpoon gun?”

“I don’t know. Marlin? Grouper? I do seem to remember lots of photos of Hemingway holding some big fish into the air,” Drake said with a grin. “Didn’t he fish a lot out here?”

“Farther south, I think. Closer to Key West,” Flint replied, still watching the boat.

The passenger swung the harpoon up. Flint saw the weapon well enough to identify it. Not a harpoon at all.

Secured on a straining bar across the boat, it was some kind of long gun.

Grips and stands and handhold protruded. It was big and bulky with a long barrel.

The guy put his head down right behind the weapon.

Adjusting his aim. Lining up.

In a moment Flint realized he was staring straight down the barrel's black void.

"Fifty cal!" Flint shouted, pointing to the right, away from the speedboat. "Dive. Fast. Go, go, go."

Drake rolled the helicopter right, tipped the nose forward, and yanked up on the collective. The engine began to spool up.

“What the hell?” Drake shouted. “Why is that fool shooting at us?”

Clouds of smoke erupted from the gun. The shooter jerked backward. The captain had moved forward, bracing the shooter, helping him to remain standing.

Even though they were wearing noise-canceling headsets, the sound of metal being torn screeched through the Robinson with deafening volume.

The engine picked up revs. Flint felt more G’s in his stomach.

Drake peeled the helo away from the boat.

More bursts of smoke came from the gun. Flint braced himself for a direct hit, but it didn't come.

Flint reached for his Glock and decided against it. Everything was moving too much and too fast. A lucky shot might take down their attackers, but he couldn't be certain. And with only one clip, he couldn't lay down much suppressing fire against the fifty cal anyway.

He glanced around the cabin for another weapon.

The captain restarted the boat. The bow leapt from the water when he pushed the throttle to the max.

"What's this bird's top speed?" Flint said.

“In theory? One thirty knots.”

“Hundred and fifty miles an hour. We should outrun them.”

“Except I’m at full power and we’re doing sixty.”

“I heard lots of metal breaking.” Flint replied. “They must have hit something.”

“Yeah. Fuel. We’re losing it big time.”

Flint craned around and saw liquid streaming from under the helicopter. Had to be the fuel. Maybe a few other fluids, too.

The speedboat was closing the gap between them. The shooter was holding on to a side rail and had lowered the gun for the rough cruising conditions.

Flint yelled, “Drop. Over them. Now. Fast, fast.”

“What?” Drake shouted, but he lowered the collective and angled the helicopter down toward the boat.

The helo dropped fast. Flint’s senses rolled and the contents of his stomach threatened to come up.

He closed his mouth, holding his lips hard together as he struggled to grab a flare gun. He pulled on the collective, steering directly over the boat.

The liquid stream coming from the helicopter poured onto the rear of the speedboat.

The captain shut down the boat’s engine and the shooter lifted the fifty cal.

Flint shoved the helo door into the wide-open position.

The boat was rolling on the waves.

The helicopter was struggling to stay aloft.

Flares were slow. Fired into the air, they took many seconds to reach their peak altitude.

Flint judged the distance to the boat to be only a hundred feet. Which should be okay. But he waited until it reached a trough in the waves before firing the flare gun.

"Go, go!" he shouted to Drake.

The helo's engine began a labored rumble and they rolled away to the right.

The flare's brilliant flash curved slightly as it traveled. Gravity was pulling it down.

A few agonizing moments passed before the flare hit the rear of the boat. It landed behind the shooter.

Fizzing and sparking, the flare grew to its full brightness.

The shooter held the long gun up and fired. Smoke pulsed from the barrel.

The Robinson took repeated hits.

Shaking with each impact, the helo became less stable with each blow.

Flint could feel the thin metal of the craft being peeled away.

The plastic door beside him shattered.

The speedboat's rear end exploded in yellow flame. The flames grew into a single great conflagration, relentlessly rising.

The Robinson could take no more. It began to rotate, curving to the right, and shook violently.

They were going down.

# Chapter 27

As the helo took hit after hit, the noise was deafening. Flint's head felt as if it might explode. He whipped his gaze in all directions, which only made the headaches worse.

With less than a hundred feet to fall, Drake had no chance of autorotating to absorb the impact.

"Blades headed toward the tail!" shouted Drake. "Brace!"

The Robinson's rotors were flexing with the rough handling. They'd reached their limit. The blades flexed so far they pummeled the tail boom, chopping it to pieces.

With a violent lurch, the Robinson began to spin.

Flint glimpsed black clouds rising from the speedboat's rear end as the helicopter corkscrewed its way down toward the Gulf. Flint grabbed the second flare from under his seat and pulled on his seat belt, cinching himself tighter.

The nose hit first, ramming him forward against his shoulder harness.

The whole machine tumbled over, slapping against the water.

Flint glimpsed sky as the helicopter rolled one last time. Then they were facing the Gulf's water again.

Cold water poured through his smashed door into the cabin.

The engine stopped.

Water hissed on hot metal. Cracks and pops filled the air.

Flint pulled the release lever and wriggled out of his harness.

Drake struggled to free himself from his seat belt.

Water continued gushing in as the helo continued to sink. The cockpit was half full already.

They would be underwater in twenty seconds. Probably less.

Flint pulled the knife from his ankle and cut the straps of his harness.

The helicopter rolled ninety degrees, forcing Flint's side into the water. The knife slipped out of his hand as he struggled to hold on to his seat. Drake half slid and half floated into the canopy.

Flint leaned over Drake's seat and pulled the lever to open the far door, which was now on the upper side as the craft lay in the water.

Air rushed out and water rushed in to fill the space.

The helicopter was never designed to float, and nature rapidly proved the point. It sank in seconds.

Flint angled through the open door and pushed with his legs to propel himself upward. Drake followed a moment later, carrying the deflated orange life raft in his hands.

They reached the surface, coughing and spluttering.

The waves rolled over them. Flint's faulty equilibrium begged the motion to stop, but his pleading was a waste of energy.

Flint glanced in all directions. He had no idea where the speedboat was now. He lay his arms on the water's surface and kicked with his legs and allowed the waves to pass. When a wave swept him up, he used the vantage point to look farther.

It was the wrong move.

He spied the boat, which was half burned. The fire was out now, but the boat was still moving. When he spied the boat, the captain must have spied him, too.

The boat turned toward Flint and Drake. The engine roared a moment then died back to a burble. Flint couldn't tell whether the captain had an attack plan or if the fire had damaged the boat, thwarting the plan before it began.

"Open the raft," Flint called.

"Now?" Drake's voice was incredulous.

"Just do it. Then dive. Stay under as long as you can."

Drake pulled a red handle and the raft burst into life. In a matter of a few quick seconds, compressed air expanded into chambers to form the circular base. The central cover rose gently, pulled taught by the raft's expansion.

Drake breathed hard, oxygenating his blood. Flint did the same and a moment later they disappeared underwater.

They swam toward the approaching boat which they could see in shadow cast by the bright blue sky above. The boat passed overhead. It was moving slowly. The engine's lazy chug was beating the water but not gaining speed.

Flint surfaced near the damaged boat on the side opposite the life raft. He bobbed his way to the rear and located a steel ladder.

The engine was still running. The boat rocked on the waves. The motion made him nauseous.

Flint pulled his pistol from his shoulder holster and prepared to board the boat.

There was plenty of noise to cover his actions, so he climbed fast, cresting the gunwale, Glock first. The fire had melted the seats and much of the rear of the craft. One man lay on his back, burned and groaning with the rise and fall of every swell.

At the front, the captain had the fifty-caliber rifle resting on a straining bar and lined up to aim at the orange life raft.

When he was ready, he pulled the trigger.

The gun bucked in his hands. The captain struggled to keep himself planted on the boat's moving deck.

The gun slid a few inches from side to side. The bullets were churning the water and tearing the raft to pieces.

The man was no amateur. He knew what he wanted to do, and he did it well. He'd had training. And plenty of it.

The burned man raised an arm and pointed at Flint.

"Here, here, here," he said, hissing through clenched teeth. Urgent. Demanding attention.

The captain turned, his eyes going wide when he saw Flint on the boat.

He swung the fifty-caliber rifle around. Sliding it off the straining bar. Bracing it with his left hand.

He was a big man. It was a big weapon. Lots of weight and inertia. The strain and urgency were obvious from the contortions of his face.

Flint didn't wait. The captain had stepped too far over the line.

There was no time to subdue him. This was kill or be killed. And Flint would not land on the wrong side of that equation.

Flint fired the Glock. Rapid. Five shots.

The first hit the man's knee. The ocean swell and the movement of the boat brought the following shots up in a line. Hip, stomach, chest, head.

The captain's bloody body lurched backward, pushed by the impact of the shots and the movement of the boat. He rolled over the side rail, the strap of the fifty-caliber gun wrapped around his arm. He fell back, splashed into the water, and the heavy gun pulled him under.

He was gone.

Flint staggered across the deck, holding on to anything he could grasp to stay upright. He kept his gun aimed at the burned man as he took a quick check over the edge of the boat.

Flint confirmed that the captain's body had been taken all the way down by the weight of the big gun.

Drake climbed aboard the speedboat at the rear ladder, the same as Flint had done. He checked on the burned man and summarized his condition.

Drake shook his head. "Guy's in a bad way."

"Would have been us if he'd been a better shot," said Flint, slumping into the captain's seat.

Drake found a large first aid kit and a Syrette of morphine.

"These guys were serious," Drake said, administering the shot to the burned man.

As the morphine took hold, the man's groans slowed, and he drifted off. Flint shook his head. The guy probably wouldn't make it, given the extent of his burns.

"How far away do you think we are now?" Flint asked as he turned the boat toward the coast. "Five miles? Ten?"

Drake shrugged. "We were eight miles out when we took the first hit from the fifty cal. So maybe about the same?"

"We'll never make it back to shore. We're taking on water. And the fuel has been leaking for a while," Flint said. "We'll get as close as we can. Maybe ride the tide. Stay with the boat until it goes down."

“And then what?” Drake asked with a grin. “Pray?”

Flint shrugged. “Whatever works.”

They limped along with the engine maxed out at a few miles an hour. Flint scanned the skies for a rescue plane of some sort. Satellite surveillance or simple radar should notice them and send a rescue vessel.

Drake nudged him out of the captain’s seat. “Take a break. You know we’ll have plenty of explaining to do when we get back. Get your story straight.”

Flint accepted the offer and found a section of seating that wasn’t charred to lie on.

His head felt better when he was lying down, but his mind still raced through disjointed and foggy moments.

Who were those guys on the fifty cal? Why were they trying to bring down the helo? How the hell did they know he and Drake would be flying around out here?

Flint felt himself dozing off when he heard the sound of a powerful helicopter engine approaching from overhead. He covered his eyes and stared into the distance.

“Friend or enemy?” Drake asked, still standing at the steering wheel, peering in the same direction.

# Chapter 28

## Miami

Flint and Drake pulled up in Gaspar's driveway late. They came in through the back gate, bypassing the front door and the doorbell, which would have started the dog barking and awakened his neighbors. Their clothes had dried, but they looked bedraggled and exhausted. Which they no doubt were.

"Sorry to be so late. Took longer than we'd expected," Drake said as they approached. "Thanks for the rescue, by the way."

"Glad to help. Maddy would never forgive me if I let Michael drown out there." Gaspar raised his coffee mug in the direction of the kitchen. "Fresh pot inside if you want it."

"Yeah, well, you might have sent the calvary twenty minutes earlier. Those guys almost took us out before we had a chance to drown," Drake replied on his way inside.

"Seriously, Gaspar. Thank you. You went above and beyond today. Truly." Flint plopped onto a chaise lounge, kneading his forehead between the eyes. "Hanna Campbell isn't even one of Scarlett's cases. No reason you should be on the hook for any of what's going on."

Gaspar shrugged. “I meant what I said. Maddy might be seven years old, but she’s a force to be reckoned with. I wouldn’t want to be in her line of fire.”

“You got that right. She’s something, isn’t she?” Flint grinned. “I’m starting to see why Scarlett hired you.”

Drake came back with the coffee, handed one mug to Flint and sat across from Gaspar.

“I do have some bad news,” Gaspar said solemnly.

“We were just shot out of the sky and nearly drowned,” Drake joked. “How much worse can it get?”

Flint replied, “That’s never a question you want to ask. Bad karma. Things can always be worse. Trust me.”

Quietly, Gaspar said, “Detective Dean Myer was killed about three hours after you met with her.”

“What?” Flint asked, as if he hadn’t heard.

“They were called out to a homicide. When she got there, she walked into a firefight between rival gangs. She was killed. Her partner seriously wounded,” Gaspar continued. “He may not survive, either. Touch and go, last report I heard.”

Drake cupped his mug in both big palms and stared into the coffee as if it might reflect his mental image of Detective Myer’s friendly face and dazzling smile.

Flint said, “No doubt they were wearing body armor. Where’d she get hit?”

“Myer took four bullets. Two to the head, one in the neck, one in the chest,” Gaspar replied. “Head wounds killed her.”

“Unlucky shots,” Drake said. “Gangbangers point, shoot, aim. Bullets go wild. They couldn’t hit a smaller female target in the head if they tried. Not even once. Certainly not twice.”

“Chest shot to the armor is okay. Hurts like hell, but not lethal. Head shots would have killed her quickly. Neck shot would have done the job a bit slower but still too soon for most first responders to arrive on scene.”

Flint sat up and gulped his lukewarm coffee. His tone was thoughtful, like he was working it through. “Myer’s partner was wounded, presumably unconscious. So he didn’t shoot her. Got a witness?”

“Other officers were at the scene.” Gaspar shook his head. “None with a clear view of Myer’s position.”

“So who says the bangers fired those four shots?” Flint asked.

“Good question. Ballistics are inconclusive. Could possibly have been unauthorized ammo. But the ordnance definitely wasn’t Atlanta PD standard issue.” Gaspar gave Drake another moment to grasp the same conclusions he and Flint had already reached.

“So preliminarily, given the ordnance, we don’t think Myer was killed by friendly fire,” Flint explained.

“They’ll need to locate the weapons actually used to kill her.” Drake replied slowly. “Any luck with that?”

“Still searching.” Gaspar paused, drained his sweet Cuban coffee, and replied. “What the ballistics show is all four shots most likely came from the same weapon.”

Flint gave Gaspar and Drake a hard look.

“So we’re supposed to believe some street punk was good enough with a gun to hit Detective Myer in the head and neck and chest with not one but four lucky shots?” Drake said, shaking his head slowly. "Not a chance in Hell."

Flint said quietly, "It's notable that Myer died within hours after talking to us. Seems like they'd have killed her before she gave us the Ella Belle Reed file, doesn't it?"

Drake's eyes widened. "You think Myer was killed for giving us that file?"

"It's a reasonable assumption. She was alive and well until she handed over those materials. Now she's dead," Gaspar said.

"Yeah." Flint felt a slow burning anger in his gut.

"I'm sorry, Flint," Drake said. "I know you liked her."

Gaspar rose to refill his coffee. "Could be coincidence or just bad luck. But that's not likely, is it?"

He put on a new pot to brew and made a quick round to check on his sleeping family. Gaspar wasn't an anxious man, but he'd seen more than his share of crime. One perk of the new job was his around-the-clock availability to protect his family. Which was a job he took more seriously than any other.

After the security check, he popped his head into his office to check on the screens he kept running around the clock. Gaspar didn't sleep well or long, and he wanted his systems up and awake whenever he was.

He'd set up extensive facial recognition searches for both Phillip Reed and Greta Campbell Reed when Drake first approached him. The only exclusions he'd put on the searches were time-based. He asked the systems to find images after the date of the boating accident when Greta and Phillip were both declared lost at sea.

Even with that limitation, he expected the searches to take a good long while.

Gaspar confirmed the systems were still running. Faces flashed rapidly on the screen as the images were checked and discarded by the software.

Eventually, if Greta and her husband were still alive, the software would find images of them anywhere in the world where cameras existed.

Question was, how long would it take? And would the images be useful once they were located?

One thing at a time. It was the best he could do given how little they knew at this point.

Drake and Flint had held off discussing the case until Gaspar returned with the steaming pot and topped off their coffee. He'd grabbed a box of guava cookies from the kitchen. Sugar and caffeine kept them all going for now.

"I looked at the flash drive's contents. The one Detective Myer gave you," Gaspar said after he settled into his seat again. "Nothing especially helpful that you don't already know."

"Did they have any suspects in the Ella Belle murder?" Drake asked. "Or was the burglar just a lucky shot, too?"

Gaspar shook his head. "They found trace evidence at the scene, but all of it was eventually identified. Most belonged to Dr. and Mrs. Reed. Everything else was tied to friends or family."

"So nothing from the killer, then," Drake said with a grimace.

"What about Phillip Reed? His behavior after his first wife died doesn't pass the smell test," Flint said. "Entirely too methodical and cold-blooded for an honestly grieving husband."

"Agreed. He finds his wife bleeding on the stairs. Sees the shooter but lets him run out. Doesn't try to chase him or stop him the way loving husbands do," Gaspar said. "Rides in the ambulance and the paramedics say he was detached and professional all the way. Not one tear. No angst of any kind. Delivering medical care to her like she was someone he didn't even know."

"I've seen guys like that in combat, though," Drake said. "They power through, hanging tough, doing the job they're trained to do. Doesn't mean they're not impacted by it all."

"True enough." Flint replied. "But taken together, the transplant operations, the lack of displayed emotions, getting remarried so soon afterward, then disappearing in that boating incident. Dr. Reed is just **off**."

Gaspar said, "He could be a cold-blooded sociopath. There're plenty of those around."

"Regardless of his psychological makeup, he's our most logical suspect. Statistically, the man closest to his female victim is the most likely killer. We'll go with Dr. Reed for now, keeping an open mind if we find a better option," Flint replied.

"Suits me." Drake yawned and shook his head to wake up. The coffee was no longer doing the job. He was wrung out.

Flint stood and stretched and nearly lost his balance. He shifted his feet to avoid falling sideways and then plopped backward onto the lounge chair.

“You guys need a bed for the night? We’ve got an empty guest room. Twin beds,” Gaspar offered. They could probably sleep right here on the patio, but the forecast called for overnight rain.

“We hate to put you out,” Drake said, like a man who wanted to accept the offered hospitality. “What will Maria say?”

“Maria loves guests,” Gaspar replied, moving toward the kitchen. “No reason to go to a hotel. You’d just have to come back here in the morning. This way.”

Once they were settled in the guest room, Gaspar returned to his office with another cup of creamy sweet coffee and a couple of cookies. He sent a few quick emails and wrote a short report to Scarlett about a different case.

He'd finished his coffee and pushed his chair back, intending to go for a refill. Which was when he noticed that one of his systems was still running, but the other one had stopped flashing images across the screen.

The facial recognition software got a hit.

Gaspar examined several images displayed on the screen.

Sometimes the software returned false positives. More often than not, actually.

The reference photo was static in the top left corner. He'd used a formal head shot of Phillip Stephen Reed posted as his public biography on several medical websites before he disappeared.

He could have used passport photos, but he'd had better luck in the past using less formal images if they were clear enough.

The faces showing now on Gaspar's screen were multiple views of another man the software had matched to the reference photo.

Gaspar sat at the keyboard and isolated the images for a closer look.

"Is that Phillip Reed?" Flint said as he approached to stand behind Gaspar, peering at the screen.

"Couldn't sleep?" Gaspar asked, working the keys, checking the reference points on the images, seeking to confirm.

"Woke up. Searching for the toilet. Saw you in here," Flint replied. Staring at the pulsing screen set off his headache again, but he couldn't pull his gaze away from the images. "Looks exactly like Phillip Reed to me."

"Maybe," Gaspar said, still working, seeking, comparing, as Flint waited for an answer.

Finally, Gaspar pushed his chair back and stood to stretch out his bad right leg.

"Is it him?" Flint asked. "If Phillip Reed is alive, then Greta could be, too."

"Can't be sure. But if I were a betting man, I'd say yes," Gaspar replied. "His name is Stephen Brand. He's a doctor. A transplant surgeon, in fact."

Flint deadpanned. "What a coincidence."

"He's within a couple of years of the right age. His background data looks reasonable, but it could have been falsified. It'll take me a while to run it all down," Gaspar said, headed back to the kitchen for more coffee.

# Chapter 29

**Atabei**

Despite his immense wealth, Ernst Hedinger enjoyed a long list of foibles. Among them was his almost pathological desire for privacy.

He rarely entertained, seldom allowed house guests, and never slept in a bed he didn't own. As a younger man, he'd been required to stay overnight in hotels and private homes for business purposes, but that was many years ago.

Like many of his eccentricities, his desire for privacy required him to own and maintain several homes around the world. The Atabei villa was one of his favorites.

One wing of his mansion was reserved for exceptionally qualified patients at Brand's hospital. Very few were offered the privilege and the current guest was the first in a long while.

The man who called himself John Smith was a high ranking official in the Chinese Communist Party. He would, some said, be General Secretary one day.

Exactly the kind of personal relationship Hedinger craved, even as he realized, in this instance, he'd allowed a scorpion into his home.

Smith was especially difficult in many respects. Which was why he had paid a large fortune for his donor heart. Smith, a man of exacting standards, required a personal interview of his Chinese heart donor prior to the procedure.

The donor was honored to meet the great man and answered all of his questions fully. Until Smith thanked him for his heart. Terrified and unwilling to die, the donor had tried to escape. Hedinger's guards pursued and subdued the man. Brand kept him alive and well until it was time to remove his heart this morning.

Hedinger enjoyed breakfast while reading his morning reports. He perused the list, located Cade's summary of special operations, and skimmed through his account of the helicopter incident quickly.

Hedinger read the summary twice, feeling his blood pressure rising to dangerous levels as he absorbed the words. He picked up the phone and dialed.

When Cade answered, Hedinger bellowed into the speaker. “What the hell happened?”

“Results were inconclusive.” To his credit, Cade didn’t make excuses. “The helicopter went down with both occupants still inside. The boat was also heavily damaged and our operatives compromised.”

“Dammit, man! Did you have eyes on the operation or not?” Hedinger demanded, barely controlling his rage.

The one thing Hedinger could not abide was incompetence. Cade had failed. Failure was never an option. Hedinger would terminate and replace him within the hour.

While Cade remained on the call, Hedinger dispatched the order electronically in disappearing text. This would be their final conversation.

“We have footage of the firefight. The bird was hit. It sank.” Cade paused. “We haven’t heard from our operatives for several hours. Both are presumed dead. No bodies recovered at this time.”

“Send me the video.”

“Already done. You have it now.”

Hedinger opened his laptop and punched a couple of keys to pull up the footage. He set the video to play and watched as the scene unfolded.

Before he had a chance to say anything else, he heard a hard double knock at Cade's door.

"Yes?" Cade said.

The door creaked open. Hedinger heard two silenced gunshots and Cade's heavy body falling to the floor.

Half a moment later, a voice on the phone reported, "It's done."

Hedinger disconnected. Cade's body would disappear before nightfall. Finding his US COO's replacement moved up on his task list.

Hedinger ran the video several times.

The helicopter had been shot down. No question.

But both men in the cockpit had survived the crash.

Hedinger watched as the life raft inflated and moved toward the boat.

Followed by the unmistakable sounds of the fifty-caliber shooting the raft.

The video ended abruptly at that point.

Hedinger refilled his coffee and slumped into his chair. He felt defeated. Which was a rare occurrence and definitely not okay. Not even remotely.

The only possible conclusion he could reach from the video was that all four men were still alive. But Hedinger's two operatives had failed to return to base. As Cade had said, they were probably dead.

Which could mean the two Americans in the helicopter had survived close quarters combat on the damaged boat.

But what happened afterward? Where was the boat? Where were the Americans?

Hedinger scanned official reports from law enforcement agencies operating in the vicinity. He found nothing from those agencies or others reporting the incident itself or the rescue of survivors.

Hedinger felt his pulse pounding in his ears. Such incompetence. His breathing was labored, and his face felt flushed.

The only good thing he knew for sure was that Cade was dead. Which was not even close to enough retribution for this colossal screwup.

Hedinger glanced at the clock. Brand would be wrapping up John Smith's transplant surgery within the hour.

He finished his breakfast and calmed himself by reading the remaining reports of worldwide operations. When next he glanced at the clock, two hours had passed.

Hedinger found the encrypted phone that connected him to Brand and pushed the call button.

“We’re finished,” Brand said wearily. “All went well. The donor has been cremated. Mr. Smith can be transferred to your villa in a couple of days.”

“Good,” Hedinger replied with perfunctory interest. He had other issues top of mind. “I need to see you. Now.”

“Can I get a shower first?”

“My car will pick you up in ten minutes,” Hedinger snapped and disconnected the call.

# Chapter 30

Brand had showered and changed before Hedinger's chauffeur collected him at the hospital for the short ride to the villa. The attractive sprawling residence, constructed with thick stucco walls and barrel tile roofs, overlooked the town and the aquamarine water of the Caribbean beyond.

Another mansion was under construction nearby. Brand had paid little attention to its progress. He was surprised to see the foundations were laid, the walls up, and the astonishingly complicated barrel tile roof almost completed. The construction teams seemed to have new artisans on site all the time. No doubt the mansion would be stunning. Brand wondered again who Hedinger had permitted to reside there.

The big sedan climbed the steep road to the driveway near the top of the hill. He turned right into the circle drive paved with crushed pink shells. The Mercedes stopped under the portico. Brand climbed out and stood in the shade for a brief moment to enjoy the view.

He adjusted his jacket, rested his hands casually in his pockets, and sauntered toward the front entrance. At the door, he pushed the button to ring the bell and heard the pleasant chimes ringing indoors.

The maid's hurried footsteps approached, tapping swiftly on the natural stone tiles. She stopped to swing the door open wearing a big smile and a crisply starched apron over her colorful house dress.

"Dr. Brand," she said, pleased to welcome him. "So nice to see you again."

"You look wonderful, Krystal," he said with a big smile as he stepped into the cool indoors. "How's your family?"

Krystal's wide grin showed one gold tooth in front. "They're all grown now, Dr. Brand. Off to college. I don't see them much."

She closed the door behind him and stood with her hands folded over her ample belly. “Mr. Hedinger is waiting in his study. I’ll bring fresh coffee. French press?”

“We’ll enjoy. Thank you, Krystal,” Brand replied as he stepped away, walking down one of the long corridors that led from the central foyer. Hedinger’s study was at the end where the room opened onto a private patio. Beyond that was a spectacular unobstructed view of Atabei and the aquamarine sea beyond.

Brand knocked on the rustic wood door before he entered. He crossed the wide room decorated with Spanish style furniture and accent pieces and outside to join Hedinger on the welcoming patio.

"How did the surgery go?" Hedinger asked, as if he actually cared about the patient's welfare.

The question was perfunctory. Full payment had cleared last night. Hedinger didn't care at all about the patient and they both knew it.

"He'll be fine. We'll bring him here in a couple of days. To the far wing of the house. And he'll have a private nurse. You won't see him or realize he's here." Brand stood with hands clasped behind his back, consuming the view for a few moments before he finally sat across the table from Hedinger.

Brand crossed his legs, taking care with the creases in his trousers. From experience, he knew Hedinger would come to the point only when he was damned good and ready. Efforts to rush the process would be futile and fruitless. He clasped his hands loosely in his lap and waited.

Krystal brought the aromatic fresh coffee and juices and water. She arranged the serving table and left again.

Hedinger waited a few minutes, expecting Brand to squirm with nerves. Which he most certainly would not do.

“You have a problem,” Hedinger stated flatly. “One that could impact me. We need the situation resolved. Immediately.”

“What kind of problem?” Brand replied as coolly as he could muster.

"Greta Campbell," Hedinger said. "Her sister has hired investigators to find her."

"Her sister?" Brand croaked and then cleared his throat. "Greta was estranged from her sister. They hadn't spoken in years. Not since their mother died."

He began to sweat. Perspiration dotted his brow and his upper lip. He felt it pooling in his armpits and running down inside his shirt.

"Seems she's back in the picture. She believes Greta is alive. You wouldn't know anything about that, would you?" Hedinger stared, his unflinching gaze harder than steel.

Brand shoved his hands under the table, stalling. What was the old despot fishing for?

When Hedinger had a problem, it was not merely solved and forgotten. Those responsible were always, always eliminated with extreme prejudice. Bodies simply disappeared, like this morning's heart donor had done.

"I have never met Hanna Campbell and never spoken to her. I wouldn't know her if she walked into this room wearing a name tag," Brand replied after clearing his throat several times.

"Why does Hanna believe her sister is alive?" Hedinger demanded.

"How would I know?" Brand clasped his hands together to control the tremors and slow his racing pulse.

"Tell me what's on your conscience. While there's still time to resolve matters," Hedinger said coldly.

When Brand failed to reply, Hedinger narrowed his eyes and continued. "Do you imagine that I don't know everything already, Dr. Brand?"

"The opposite. I'm certain you know everything worth knowing in the world." Brand cleared his throat again, shaking his head. "I told you. Repeatedly."

"Tell me again."

"I dumped Greta out of the boat without a life jacket. I watched her sink. We were ten miles out into the Gulf. It was dark, cold, storming. There's no way she survived. How could she?"

Hedinger cocked his head, narrowed his eyes, and stared, as if he were a human lie detector. After a while, he said, “Okay. Maybe you’re right. Let’s say Greta died that night the way you’ve described. Why does her sister believe otherwise?”

“Hanna’s crazy. Guilt? Drugs? Hallucinations?” Brand said, dredging up his own fear-based anger for emphasis. “How should I know?”

Hedinger chuckled like a rabid hyena before he demanded, “Why are you concerned that Hanna Campbell could be right about her sister?”

“I’m not really **concerned**, exactly.” Brand took a few deep breaths. “You know this already, too. Greta found out about my first wife, Ella Belle. I don't know how she figured it out, but she did."

"Figured out what?" Hedinger asked coldly.

"That the home invasion was a setup. That I'd sold Ella Belle's heart," Brand replied. "To you."

"Go on." Hedinger's stare was unwavering.

"We were arguing. In the heat of it, she called me a cold-blooded killer."

Hedinger's lips pressed into a hard line, but he didn't interrupt.

"Greta said she'd go to the police. She said my license to practice medicine would be revoked. She said

I'd go to prison at the very least," Brand whispered. "She'd discovered that the heart recipient had died soon afterward. That made Greta wild. Uncontrollable. She came at me with a knife. What was I supposed to do?"

"So you panicked," Hedinger stated flatly. "Decided to kill her and leave the country."

Brand stared into space. "Greta was a mean and vicious woman. She'd have done everything she threatened and more if she could."

"You should have told me this at the time. It would have been easier just to eliminate Greta in a provable way," Hedinger said without sympathy. "Now we've got a situation that could ruin everything you've built here."

"Only if Greta really is alive. And how could she be? **I watched her drown**." Brand sounded truly desperate now, even to his own ears.

Hedinger allowed the silence to linger for a while before he asked, "All of this bothers you too much. You don't truly believe Greta is dead. Which means you have more than mere doubts. Tell me."

Brand lifted his head, guilt fairly oozing from his pores. He looked straight at Hedinger and confessed. "There was a royal wedding a few weeks ago in London."

He described what he'd seen. "Afterward, I scoured the internet until I found the footage of the crowd and the child and the balloon. I downloaded the video and watched it many times."

Brand could describe the woman in vivid detail, but they both knew what Greta looked like.

Hedinger didn't interrupt until Brand finished his confession. After a few moments of thinking, Hedinger said, "Look, it's not likely to be her, is it? You saw Greta drown. She's been gone for years. If she were planning to resurface and make trouble for you, she'd have done it already."

Brand felt the knot in his belly loosen slightly.

"But I can understand why both you and her sister want to confirm. Give me the video. I'll look into it," Hedinger said.

Relief flooded Brand's body, relaxing his muscles and leaving him wrung out. He felt as though he might pour like liquid mercury onto the ground. "How will you do it?"

"Leave it to me. I've got resources. I'll let you know what we find out."

"What if it turns out the woman **is** actually Greta? Will you kill her?" Brand asked because he couldn't stop himself.

He wanted Greta dead. He'd wanted her dead four years ago, and he still did.

Hedinger gave him a level stare. "Let's cross that bridge if we come to it, shall we?"

# Chapter 31

### Houston

Flint and Drake had returned to Houston on a nonstop commercial flight. After a meal and some sleep, they joined Scarlett in one of her conference rooms at Scarlett Investigations. Gaspar participated remotely from Miami.

Flint had leaned on Scarlett to persuade her to help. She wasn't thrilled about it, but she agreed. Probably because he was still suffering residual effects from his concussion, and she didn't want to be responsible for him cracking his head open again.

Whatever. He'd take what he could get at this point.

Gaspar had brought Scarlett up to speed and Drake had reported everything to Hanna. Hanna had caught a bug the day before and wasn't strong enough to join them, either physically or emotionally. So Drake had left her back in the hotel room.

Flint walked into the conference room just as Drake mentioned Hanna was up to speed.

Scarlett glanced toward Flint and flashed a glare brighter than Houston's noonday sun. Flint shrugged. "I'm feeling better, thanks for asking."

Scarlett didn't reply and she didn't soften her steely frown, either.

Gaspar took the lead. "Now that we're all up to speed, let me report what I learned while Flint and Drake were winging it back to Houston."

Flint's headache was improving. A big steak for dinner and a solid forty winks in his own bed helped. A gallon of strong black coffee helped, too.

He slid his open palm over his face and rubbed the back of his neck to ease the muscle tension. He glanced across the table and nodded pleasantly toward Scarlett.

She must itch to hassle him about the bones he took from the Marilyn Baker corpse, but Flint wasn't ready to move on that issue yet.

He had known nothing about his mother for thirty-four years, and the ignorance hadn't harmed him any.

The woman was long dead. No reason to rush the DNA now. No reason at all.

Despite what multitaskers claim, Flint worked more efficiently and effectively when he focused on one thing at a time. Even when he wasn't suffering from a concussion.

When Flint tuned in, Gaspar was talking about Detective Dean Myer. "No new intel on her death. The feeling in her unit is that she was killed by a gangbanger."

"That's crap," Drake said flatly.

"Agreed," Flint said. "Myer was executed. Probably for something she knew or something she did. Could be unrelated to her giving us the murder book on Ella Belle Reed. But what are the odds?"

"Why does it matter? Solving Detective Myer's murder isn't our job. Wasting time on that murder will delay our search for Greta Campbell," Scarlett said. "We all believe Ella Belle Reed's murder is tied to her husband and that organ transplant surgery he did the next day. Let's just use that as our working hypothesis and move on for now."

Gaspar began to brief them on the recipient of Ella Belle's heart. "The man was beyond wealthy. The kind of money greater than the GDP of third world countries. None of us in this room is ever likely to see that much wealth in our lifetime. He was the rich spoiled son of a rich spoiled father of a rich spoiled grandfather. Buying a human heart would not have seemed the least bit odd to him."

"Man, that's cold." Drake shuddered like an evil spirit had walked across his grave. "Seems fair that he died soon after he got that new heart, doesn't it?"

"Seems like a total waste of human life to me," Flint replied. "Ella Belle Reed was a wonderful person, by all accounts."

“Married to a total bastard, by all accounts,” Scarlett said angrily. “Why do women never see the truth about men like Phillip Reed until it’s too late?”

“You know, that’s a good question. Because Ella Belle and Greta Campbell had that in common, didn’t they?” Flint cocked his head. “Both were duped by Phillip Reed. What was it about him that caused two intelligent women to stand right in his scope of destruction?”

“Kind of like that lawyer in South Carolina who duped everybody he knew and finally killed his family, too,” Drake said. “It’s a pattern. Part of being a despicable human, I guess.”

"This photo was taken at his wedding to Ella Belle." Gaspar flashed a photo of Phillip Reed on the screen. "The happy couple looks like a **Vanity Fair** photo shoot. Beautiful people. Up and coming. Talented. Successful. Going places. You know the type."

"Yeah, there're thousands of couples just like that here in Texas every week," Scarlett said, shaking her head. "Without the murder and selling organs thing, of course."

Flint sat up straighter and refilled his coffee. "That's a good point, though. Murder is not that uncommon. But selling human organs certainly is."

"That's a whole new level of depravity," Scarlett said, nodding.

"Yeah, but it's a whole new level of difficulty, too." Flint continued. "Think about it. There're thousands of people in this country and around the world who need a heart transplant every day."

"And there're thousands of people who die every day, too. Every one of them has a beating heart right up until the moment it stops," Scarlett said. "What's your point?"

"Logistics," Flint replied. "A heart is only viable for transplant for four to six hours after death. And transplanting a heart isn't exactly a quick thing. Say a tissue match is found in a car accident victim in Los Angeles for a patient who needs a heart in New York. No way that heart makes it across the country in time for the surgery."

"Right. That's one reason it's hard to get a heart transplant and why so many people are on the waiting list. So?" Scarlett asked.

"This is all so much worse than you're thinking, Scarlett, because you're not a psychopath," Gaspar said easily. "What's the most reliable way to make sure that the sick man gets his transplanted heart within the viability window after the accident victim dies?"

Silence settled on the room as Flint and Gaspar waited for Drake and Scarlett to come to the only logical answer.

Almost instantly, Scarlett narrowed her flashing eyes and flared her nostrils like an outraged bull. "The bastard."

Drake took another couple of seconds to figure it out. “You’re saying they killed Ella Belle right at that time for the purpose of taking her heart and transplanting it? Like a murder for hire?”

Flint looked at the carpet and shielded his eyes from the strobe effect of the computer screen. “With a sick, perverse purpose. Not the usual motives for murder, like revenge, jealousy, rage.”

“Money,” Scarlett said flatly. “Murder for organs is about money. Greed.”

“And probably leverage.” Flint pointed out.

“Leverage?” Drake asked.

“Wealthy guy buys a heart and someone is killed so he can have that heart," Gaspar said with a shrug. "That stupid schmuck will be a blackmail target for as long as he lives."

Flint said, "And I'm betting Greta found out about Ella Belle's murder and the motive for it. Somehow she discovered what Phillip had done and probably confronted him."

"And then he had to kill her," Scarlett said quietly. "Because he'd be lucky to go to prison for the rest of his life when Greta revealed his crimes. Georgia has the death penalty. So does Florida. Either way, the scumbag dies."

"Unless he kills Greta to keep her quiet before she has the chance to turn him in," Flint said.

# Chapter 32

Before Flint finished speaking, Drake's heavy brown eyebrows dipped low over the bridge of his nose. Combined with his size and the combat skills he carried in his powerful arms and shoulders, he looked like a vicious brawler.

"My mama always says a leopard doesn't change spots," Drake growled. "What if Phillip Reed killed Greta for the same reason he killed Ella Belle?"

"To steal her heart and sell it, you mean?" Scarlett asked, incredulous.

"Why not? He did it once. He'd do it again. Everything's easier the second time," Drake replied gruffly.

"Before or after he dropped her into the Gulf for the shark food?" Scarlett said, shaking her head as if the story didn't track and she didn't want it to. "How'd he get away after the boat sank with the two of them in it?"

"Same way we did." Flint agreed, having already thought it through. "Somebody came and picked him up."

"**Somebody**? **Somebody** picked him up but not her?" Scarlett asked, nostrils flaring. "So Greta's death was a sick premeditated murder?"

"It's looking that way, isn't it?" Drake said.

Gaspar shrugged. “Maybe both Greta and her husband were picked up by the same guy who killed Ella Belle in the home invasion. Or another goon hired by the same guy who paid the invader.”

“You’re suggesting a massive criminal enterprise, which is wildly expensive to pull off,” Flint said with no trace of incredulity. “Phillip Reed doesn’t have that kind of money, does he?”

Gaspar shook his head. “He was worth a few million at one point. But at the time he and Greta disappeared, his bank accounts were empty.”

“A few million is not nothing,” Drake stated.

"How did a few million just disappear? No trace of the money?" Scarlett asked.

"Seventeen million dollars from Phillip Reed's bank accounts was transferred to the Caymans. The transfers happened over a period of several months. Installments. To keep under the legal transfer reporting limits," Gaspar explained. "But the money's no longer there. It was transferred out again. Long before Greta disappeared."

"Transferred where?" Drake asked.

Gaspar shrugged and said nothing.

Flint stretched his neck and shoulders and kneaded the pain between his eyes. "Tell us about the guy you found on the facial recognition search. Is it Reed? Or not?"

"Name is Stephen Brand. He lives on a private island in the Caribbean owned by Ernst Hedinger," Gaspar began.

Flint interjected. **"Ernst Hedinger?"**

"Yeah. Do you know him?"

Flint pursed his lips. "Go on."

Gaspar continued. "Brand has been the Chief of Surgery at the Atabei Transplant Center for the past four years. The hospital specializes in organ transplants for patients with the money to buy whatever they want. Brand's biography claims he was born in South Africa. Trained there in cardiothoracic surgery and then specialized in heart transplants."

"South Africa? They have excellent medical training and facilities there. Why would he leave a practice like that for a small island country like Atabei?" Scarlett asked.

Drake replied, "Good question."

"Brand lives in Atabei. He rarely leaves the island," Gaspar continued. "In fact, I could find no evidence that he's left Atabei at any time. Brand's South African passport has expired. I can find no evidence that he's acquired another passport issued by any country."

"Since Atabei is a private island, records are limited. What can you access?" Scarlett asked.

"Almost nothing is publicly available. There are internet search results that pop up, but it's like they've been created specifically for casual searchers," Gaspar said. "No criminal records seem to exist on Atabei. There is no judicial system."

"Brand has no criminal history in South Africa or anywhere else that you've located so far?" Flint asked.

"Nope."

Flint exhaled loudly. "So we believe this guy Stephen Brand is actually Phillip Reed?"

"Ninety-five percent sure," Gaspar said. "We need fingerprints, DNA, or a confession, or all three to be certain."

"What about Greta?" Drake asked.

"Three possibilities." Gaspar held up one finger at a time as he ticked off the options. "Either she died at sea, as folks were told at the time, or she didn't. And if she didn't, then either he killed her afterward or she's still alive."

Flint asked, "Has your facial recognition come up with a match for Greta?"

"No match for her so far. I did find the actual video Hanna saw of the crowd at that royal wedding. But the woman's image is not good enough to match to Greta either," Gaspar said. "My programs are still running. But we've been through most of the databases. It's not looking likely that we'll find a match for Greta."

"Is there any other angle you can work?"

"I tried matching the woman's image to Greta's official passport photo in the US passports database. It's close. But not close enough for a definitive match," Gaspar said. "I also tried the man and the boy who were with her. The system is still working on those."

"How about Brand's sex life? Could we get lucky and find Greta has been living with him on Atabei all along?

Maybe they escaped together?" Drake asked.

"Guy like that usually latches on to another woman sooner rather than later. As a man told me once, a guy doesn't usually leave home unless he's got somewhere to go." Scarlett sneered. "Probably had Greta's replacement in the wings before he killed her."

"Agreed," Gaspar said with a shrug. "But Brand never shows up with a woman on his arm in any of the photos I've been able to find. So it's not likely but possible that Greta's still with him, I guess."

Flint stood to stretch and walked around the room a bit. "Which means the only way we can know for sure is to confront Brand."

“How do you propose to do that?” Drake asked. “It’s not like we can book a flight over there.”

Gaspar said, “It’s a valid question. Atabei is about as closed to visitors as a country can get. There’s an airport, but it’s private and guarded and requires permission to land anything larger than a songbird. Same with the boat docks. No one goes in or out of there without the approval of local security. Which we’re not likely to get.”

“Never seen a security guard I couldn’t beat in a fair fight,” Drake said, opening and closing his fists as if he were itching to prove it.

“Not like that,” Flint said, shaking his head. “Hedinger uses ex-Mossad for security. Those guys would kill you before you had a chance to take them out. Hedinger's got several mansions around the world and every one of them is a fortress. Even if we could get into Atabei, getting out will be equally difficult."

"And you know this how?" Scarlett asked, arching her eyebrows in his direction.

"Don't ask," Flint replied.

A brief silence settled over the room.

"So let's get to work," Gaspar said after a bit, loading an image of Atabei from the air onto one of the screens. "Here's the island country we're talking about. It sits in the Caribbean near the Bahamas. The island was sold to Ernst Hedinger about ten years ago. Since then, he's poured money into improvements and built a paradise that's also, as Flint said, a 'fortress.'"

"Can't get onto that island from the air without Hedinger's goons shooting you down or shooting you after you're down. So any sort of drop-in attempt would fail. The airspace is monitored tighter than every military base you can name," Flint said. "They probably have anti-air weapons of some sort. Man-portable air-defense system, most likely."

"You think so?" Drake asked, incredulous. "If they used MANPADS to take down an aircraft, governments would find out about it.

That would be the end of Hedinger's idyllic island, surely."

"Good point. But do you want to be the one to test that theory?" Flint asked. "If they're watching the airspace, we can't use it to get onto the island. Maybe they wouldn't shoot us down, but they would spot us and come after us. I'd like to avoid all that if we can."

"Right," Drake mumbled, still spoiling for a fight.

"Can't go in by boat, either," Scarlett pointed out reasonably when Gaspar flashed an image of the docks on the screen. "The harbor is closed and armed guards to keep the riffraff out."

Gaspar said, "Atabei is small geographically. Population is only about two thousand, give or take, if you include the locals who mostly do all the labor. Very few guests. All guests are invited, monitored, and escorted for the entire time they're allowed to stay on the island."

Flint rolled his shoulders to loosen the tension that the mention of Hedinger's name had settled on him. "Yeah, and when Hedinger is in residence, the place will be locked down tighter than the Kremlin. Security staff size when he's not in residence is probably smaller."

"There's no official numbers. But if we assume crews of two running shifts around the clock at the airport and the docks, that's at least twelve guards," Gaspar replied. "We should assume maybe fifteen, at a minimum. Give or take."

"Seems like a lot," Drake said. "You're saying he's got one security officer per fewer than one hundred fifty people? Normal ratios of cops to civilians are a lot lower."

"Fair point." Flint nodded. "There are probably closer to ten members of the team when Hedinger's not in residence. Maybe less. But it's smart to plan on fifteen or more."

"So what do you propose we do?" Scarlett asked with a hard edge to her tone, which Flint was glad to hear.

Because if Hedinger was the mastermind they were dealing with here, which was looking more likely by the minute, Flint's small team was seriously outmanned and outgunned.

With Scarlett on board they'd have easy access to Gaspar and all of Scarlett's resources.

Drake, of course, had always been fully committed.

Flint could only hope his small band of warriors would be enough. "Gaspar, can you pull up the most recent satellite video of Atabei again? I saw some unusual activity on the northwest side of the island. Let's take a closer look."

# Chapter 33

Flint donned his dark glasses and kept his eyes lowered until Gaspar had the video focused on the construction activity he'd noticed earlier.

"What is that?" Drake asked. "The footprint seems huge for a private residence, doesn't it?"

Flint looked at the screen's pulsing lights in brief spurts. "Can we get a closer look?"

"We can peek under their underwear if you want," Gaspar deadpanned while increasing the size of the images on the screen. "Hard to tell what the owner plans to use the place for. Could be a home or a small hotel, perhaps. There's no building department or permitting requirements in Atabei. So no systems I can breach to get floor plans or applications for construction."

"Right. But it looks like residential living of some kind. Multiple suites with en suite baths. So a hotel isn't a bad guess. Could also be one of Hedinger's mansions."

"How many mansions does Hedinger need on one small island?" Gaspar shook his head as he continued manipulating the video to achieve closer views. "He already owns the biggest residence on Atabei. And they've got the country club. And the hospital."

"Fair point," Flint replied again. "So it's a mansion but not one Hedinger plans to live in. Still, he'd have given approval for the build."

Scarlett leaned against the desk with her arms crossed. "Not likely any building would happen on that island without Hedinger's approval, is it?"

"Definitely not," Flint said. "You can pull video of that construction for the past few months, I assume?"

"Sure. But why?" Gaspar asked, already flashing backward through a time-lapse version of the main phases of the project.

"Because building a place like that requires special expertise. Special equipment. Big crews to do the work," Flint mused, refining his plan as he watched.

The images on the screen morphed from the original vacant lush island vegetation and ran forward as the land was cleared, foundations were poured, substructure completed, and the outer walls constructed.

An immensely complicated decorative barrel tile roof was eventually installed atop the roof, which must have taken weeks to complete.

The walls were constructed, the roof installed, and the windows and doors were placed. From that point forward, a constant stream of workers moved around the mansion.

The images on the video were almost comical. Artisans of one sort or another moved rapidly from one task to the next as the sunrise and moonrise followed the passing of the days. Plumbing, electrical, floors, ceilings, cabinetry, surfaces.

The house seemed to grow to monstrous proportions until progress stopped abruptly.

"That brings us up to the present," Gaspar said. "Looks like they're working on various aspects of the interior. Applying thermal imaging, I can identify maybe two dozen workers on site right now."

Flint asked, "When and how did they get to the jobsite?"

Gaspar zoomed out for a broader view and reversed the video slowly until the workers seemed to march backward into a luxury motor coach parked in one of the driveways. He traced the motor coach as it reversed to Atabei's private airfield.

At the airfield, the workers backed off the coach and up the jet stairs to a private charter. A turboprop. The unmistakable T-shaped tail of a Bombardier Dash 8.

"Where did that flight originate? Can you find out?"

"Sure," Gaspar replied, clacking his keyboard for another few seconds. "Looks like it flew into Atabei from a private airport in Miami."

Flint nodded. “So the construction crew commutes from Miami every day?”

“Seems a little extravagant. And time consuming. But since there’s no hotel on Atabei and no temporary housing for workers on site, Hedinger might have no alternatives,” Scarlett said. “And I don’t like it. One way in, one way out. You’d be at Hedinger’s mercy if he discovered you. I’m pretty sure the man would kill you without a moment’s hesitation. His goons have already tried twice. Third time’s the charm.”

“Which is why I’ll have a solid escape plan before I do it,” Flint replied with a grin.

Drake was still frowning. "I should go. At least I know how to wield a hammer. You're useless at construction work. I've seen you try."

Before Flint could deliver a snappy comeback, Gaspar returned to the screen. "Okay. The construction workers seem to be staying at a Miami hotel near the private airport where the Dash 8 picks them up and drops them off."

Flint said, "Can you get intel on all of them? We need to know names, background checks, areas of expertise. The whole Megillah. Goal is to find at least one reasonable candidate. Two would be better. I like choices."

"You'll never learn. You can barely function." Scarlett narrowed her gaze and clicked her tongue against her teeth. "So you're going into a dangerous situation, on your own, with no back up? You're half loco."

"Only half? That's nicer than what you usually say about me," Flint teased. "But if you'd like to come along, maybe we can find a construction gig for you, too."

Before they had a chance to escalate the argument, Gaspar interrupted. "She's right. You're far from one hundred percent. You should wait until a couple of days after your concussion clears."

"You're acting like this is some sort of suicide mission," Flint said with the kind of steely determination that brooked no argument. “It’s a witness interview. I could do it on one leg with my eyes closed.”

Gaspar said, “Who are you kidding? You can’t even stand on one leg without falling over.”

Flint stood up and posed like a flamingo with his palms together above his head to make the point. He wobbled, but he managed to stay upright.

“Hey, it’s your funeral.” Scarlett shrugged and gave up the effort. “You still need backup. Take Drake. Maybe he can keep you alive. We can extract you both when you’re ready to leave.”

Flint glanced at Drake. “You up for this?”

“No doubt. Already volunteered, didn’t I?”

“Okay, then. Let’s do this.” Flint sat down and glanced at his watch. “Two candidates. One plan. Everybody lives to tell about it.”

A quick nod from Drake, but his tone was hard when he replied, “Except Brand. I’m not willing to trade our lives for his. No matter what.”

“You think it’ll come to that?” Scarlett asked.

“With men like Brand, it always comes down to him or me,” Drake replied. “Can’t be any other way.”

# Chapter 34

## Atabei

Ernst Hedinger glanced at his watch. His private plane was scheduled for wheels up two hours from now. Which was enough time for a bit of relaxation if he didn't dawdle.

He pushed a button on his speakerphone to talk as he changed into his shooting clothes.

"Yes, sir," his right-hand man answered instantly.

No one kept Hedinger waiting. Not if they wanted to remain employed.

Working for Hedinger was a lifetime commitment. The point was made clear before any employee was hired. No exceptions for any reason.

“Send the car around to the skeet range in an hour, Meier. I’ll shower and dress there. Wheels up as scheduled,” Hedinger said, slipping into his trousers and shoving his feet into supple leather boots simultaneously.

“Yes, sir,” Meier replied as expected. “Do you require my assistance now?”

“No.” Hedinger disconnected, pushed both arms into his lightweight shooting jacket, and headed through the house, outside, and toward the range.

A brisk walk through the gardens in the sunshine would do him a world of good.

The business with Brand's wife was troubling and weighed on his mind. He planned to picture Greta Campbell's face on the clay pigeons and shatter the pall she'd cast over his operations with several well placed shotgun blasts.

Hedinger enjoyed shooting. He'd fired his first gun at the age of five at a thieving beggar and never looked back.

Hedinger's father served in the French Zone of occupied Germany after the war. It was a difficult life for him, no less than the deprivation his wife and son endured.

Many nights, young Ernst dried his mother's tears. They had precious little food and no luxuries of any sort during those extremely lean years.

When a dirty, half-clothed man came to the door late in the afternoon, Ernst's mother had tried to be kind. She'd explained in French, her only language, that she had no extra food to share.

The beggar refused to listen. He lashed out, screaming violent profanity. When Ernst's mother tried to step inside and close the door, he grabbed her wrist and twisted it cruelly, making her cry out in pain.

The pistol was loaded and ready on a small table near the door. Terrified and outraged, young Ernst ran to pick it up. He'd never held the pistol before, and it was large and heavy in his hands.

Ernst did not hesitate. He stepped forward and screamed, “Let my mother go!”

Before the beggar had a chance to comply, Ernst pulled the trigger.

Lucky shot. For the beggar. The bullet missed.

The beggar dropped Ernst’s mother’s hand and ran away. Ernst shot again, but his second attempt was as inept as the first.

His mother crumpled to the floor, crying inconsolably. Ernst tried to get her into the house and close the door, but she seemed incapable of movement.

After a while, one of the neighbors came and helped her into bed. His mother stayed in bed for days afterward.

Ernst locked the front door when the neighbor left and waited until his father came home.

His father was pleased and proud of his son. Hugged Ernst and told him so, over and over again. And the next week, the shooting lessons began.

Shooting was one of the joys of Ernst Hedinger's life.

Living in that rough neighborhood formed the bedrock foundation of Hedinger's character. He'd become hard and strong and unflinching in the face of every threat.

From that moment on, he kept his shooting skills sharp and current.

Hedinger did what needed to be done.

He sought neither recognition nor approval.

From anyone or anything.

Along the way, he'd realized he enjoyed shooting too much to limit himself to inanimate targets. Hunting live prey was the next step.

From his first hunt, the sport filled him with a kind of satisfaction deeper than accumulating money. Which had been his first love but fell quickly into second place.

Shooting skill, instant results, watching targets fall where he placed his bullets. All of it was immensely satisfying on a primal level he enjoyed and didn't try to analyze too much.

He'd hunted game of every sort over the years, but his favorite prey was big cats.

Lions, leopards, and tigers were some of the most dangerous and challenging game to hunt. In three to four seconds, big cats could cover a hundred yards and shred a man to pieces before he had a chance to shoot.

When he was ten years old, Hedinger had seen the big cats take a hunter down before his companions could save him. On a safari in Africa with his father, Hedinger had watched his father's friend make a classic mistake. He'd gone after a wounded leopard.

The man had been warned.

Leopards don't simply slink away to die when they're wounded.

Instead, sleek, beautiful leopards lie in wait. Like Greta Campbell. Wounded and dangerous. But not dead. Not yet.

They want payback first.

The man had been told. He hadn't taken the warning to heart. He pursued the leopard hoping to complete the kill.

He failed.

The blindingly fast leopard got the last kill before he died.

Young Hedinger had absorbed the lesson. He'd learned the value of honing his reflexes to lightning speed.

Coupled with developing his unerring aim, Hedinger conquered the wounded leopard problem long ago. The solution was simple. Shoot to kill. Every time.

Big cats, like their common house cat relatives, were also nocturnal animals with exceptional night vision. Neither Hedinger nor any commercial equipment he'd tested could compete with the big cats' natural ability to see in the dark.

A problem simple to solve. Only hunt in daylight.

Thus had Hedinger's shooting skills developed over time from trauma to expertise.

Greta Campbell might be a wounded leopard, lying in wait for the hapless Brand. But she would not succeed. Hedinger would deny her the final kill.

He could see his private skeet shooting range now. Located at the edge of his property, it abutted the Caribbean as a precaution. If a shot went wild or sharp shards of the clay pigeons sheared off, neither humans nor animals would be inadvertently injured.

Hedinger had worked up a patina of sweat on his body by the time he reached the clubhouse. The stucco building with the barrel tile roof was a style consistent with other buildings on his Atabei estate. A casual observer might assume the clubhouse was a small home near the sea.

The clubhouse was large enough to accommodate teams of skeet shooters. Hedinger had hosted tournaments here over the years. The open floor plan contained comfortable seating, a dining room, kitchen, two locker rooms, and more. Outdoor seating areas amid the tropical plants and flowers added to the exotic ambience and provided stunning views of Atabei and the surrounding sea.

Of course, the clubhouse was locked and guarded and under constant surveillance, like all Hedinger's properties. Yet, as he approached, the place seemed abnormally deserted.

Hedinger marched to the front entrance and punched the keycode into the pad on the heavy wood door to release the lock.

# Chapter 35

The clubhouse door lock clicked open, and he pulled the handle. A refreshing rush of cool air bathed Hedinger's face and enveloped his overheated body when he stepped inside.

He was pleased to see that Mario, the young man he'd recently hired away from the Italian Olympic skeet shooting team, had every surface shining and clean. Mario was inexperienced, but he possessed passion for the sport that Hedinger demanded. The rest would come in time.

"Mario," he called out. No reply. He tried again. Same result.

Where was Mario, anyway? The skeet ranger should be here at all times other than preapproved absences. Mario lived on the premises. There was no excuse for absenteeism. He'd made that plain to the boy, hadn't he?

Hedinger strode to the back of the clubhouse where Mario's living quarters were. He knocked on the bedroom door. No answer. He turned the knob and stuck his head inside. The rooms were unoccupied.

The bed was a mess. Hedinger shook his head, clicking his tongue. "Unacceptable," he said aloud. Orderly, self-controlled, discipline in all things was the essential bedrock of Hedinger's successful enterprises.

A disheveled bed indicated a level of sloppiness that Hedinger could not abide.

He closed the door and walked back to the common rooms, shaking his head.

Hedinger made a mental note to reprimand the kid. Training was a job that should have been done by Mario's predecessor. But the old man had died unexpectedly in his sleep a few months back. He'd been a true master of all skills. Hedinger was surprised to realize he missed the old coot.

He shrugged. Mario would grow into the job. He possessed the foundation of talent, skill, personality, and the kind of rabid devotion Hedinger demanded. Mario would be okay. Eventually. He could tell.

Maybe Mario was working outside. Keeping the grounds in tiptop condition, all the equipment gleaming and fully functional, was Mario's primary responsibility. Hedinger was likely to find his employee on the field.

He'd already dressed for shooting, but he needed a weapon. Hedinger made his way to his collection of shotguns, which were stored in a locked cabinet along the back wall of the ranger's office.

He spied his favorite Citori shotgun gleaming and ready.

Briefly, he considered pulling two shotguns from the cabinet. He owned so many, and he enjoyed shooting them all.

He shrugged. No time for that today. He should have started earlier if he'd wanted more time here.

He relocked the cabinet and dropped the key into his pocket.

Hedinger searched for the specific shells stocked and reserved only for his personal use. Not the usual skeet shells filled with small pellets which he considered useless. He preferred more powerful ammunition with greater stopping power.

He snagged two boxes of his personal shells, loaded two into the shotgun, and stuffed both boxes into his pocket. He should have time for two rounds of shooting if he didn't dawdle.

Then he flipped the switch to turn on the two traps that would launch the clay targets out on the range, one in the high house and one in the low house.

He left the building through the front door, striding quickly toward the skeet field.

Again, Hedinger wondered where Mario could be. Maintaining Hedinger's skeet field and everything related to it was Mario's only reason for existing in Atabei. He knew no one, lived here on the grounds, and spoke only Italian. Aside from Hedinger and his staff who were all multilingual, Mario might be the only current resident of Atabei who spoke Italian, in fact.

All of which meant Mario should be here.

But he wasn't here, and his absence had become increasingly irritating. Hedinger would have required Meier to accompany him for the shoot if he'd realized Mario was missing.

When he rounded the corner of the clubhouse, a clear view of the field and the Caribbean beyond opened before him.

The eight shooting stations and two trap houses at either end of the skeet field were ready and waiting.

No Mario. The field was abandoned.

“Dammit!” Hedinger enjoyed solitude and the beauty of his surroundings, but he also expected his employees to do their jobs.

Mario’s absence was unacceptable.

He made a mental note to replace Mario on his way to the airport. The boy was good, but he wasn’t essential. No one in Hedinger’s organization was irreplaceable. High time Mario learned the lesson.

He scanned the field. Everything else seemed to be in order. Hedinger preferred the international version of the game, and his field was constructed to suit his demands.

The event was constructed to simulate bird hunting. The shooter shoots from eight positions in a semicircle. Two houses—the high house on the left and the low house on the right—perched at each corner of the semicircle, hold traps that launch the targets. The traps launch clay targets at two different heights on a specific rotation. The shooter's goal is to hit all twenty-five of the targets to achieve a perfect score.

The game required skill, accuracy, and speed. The Olympic version was slightly more difficult and could be breathtaking to watch when played by such high-caliber athletes.

Hedinger, aggravated now by Mario's failures, approached the field and Station 1. With no assistant to perform the service, he opened the first box of shells and poured them into his shell holder. He tossed the box onto the ground.

Mario would show up eventually. When he did, he'd damned well clean up the field.

Hedinger settled into position, stuffed his earplugs into place, and prepared to shoot the first target.

He called for the bird and the trap flung the first target from the high house. He aimed and hit the single to begin the round. Second was the low house single, which he also hit. Quickly, he reloaded two shells.

Before he could begin to shoot the high house and low house pair, he heard a woman scream as if she were being flayed alive.

"What the hell?" Hedinger pulled the earplug from his right ear and shoved it into his pocket. The bloodcurdling screams came from behind the high house.

He stomped in that direction. When he rounded the corner, he stopped abruptly.

The screaming banshee of a woman was stark naked. She was attacking Mario with her entire body. She kicked and pummeled him fiercely and furiously. The screaming stopped briefly while she bit off a chunk of his cheek and spat it on the ground.

Which was the last thing she ever did.

Mario yelped in pain and shoved the woman away from him. He turned his back, trying to stanch the bleeding from his cheek.

She fell backward but somehow stayed on her feet. She was scrawny. Hedinger had seen residential PCV pipes larger in circumference than her arms and legs.

Her brown hair stood up all over her head like it had been glued vertically.

Her face was positively horrifying. Mascara blackened her eyes and streamed down to the purple glitter lipstick surrounding her wide-open pie hole.

She never shut up. The screaming was earsplitting.

“Enough!” Hedinger changed his position, raised his shotgun, and blasted the damned fury’s face off.

# Chapter 36

Instantly, the harpy's screaming stopped. Hedinger wished he'd taken the time to replace the earplug before he'd killed her. His hearing would suffer for the rest of the day. Something else to feed his anger.

He lowered the shotgun and turned his attention to Mario. The boy was standing with one bloody hand pressed against his damaged cheek and the other covering his gaping mouth.

"You killed her." His eyes were wide and his tone breathy, incredulous. "She's dead."

“Tell me who the hell she was and why she’s here on my field,” Hedinger demanded, in no mood for mollycoddling spoiled, defiant employees.

Mario was also out of uniform, Hedinger noticed. Yet another outrage. He was dressed in sloppy jeans and a ratty oversize polo shirt. He wore canvas shoes on his feet. No socks. Blobs of blood had run from his cheek down his chin and onto the wrinkled turquoise cotton.

Because his back had been turned and she’d been downwind from Mario, none of the harpy’s bloody face had splashed onto the front of Mario’s clothes. He simply stood there, holding his cheek, looking helplessly at the dead woman.

"Mario!" Hedinger bellowed.

As if he'd been called back from a great distance, Mario turned his head slowly toward Hedinger. He said nothing.

"Who was that woman?" he demanded in harsh Italian.

Mario shrugged and explained haltingly. "Her name is Patty, she said. I met her last night over in Grand Turk. She wanted to come here. She'd never seen beautiful Atabei."

Hedinger's anger mounted with every word out of Mario's mouth until he thought his head would explode. "No unapproved visitors, Mario. No exceptions. I made that very, very clear when I allowed you to come here."

Mario sorrowful, horrified gaze was still glued to the dead woman.

"Was she a prostitute?" Hedinger demanded.

Mario nodded again.

"Anyone come here with her?"

Mario shook his head.

"How did you get her onto the island? She didn't have approval. She should not have been admitted." Hedinger's outrage had not abated. He wanted to choke the life out of this kid. He tightened his grip on the shotgun to restrain his hands.

"She had no one. No family. No friends. She needed a place to sleep. I liked her. Told her she could stay with me for a few days. That's all," Mario said quietly, almost whispering. "I didn't think you'd see her. She'd be gone before you returned."

Hedinger's anger was smoldering. Mario's answers both inflamed and satisfied. The girl was alone in the world. No one would notice she'd gone missing.

"How did she get here?"

"She—she flew over with me."

"And why wasn't she turned away before she boarded the plane?"

"Schmid. The copilot. He sometimes lets us bring dates back to Atabei. He says he knows how lonely it can get," Mario said, still in shock, still staring at the faceless woman.

"So you've done this before? Brought women back to my clubhouse?" Hedinger's tone grew harder than granite. "Even though you knew you were forbidden to bring them here."

"Schmid said it was okay." Mario whispered. "Twice. Only for a few hours. When you were away so they would not bother you. I'm sorry."

"Yeah, I can see that," Hedinger said angrily, raising the shotgun.

Mario raised his face to look at his boss for the first time since Hedinger rounded the corner of the high house and found the screaming woman attacking the kid.

Mario saw the gun.

His big brown eyes rounded and widened even further.

When he understood what Hedinger intended to do, Mario removed his palm from his cheek and began to shake his head, holding his bloody hands out in front of him.

Hedinger was not deterred by Mario's silent plea. He aimed and fired the powerful weapon.

The close-range shotgun blast almost took Mario's head clean off his neck.

His body fell to the ground in a heap. Hedinger noticed bits and pieces of Mario had landed a few yards away.

“Stupid kid,” Hedinger growled as he reached into his pocket for his cell phone and pressed redial.

Meier answered immediately.

“Bring the car to the clubhouse. Now. Just you. Alone.”

“Yes, sir,” Meier said. “On my way.”

Hedinger placed a second call. This one to his head of security. He explained the situation.

“We’ll clean up as soon as you leave,” Bauer replied.

“Is Schmid on duty at the hangar right now?” Hedinger demanded.

Bauer hesitated half a moment. “He is.”

"Detain him until I arrive."

"Of course."

"Advise the pilot we'll be leaving earlier than planned."

"Of course," Bauer said again.

Hedinger disconnected the call.

He placed the shotgun and the shells on the ground. Bauer would dispose of them.

Which was practically a crime in itself.

The gun had performed perfectly as it had been designed to do. Hedinger had no complaints about the firearm or the shells.

The gun would be replaced. Perhaps the new one would function as well as its predecessor.

Perhaps not.

New didn't always mean improved, of course. One needed only to consider Mario as the most recent example.

Hedinger had had such high hopes for the boy. Foolish hopes, as he now realized.

Still, Mario's treachery was a gift.

If not for whimsy or serendipity or whatever name one wished to attach to such unexpected fortune, Hedinger would not have discovered the hole in his security.

Now that he knew, he could plug it and stop Schmid before something much worse than a screeching harpy invaded his paradise.

By the time Hedinger returned to the driveway in front of the clubhouse, Meier was waiting with the Rolls.

"Directly to the airport?" Meier asked after Hedinger was settled into the back seat.

"Yes."

The drive from the back of Atabei to the airport was short and easy. The island wasn't huge, and the roads were as perfect as roads can be.

Meier was an excellent driver, and the Rolls was perhaps the best car on the planet for passenger comfort, in Hedinger's opinion. Which was the only opinion that mattered.

Hedinger had not a complaint in the world at the moment. Except that he'd been looking forward to his round of skeet. Disappointed to miss it.

"Next time," he said aloud as he watched the sparkling turquoise Caribbean Sea wash gently against the island's beaches.

Meier turned into the long driveway toward the airfield hangar that housed Hedinger's private jet.

Bauer had passed along his orders.

The gleaming bird was waiting on the tarmac.

Meier pulled up near the jet stairs and exited the Rolls. He opened the back passenger door to allow Hedinger to climb out.

“Your bags are in the trunk. I’ll bring them up to the cabin with me after I park the Rolls inside,” Meier said.

“Excellent.” Hedinger glanced around the tarmac for his staff as Meier pulled the Rolls away toward the garage.

Bauer and Schmid strode purposefully forward from the hangar’s office fifty yards away. Hedinger waited near the jet stairs, allowing them to clear various equipment and personnel buzzing around the area.

The sun was high and bright now. Hedinger pulled sunglasses from the pocket of his shooting jacket and slipped them over his eyes. The polarized lenses allowed him to see the two members of his inside security team clearly as they approached.

Bauer stopped five feet from Hedinger.

Schmid took his cues from his boss and stopped as well.

“You wanted to see me, sir?” Schmid said directly to Hedinger.

The noisy jet engines were running behind him. With the damage to his hearing in his right ear after the shotgun blasts, Hedinger could barely hear the question.

Schmid shifted his feet and clasped his hands behind his back, waiting. Bauer stood a respectful distance to Schmid's left.

Hedinger said, "You know Mario, don't you, Schmid? The Italian boy?"

Schmid replied, "Yes, sir. I do."

"Mario tells me you allowed him to bring a woman onto Atabei without proper permission. Mario says you've done this before. For him and for others," Hedinger said, looking directly into Schmid's face, watching his eyes. "Is this true?"

Schmid flinched. He glanced toward the pavement. He cleared his throat.

Hedinger didn't need to hear the response. He knew the answer. His evidence was still on the ground at the skeet field.

“Do you have your pistol, Schmid?” Hedinger held out his right hand, palm up.

Schmid pulled the pistol from its holster and passed it to Hedinger with the grip extended.

Hedinger took the gun, gripped it tightly. He continued to look Schmid directly in the eyes. He wondered briefly whether Schmid would offer excuses or ask for forgiveness.

He did neither.

He simply stood ramrod straight, shoulders back, hands clasped behind him.

Knowing.

Waiting.

Hedinger raised the pistol and fired one shot directly into Schmid's forehead.

Hedinger handed the pistol to Bauer.

"No one. Absolutely no one enters Atabei without my permission. Remind your team of the rules," he demanded, shifting his steady gaze to the senior command officer.

"Understood," Bauer said.

Hedinger gave a quick nod before he turned and climbed the stairs into the cabin of the jet.

# Chapter 37

## Miami

Predawn temperatures in Miami were pleasant enough. The day would become hot and muggy by midafternoon, but Flint didn't need to worry about that now.

"So far, so good," Drake muttered quietly but loud enough for Flint to hear.

"Get in. Get out. Nobody gets hurt," Flint reminded him tersely. "No heroics. No vengeance."

The Bombardier Dash 8 was warming up at their outdoor gate as the ground crew prepared the bird for flight. An easy breeze blew in from the Atlantic moving the fuel fumes away from the boarding area.

Construction workers were flown back and forth from Miami to the job site on Atabei daily, six days a week, until the mansion was completed. Early mornings, long and exhausting workdays, late nights. The hours and the project were grueling. Which fortunately left little time for the crew to become overly familiar with each other.

A man wandered past, and Drake gave him a friendly nod. The man didn't respond.

Flint quickly counted heads. Fifty-two men milled about, shifting their weight, hands in pockets, waiting to board.

Flint and Drake were indistinguishable from the others. They sported the same heavy jeans and work boots and long-sleeved cotton shirts. The informal uniform of construction workers everywhere. They'd be issued hard hats, gloves, and other equipment as necessary once they arrived at the job site.

Flint and Drake stood on the tarmac waiting as the ground crew loaded cargo and supplies. Miami Marlins baseball caps were pulled low to shield their faces from curious stares and security cameras.

Clipped to the breast pocket of their flannel shirts was a temporary work badge. Each worker was identified with a photo, number, and job function. Flint was Biscayne Bay plumber number two. Drake was South Beach electrician number four. Their crew's job was the installation of whirlpool bathtubs in three of the mansion's guest bathrooms.

The project was starting today, and the entire crew of necessary artisans was flying to Atabei for the first time. Which meant Flint and Drake could more easily blend into the ten-man crew without being spotted as outsiders. Soon they'd trudge up the jet stairs and enter the cabin along with the others.

Flint wasn't expecting trouble. Not here, anyway.

All workers were fully vetted and required preapproval. The counterfeit badges and accompanying falsified paperwork had been sufficient to get Flint and Drake a seat on the Atabei-bound Dash 8. The assumption made by the security team was that no one would be among the crew without approval. Which meant security was somewhat lax now.

Flint scanned the area and noticed nothing alarming. The mission seemed simple enough.

Blend in with the construction crew to gain access to Atabei. Once on the island, locate Dr. Stephen Brand. Confirm his identity. Interrogate him for intel about Greta Campbell.

If Greta was located on Atabei, find her and get her back to Houston to meet up with Hanna.

If Greta wasn't on Atabei, then find out where she was and go there.

Flint was acutely aware there's many a slip twixt the cup and the lip. Planning and execution could be miles apart.

Two armed security guards had stationed themselves at the bottom of the jet stairs. The construction workers began lining up to board. They'd been told not to bring weapons. One guard wanded each man with a metal detection device. The second guard snapped a photo of the worker's face and badge and required a thumbprint before he was allowed to climb the jet stairs and board the plane.

Finding a corrupt security guard who would pass them through without flagging their counterfeit credentials had not been easy. Without Flint's covert connections, the ex-Mossad agents Hedinger employed would have been impenetrable.

Even so, the guards seemed nervous and especially diligent. The guard with the wand covered each man thoroughly before allowing him to pass.

"Hey, what's the problem?" Drake demanded when he was asked to spread eagle for the third time. "If we had weapons that thing would be screeching loud enough to wake the dead."

"Shut up." The guard shoved Drake roughly against the stairs. "I'm not taking a bullet in the head because you've brought along so much as your favorite nail clippers. Spread your arms. Do it now."

"What the hell are you talking about, man?" Drake whined and did as he'd been told.

Flint moved into line behind Drake and made a show of cooperating. Then he approached Peretz, the fidgety guard checking credentials and thumbprints.

Flint looked directly at the camera as Peretz pretended to snap his photo and offered the phone's flat surface.

When Flint pretended to leave his thumbprint, he murmured, "What happened? Why are you guys so twitchy?"

"Hedinger killed one of the guards yesterday before he left," Peretz replied.

"Why?"

"Failure to comply with security policies. We're all on edge. Keep your head down," Peretz explained under his breath as he waved Flint toward the plane.

Flint trudged up the stairs and ducked his head to enter the cabin of the Dash 8. Rows of seats, two on each side of the aisle, were almost full of tense construction workers. Overhead bins were closed. Oversize windows offered a wider view than many regional jets.

He followed Drake toward the first available row of empty seats. They settled into aisle seats across from each other, but they didn't talk. The typical noise cancelling technology employed in the Dash 8 would have kept the cabin relatively quiet even if the workers were a chatty bunch. Which they weren't.

The two security guards boarded the plane, closed the jet stairs, and sealed the door. The plane pushed back and taxied to the runway. Very soon, they were airborne.

Flint leaned his head back, lowered the bill of his cap, and closed his eyes. They'd been up most of the night working out the plan and he was bone weary. His concussion symptoms had improved, but the throbbing headache was still there. He'd stopped swallowing Tylenol every hour, but only because of concern for his liver. During the short flight, he hoped to catch a few winks.

Drake gave him a nudge. When he opened his eyes again, the Dash 8 was preparing to land in Atabei.

Flint looked out the big windows to catch a breathtaking view of the spectacular crescent-shaped island. White sand sparkled in the sun like brilliant diamonds surrounded by the turquoise water of the Caribbean Sea.

As the Dash 8 descended, coral reefs and schools of tropical fish were visible through the clear water.

The island's hilly terrain and lush vegetation reminded him of Turks and Caicos.

Flint had been unable to unearth the sum Hedinger paid for the spectacular island. Rumors were that he'd performed a stunning favor for the former owner and received Atabei in exchange.

Flint assumed whatever Hedinger had done to inspire that sort of largesse was not only illegal and immoral but beyond unethical as well.

The Dash 8 hit the runway with a hard thump and strong brakes slowed it down before it sped off the runway into the sea. The pilot taxied the plane to the hangar and brought it to a stop. The two security guards unbuckled their seat belts, opened the door, and extended the jet stairs.

Peretz hustled down the stairs while the other guard stood at the exit to watch the workers file out.

Flint glanced out the window where a bus waited to collect the workers and drive them to the construction site on the other side of the island. He unbuckled his seat belt and stood in the aisle, stretching the kinks from his body.

As the workers ahead of him left their seats and filed out the door, Flint and Drake followed. Outside at the top of the stairs, he took a whiff of fuel-scented air and glanced toward the hangar. He counted six armed security guards from his vantage point, not including the two who had traveled from Miami on his flight.

Hedinger was serious about security for damned sure.

The construction crew hustled down the stairs and across the tarmac to the bus, where their badges were rechecked and they were wanded again before they were allowed to board.

Flint needed room to move. The first order of business was to escape the constant surveillance. Time was running faster than he'd planned.

They had seven hours to locate and interrogate Phillip Reed, including whatever follow-up was required after first contact. If Greta was here on Atabei, finding her would be the second order of business.

Drake increased his stride to join Flint on the walk to the bus. “Stay sharp. We don’t make it back for the return plane ride to Miami, Hedinger’s goons will hunt us down like killing rabbits.”

“No questions asked,” Flint replied, nodding in agreement.

# Chapter 38

**Atabei**

Drake and Flint had avoided detection because Peretz, the same guard they'd dealt with back in Miami, checked their badges before they boarded the bus with the others. Tension was so thick Flint could barely breathe.

The driver climbed into the driver's seat and the two guards boarded the bus for the ride to the job site.

Flint had assumed the guards would rotate at different checkpoints.

Now he realized both guards would be with them for the entire day.

A lucky break.

Peretz could run interference for Flint and Drake should they need it. Which they probably would at some point.

For cover, Flint had chosen two skills for which there would be several men qualified on the job site. Electricians and plumbers were essential for installing high-end whirlpool tubs.

The construction plan was to install four tubs during today's work hours.

Which meant the crew boss had allocated four electrician/plumber duos in his budget.

Flint and Drake had been paired together and assigned the installation at the far back wing of the building. The money he'd paid Peretz had been well spent. So far, so good.

The bus rumbled along the paved roads toward the enormous mansion Flint had seen on the satellite photos of Atabei. A truck followed along behind them carrying supplies and equipment. When the bus reached the long driveway still under construction, the driver stopped to drop off workers.

Another armed guard entered the bus and called for a dozen workers to follow him. They filed out behind the guard like a line of goslings following their mother.

The driveway site had previously been prepared and graded for proper drainage. Huge piles of crushed shells had been dumped at regular intervals along the expansive circular drive from the road to the mansion's entrance by large trucks.

Front end loaders were poised and ready, waiting for drivers to move the shells and spread them evenly along the surface. As they stepped off the bus, the first five went directly to their assigned stations, fired up the machines, and began to spread the crushed shells.

Five more workers quickly climbed aboard compaction machines to begin compacting the shells that had been spread yesterday.

Flint estimated the work on the driveway would take at least another week to complete at the rapid pace the workers were moving. The job was hot and heavy, and the pressure added by working under armed guards had to be intense.

The bus driver closed the door after the last man stepped off. He drove along the road adjacent to the mansion's property to the east wing. He pulled the bus to a stop again. Peretz rose from his seat, through the open door, and down three steps to the ground.

The second guard gestured toward the door and barked, "This is where you exit."

The remaining workers filed out, one row of seats at a time. Flint and Drake were at the back of the bus and the end of the line. Peretz waited with a clipboard, passing out assignments. As expected, Flint and Drake were told to report to the suite at the back of the house overlooking the Caribbean Sea.

They walked along a path through the lush tropical plants, keeping a sharp lookout for snakes and other wildlife until they rounded the corner of the building out of sight of the security guards.

Flint stopped under the shade of the coconut palms scanning for the two silver Vespas he'd paid Peretz to procure. He spotted them parked below his sight line near the bottom of the hill at the shoreline.

"This way," he said as he set off quickly with Drake close behind.

He rushed down the incline, slipping on the rocks and plants all the way to the bottom. From the locked under-seat and glove compartments, they retrieved weapons, ammunition, encrypted satellite phones with chargers, sunglass goggles, helmets, chronographs, and water bottles.

They stripped off their Marlins caps and long-sleeved shirts and stashed them in the empty under-seat compartments and left the remaining items for later.

"We'll start with the hospital. He should be at work by now. If he's not there, someone is likely to know where he is," Flint reconfirmed as they started the Vespas and rolled away from the mansion. After a mile or so, they picked up speed.

Using the satellite images, Flint had memorized the layout of the island. The hospital was located near the small residential section of Atabei Town, about five miles north of the mansion. Most of Atabei's two thousand residents lived near the town.

Atabei Town was clustered around two intersections and four blocks of commercial businesses. Behind those businesses in all directions were conch houses built on narrow residential streets.

The conch houses were built of wood and set on posts which allowed air to circulate underneath the floors. Most were one story with a porch across the full width of the front of the house.

Clad with horizontal weatherboards, the conch houses sported gabled metal roofs and double-hung sash windows. The homes were painted cheerfully in bright, pleasant colors.

But as with the homes in most Caribbean islands, hurricanes could easily demolish them and had done so several times over the years.

When they pulled into Atabei Town, Flint slowed the Vespa and took the first right turn onto Atabei Street to approach the Atabei Country Club. The hospital was directly across the boulevard from the country club.

Flint drove past the hospital and down the block to the first alley. He turned right and found the cubby behind two large dumpsters. They parked the Vespas side by side, out of view of the hospital's front entrance.

He removed his helmet and placed it on the handlebars. He ran his fingers through his hair and straightened his clothes.

Drake parked beside Flint, pulled the keys, and dropped them into his pocket.

Flint said, “You really think anybody around here is going to steal anything?”

"Nope." Drake shook his head. "Hedinger would chop off their hands if they tried."

"Exactly."

"Before we go in there," Drake said, "are you sure you want to be so obvious about what we're doing? If this guy really is Phillip Reed, he's not gonna be very happy."

"We talked about this. If he's here, going right to the source is the fastest way to get what we came for. If he's not here, we need to flush him out as soon as we can. We've only got a few hours to find Greta and get her off this damned island," Flint replied.

"Assuming she's alive. Assuming she's here. We have no evidence to prove either," Drake said, shaking his head. "The security staff looked exceptionally competent to me. We're painting a big target on our backs."

"That's what our guns are for. We'll shoot back." Flint grinned and turned to stride across the pavement and along the sidewalk toward the hospital's main entrance, Drake at his side.

The building looked like the mansions he'd seen on the east side of Atabei. White stucco walls, barrel tile roofs, lush tropical landscaping, waterfalls. Cheerful colors and well tended grounds everywhere.

No sea view from the hospital windows because it was located in the interior of the island.

When Flint stepped under the portico toward the entrance, the sliding glass doors opened wide, silently welcoming visitors with a feeling of grandeur and elegance.

A splashing waterfall adorned the lobby creating a sense of natural tranquility. Sparkling chandeliers and slow-moving fans hung from high ceilings. Seating groups dotted the gleaming marble floors like lily pads. Richly colored murals depicting tropical scenes covered the walls.

The air was fragrant with the scent of exotic blooms and sea salt and the place was filled with natural light from oversize windows.

In short, nothing about the place resembled a hospital. Instead, the place felt like indulgence and relaxation.

He saw not one wheelchair or handrail. Smelled no antiseptic. No physicians or nurses wandered the halls dressed in surgical garb.

Atabei Hospital was more like the private concierge floor at the world's most luxurious hotels.

And unlike American healthcare centers, this one had no security officers monitoring the lobby.

Flint scanned the premises for surveillance equipment. No cameras were immediately identifiable by an untrained eye. A normal visitor might believe the lobby was not secure.

But on Hedinger's properties, everything was constantly watched. Which meant that there was plenty of security, whether he could see it or not.

Flint walked deeper into the lobby, all senses on alert. Drake did the same.

There were no signs identifying the admissions or records departments. No indications that an emergency room existed. Which, perhaps, it did not.

Drake said, "Wonder where they keep the sick people."

Flint's constant wariness was rewarded when a stunningly beautiful young woman entered the lobby from behind closed doors opposite the entryway. She came walking across the marble floors, her heels tapping a quick tattoo.

Wearing a lovely floral dress and a white blazer befitting a tropical hotel, she had no name tag, but it was obvious she worked here. Her entrance was purposeful. She was fully aware Flint and Drake had entered the building.

“I’m Genevieve Sweeting, hospital CEO. May I help you gentlemen?” she asked as she approached, her gaze sharper than a full body scan.

“We’re meeting Dr. Stephen Brand,” Flint said, getting straight to the point. “Please direct us to his office.”

She smiled pleasantly. “Is Dr. Brand expecting you?”

Flint flat out lied. “He knows we’re coming.”

“I see.” Her smile faltered slightly as she reached into a deep pocket for her cell phone. “Dr. Brand is usually in surgery most mornings. You may need to come back this afternoon. I’ll check with his assistant. Just one moment, please.”

Sweeting made the call. A few moments later she said pleasantly, “Hi, Mary. It’s Genevieve. Is Dr. Brand available? He has visitors in the lobby.”

She paused briefly to listen and then looked directly at Flint. “I’m sorry. I didn’t get your names.”

"John and Joseph Campbell. We're here about our sister, Greta Campbell," Flint said evenly, but Genevieve didn't flinch. The names meant nothing to her. "She's missing and Dr. Brand was one of the last people to see her."

The missing sister comment prompted a concerned frown. Genevieve repeated the information to Brand's assistant.

She listened to a brief reply and then asked Flint, "As I suspected, Dr. Brand is in surgery. How about two o'clock this afternoon? Will that work for you?"

He glanced at his watch as if he were actually checking the time. "Sure, we can come back."

Genevieve confirmed the time with the assistant and disconnected the call. "There's a lovely restaurant two blocks from here, if you need somewhere to wait."

Drake shook his head. "That's okay. We're staying with a friend."

Flint and Drake thanked her for the help and turned to leave. Genevieve watched them go, frowning.

When the glass doors parted silently and they walked out onto the portico, she was still standing there.

# Chapter 39

Hedinger's jet cruised comfortably at thirty thousand feet. He'd showered and changed from his shooting clothes. Distance, time, and eliminating two employees guilty of gross insubordination had improved his mood somewhat.

"Meier, get Bauer on the phone, please," he said politely, as if Meier had the option to refuse. Which, they were both well aware, he did not.

"Yes, sir," Bauer said when he picked up the call.

"I will send a replacement for Schmid from my staff at Château

Loggerhorn. He'll arrive next week. You will cover his job personally until the replacement arrives," Hedinger stated flatly.

Bauer cleared his throat to reply. "Yes, of course."

Hedinger heard something. Bauer was off. He narrowed his eyes. "Is there a problem?"

"With replacing Schmid? No. Not at all," Bauer said.

"What, then?"

Bauer cleared his throat again. "We moved Mario and the girl to the morgue at the hospital. Schmid's there, too."

"Again, what's the problem?"

"Brand wants to use them. As donors. He says he has patients waiting," Bauer replied.

Hedinger shook his head. "Whatever. It's a medical decision."

"I'll relay your decision," Bauer said.

"Anything else?" Hedinger asked impatiently.

"No, sir," Bauer replied.

Hedinger disconnected the call. He pressed the call button for Meier.

"Bring me a fresh encrypted cell phone," Hedinger said, leaning back in his desk chair, eyes closed, expecting his every whim to be answered. Which it always was.

Meier left the cabin and returned shortly with the requested item. “Shall I bring your lunch?”

“After I make this call. Half an hour. No more,” Hedinger said, firing up the phone.

He connected it to the device that would confirm identity by voice analysis. Next, he punched the memorized number into the keypad.

“Call you back,” the man said after the second ring. He disconnected.

A few seconds later, the encrypted cell rang. Hedinger picked up.

“Otis Jarsdel,” the caller said. “It’s a right nice night for ice cream. Four score and seven years ago.”

Hedinger watched the device as it analyzed the man's voice. After a few moments, a green light flashed, indicating a total match.

Otis Jarsdel. Certainly the best operative Hedinger had ever employed.

“How can I help you?” Jarsdel asked.

“Have you located the missing woman?” Hedinger asked.

Jarsdel didn't ask why Hedinger wanted to find the woman. He didn't care. And Hedinger wouldn't have told him anyway.

“We have a video image captured during a crowded street scene. Nothing else to go on,” Jarsdel said.

"London. Near Buckingham Palace. During the last royal wedding," Hedinger said.

"Which didn't narrow things down," Jarsdel replied. "So many tourists in town when the royals have their celebrations."

"Exactly," Hedinger said.

Jarsdel said, "We checked the databases. No record of the woman entering or leaving the country within ninety days either side of the video. Not under her real name or using her US passport, anyway."

"You think she came in illegally and she's still there," Hedinger stated.

"Limiting the search to Wales, Scotland, and England, you're looking at seventy-six million people. It'll take a while to canvass them all," Jarsdel said sardonically. "England alone is sixty-eight million."

"I didn't expect to hear excuses from you," Hedinger stated flatly.

"We're working on it. How soon do you need this done?"

"As quickly as possible."

"As a US citizen, she would have a biometric passport. We can pull the fingerprints and iris scans from there and compare them to potential matches, once we have comps," Jarsdel said.

"We know her real identity. But we have no idea what she's calling herself now." Hedinger paused to sip his coffee. “You’ll need to be creative and clever. If she could be found with a simple database search, we wouldn’t be having this conversation.”

“What more can you send me to work with?” Jarsdel asked. “I have photos, fingerprints, date of birth. How about DNA?”

“No. Just the video you’re working from,” Hedinger said. “The situation is simple. We thought this woman was dead. Turns out she might still be alive. We need to fix that.”

Jarsdel paused. Hedinger waited.

“That’s not my usual line of work,” Jarsdel said. “I’m not a fixer.”

“First time for everything,” Hedinger replied. “This is a chance to broaden your skill set. You can charge higher fees.”

Jarsdel paused again, longer this time.

Hedinger became impatient. Partly because this was an offer Jarsdel was not allowed to refuse. He should have known as much.

Jarsdel inhaled deeply and said, “I’ll send materials as soon as I have them.”

Hedinger said, “Call me on this number when you have something to report.”

“Will do.”

"And to be crystal clear, this matter is for your eyes only," Hedinger said before he hung up.

He slipped the phone into his pocket where he could feel it ringing when Jarsdel called.

Then he pushed a couple of keys on the laptop and watched the woman in the London video again while he waited for his lunch.

Hedinger had never met Greta Campbell. But he'd seen this brief video clip at least fifty times since Brand brought the matter to his attention. She was a handsome woman, even now.

Unlike Brand, Hedinger refused to succumb to self-delusion.

Ignoring trouble had never, in all his years, made trouble disappear.

Quite the opposite.

For Hedinger, trouble was like a nuclear bomb.

Trouble detonated and mushroomed until it enveloped and destroyed everything within a one-mile radius. And then it ignited fires that scorched the earth for another mile.

The best thing to do with trouble was to find it and destroy it.

Before it had the chance to destroy you.

# Chapter 40

### Atabei

Flint and Drake walked away from Atabei Hospital as if they had somewhere specific to go. They crossed the street and walked half a block to the alley where they'd stashed the Vespas.

“Brand knows we're here now. If he reports us to Hedinger, they'll be looking for us soon,” Drake said as they donned the helmets.

“Hedinger has limited security staff on the island. And we know they're at least one man down because Hedinger killed him yesterday,”

Flint said. “We can take more players off the board if we need to. Replacements can’t get here for a few hours, and we’ll be gone by then. We’ve got plenty of time.”

“You think he’s really in surgery right now? Or is he frantically contacting Hedinger?” Drake asked.

Flint shrugged, ignoring his pounding headache. “You’re greatly exaggerating my mind reading capabilities.”

“Okay. What now?” Drake sounded unsure, but he’d followed Flint into worse places. Too late to turn back now.

“If Greta’s still with him we could find her at Brand’s home. Unless

Genevieve lied, we know he's not there. We might find something useful," Flint replied. "We're looking for DNA on Brand to prove he's Phillip Reed. We've got time to kill, and we should make good use of it."

Drake shook his head. "His home is likely to be locked down tighter than Fort Knox."

"I doubt he needs that kind of security. Hedinger rules this place with an iron hand. No one would dare commit a crime of any kind here, I'll bet. Atabei could be the safest place to live on the planet." Flint started the Vespa.

"Yeah, if you want a ruthless gangster enforcing the law," Drake replied, rolling away from the hospital behind Flint toward the opposite end of the alley.

The drive to Brand's home was only a few blocks. Like everything they'd seen so far on Atabei, the streets and sidewalks were pristine. Widely spaced stucco homes with barrel tile roofs were set back from the curbs. The pungent scent of jasmine and gardenias filled the air. The only people Flint saw along the way were gardeners tending to the lush tropical landscaping.

Flint parked the Vespa across the street and two doors down from Brand's residence. He scanned for security cameras and didn't see any.

Brand could have invisible security installed, but that would defeat the purpose.

Deterrence of opportunity crimes relied heavily on obvious security. Which was why people placed signs in the yard announcing active security systems.

Drake parked alongside Flint's Vespa. They left the helmets and walked toward Brand's home. Gaspar and Scarlett should be able to see them on the satellite cams.

Flint wasn't comfortable with constant surveillance. He had agreed to it because of the concussion. And because it made the rest of the team feel more secure.

Flint and Drake peeled off to circle the house and reconnect at the back entrance, pulling on surgical gloves as they moved. When they were no longer in view of the neighbors, they donned black ski masks to cover their heads and faces.

They had studied the house and its surroundings thoroughly and concluded that breaking in through the sliding glass patio door was the best option.

Flint quickly confirmed the door had no blocking bars, security pins, shatterproof film, security decals, or glass break sensors installed.

Drake pulled a steel stake from the garden to use as a pry bar and knelt down near the bottom right corner of the door. He inserted the stake into the bottom and simultaneously pried the door as he lifted the handle to open it.

Less than a minute later, they stepped inside to the cool, dim interior of Brand's home. Flint paused to listen for activity while Drake returned the sliding door to its track and closed it.

The only noises he heard were the frosty air-conditioning and the refrigerator.

He flashed Drake a thumbs up. They fanned out, moving deeper into the house.

The kitchen was polished to a high shine. The dishwasher had never been used. The refrigerator contained nothing but bottled water. Flint opened a few cabinet doors and found nothing stored inside.

Indeed, Brand's home seemed as cold and sterile as an operating suite. The glossy marble floors showed not a speck of dust or cat hair or anything suggesting life was well lived here.

In the den, Brand's furniture resembled a luxury hotel room. The upholstery was spotlessly white and the occasional Parsons tables were unmarred. An oversize television was mounted on the wall across from a single easy chair. Flint had the impression that neither the television nor the easy chair had ever been used.

Across the right side of the house, there were three bedrooms. Two were properly decorated but unoccupied. Only the master was being used. Even here, the king-size bed had been made with military precision and the bedside tables were uncluttered.

Flint walked through to the master bathroom. The gleaming glass enclosed shower took up half the room. There were no toiletries on the shelves inside the shower. The glass sparkled as if the maid had polished it an hour ago. Perhaps she had.

Drake's heavy footfalls came toward Flint across the marble. "Find anything?" Drake asked.

Flint was opening and closing drawers in the vanity. "Not yet."

"I don't think he lives here," Drake said. "No human male could be this clean and tidy. It's not possible."

Flint had found the drawer containing toothbrushes, hairbrushes, and dental floss. He pulled out an evidence bag and placed two toothbrushes and one hairbrush into it. He resealed the bag and stuffed it into his pocket.

“You think those are his?” Drake asked.

Flint shrugged. “Can’t say for sure. I was hoping for a source we could positively identify. Didn’t find it. We’re going to need a sample directly from Brand.”

“So I hold him down while you pull his hair out?” Drake grinned.

“Something like that.” Flint smiled back. “You find anything helpful?”

"If this guy is actually living here, I'll eat my hat. There are no photos, no books, no mail, even. I think this place is just for show. Or maybe he sleeps here. But that's it," Drake replied.

"No sign of a woman either, I take it," Flint said.

"Nothing. No makeup, no clothes in the closets. No plants. No personal photos. None of the stuff women usually like, in my experience," Drake said. "Greta's not here. I'd bet she's never been here, either."

"Agreed." Flint cocked his head. His thinking was slow and sluggish, which annoyed him to no end. So he ignored it. "Okay. So he's a single white male. Lives alone. Eats elsewhere. Sleeps here, possibly. Probably doesn't even shower here."

"There are clothes in his closet, but not many. He probably gets dressed at the hospital and takes his meals at the country club," Drake said.

"Or he has a mistress, and he lives at her place. All of which means we need to find him," Flint replied. "And we're short on time. Let's go."

When Flint stepped into the hallway a gust of warm air blew through the sliding door in the kitchen. His increased sensitivity to lights, sounds, and distractions alerted him long before Drake noticed.

The hairs on the back of his neck stood up and his heart pounded faster.

He stopped abruptly and Drake screeched to a halt within inches of knocking him over. Before Drake could say anything, Flint lifted his hand to the stop position.

He paused to confirm, to be sure he hadn't imagined it. The warm breeze continued to blow inside.

Now that he was listening intently, Flint heard a distant lawn mower as well.

No question. Someone had opened the patio door.

Flint closed his eyes, focused on the breeze, and filtered out the sound of the lawn mower.

Which was when he heard the soft sliding of the door on the track followed by a quiet click when the door lock was gently reengaged.

# Chapter 41

Flint signaled Drake, gestured toward the kitchen, and put his index finger over his lips. Drake nodded in silent agreement.

Hedinger's security team had been watching the house.

Or watching the two of them.

Or all of the above.

Brand's house was spacious enough for normal living, but fighting a highly trained Mossad operative would destroy the place. Flint leaned against the wall and swiveled his head slowly, scanning for options.

The intruder moved like a gymnast, wiry and flexible.

He was dressed in black, head to toe, including black leather gloves and a tight-fitting black cap that also covered his face. At night, he'd be almost invisible.

But against the bright tropical decor of Brand's home, he was easier to watch than a snake in the garden.

From Flint's current vantage point, even with his blurred vision, he could have dropped the intruder with one shot. But he gestured Drake to holster his weapon. Gunshots would draw too much of the wrong kind of attention.

Flint drew his knife and waited for the enemy to come to him.

Drake positioned himself on the opposite side of the door.

The stealthy intruder crept through the open floor plan from the back of the house to the front, twisting his body to scan the room's obvious hiding places.

Quickly, he reached the short hallway to the bedrooms.

He opened each door as he came to it, slipped inside, and finding each room unoccupied, slipped out again.

Observing the intruder was like watching a master class in outdated Mossad techniques. Flint had studied Mossad training videos over the years. This guy's operation was textbook perfect. Which made his movements predictable.

Flint flattened his back against the wall and strained to hear the nearly silent footsteps on the slick marble floors as the intruder came closer to the master suite.

Drake was positioned to be seen first.

The intruder should have been alert to two remaining options since he'd eliminated all other possibilities.

Either the house was unoccupied, which he should have assumed could not be true since he'd most likely been dispatched because Flint and Drake were seen entering the home.

Or, by process of elimination, his prey would be lying in wait in the master bedroom.

Which meant he should come in hot with intent to kill.

Four seconds later, the intruder pushed the door. It moved a few silent inches inward.

The intruder crept into the room.

When he saw Drake poised to tackle him, the intruder raised his knife with his right hand, intending to plunge it into Drake's gut.

He moved forward.

Drake blocked the knife, holding the intruder in place for a split second.

Which gave Flint all the time he needed.

Fighting dizziness and fueled by adrenaline, Flint clamped his jaw to hold back the nausea as he came from behind the intruder.

He plunged his Ka-Bar straight edge deep into the intruder's kidney with all his weight and momentum.

He gave the knife a hard twist for good measure.

Before the intruder could escape, Flint withdrew the knife and then forcefully jabbed the other kidney.

The intruder cried out just as Drake hit him hard in the belly and knocked him to the ground.

The wiry man refused to give up.

He fought against Drake with what remained of his strength.

But the scuffle was short and bloody.

The intruder's wounds opened wide and poured his life all over the marble floor.

While Drake was finishing the job, Flint won his battle of wills with nausea.

He strode quickly to the master toilet and splashed cold water on his face and rinsed his mouth. For the moment, he felt slightly less dizzy.

"You okay in there?" Drake called out.

"Yeah. Fine."

Returning to the room, careful to step around the large pool of blood on the floor, Flint reached down and pulled the man's knitted mask off.

He swiped it in the man's blood, collecting enough to test several times over. He stuffed the soggy mess into an evidence bag and sealed it.

Next he yanked the man's glove off his left hand and captured his fingerprints on his phone app.

Finally, he snapped a few photos of the man's face, frozen in horror the moment he died.

Flint punched a few quick buttons on the phone to send the prints and photos off to Gaspar.

Then he dropped the phone into his pocket and handed the evidence bag to Drake.

"Do you recognize this guy?" Drake asked.

“We’ll use the DNA to confirm identity when we get back. But I’ll bet you ten bucks now that this guy got burned at least five years ago. No way an active Mossad agent makes mistakes like that,” Flint said. “If he’d been a solid performer, we’d be dead. Simple as that.”

“Lucky for us, then,” Drake replied, breathing heavily. “Now what? I vote we get out of here before his pals show up.”

“What makes you think they’re not waiting outside?”

Drake snapped his gaze back to Flint. “Are they?”

“Not likely.” Flint shook his head carefully. “There’s two of us and maybe they knew that. But only one of them came inside. Which probably means he didn't have a partner with him."

"Probably," Drake replied sourly. "So if he'd been authorized to take us out, he'd have had backup. If he wasn't tasked to eliminate us, then he's rogue."

"Let's not wait until reinforcements arrive to find out which it is," Flint said. "How did he communicate with his team? He's not wearing a headset. Check his pockets. See if he has a cell phone or a tracking device on him."

Drake patted the dead man's pockets. He pulled out a holstered pistol and a cell phone.

"Keep the gun. We might need it," Flint said.

Drake stuffed the pistol into his pocket. "What about the phone? They can track it easily enough. And us, too, if we keep the phone on us."

"Bring it along. We'll download the data and find a clever place to stash it," Flint replied on his way through the house.

At the front entrance, Flint looked through the window blinds, scanning for security personnel. A few cars were parked along the curbs. He counted six groups of pedestrians, all civilians, strolling the sidewalks. Traffic on the street moved at or near posted speeds.

# Chapter 42

“Now what?” Drake asked, stuffing the dead man’s weapon into his waistband. “The battery’s not removable unless I destroy the phone to get it.”

“Turn the phone off and take the SIM out. They might still be able to track it, but we don’t want to destroy the phone.” Flint’s thinking felt sluggish, and his head buzzed with dizziness. “We’ll exit through the front door. If they’re out there, they won’t attack us in full view of the neighbors.”

“You hope.” Drake gave him a level stare for a couple of seconds before he replied. “We go out through the front. Then what?”

“Find the mistress,” Flint said.

“Be a lot easier to pull that off if we knew anything at all about her,” Drake said sardonically.

“That’s why Hanna hired such high-priced talent like us,” Flint deadpanned.

Drake grinned. “Because we’re not clairvoyant?”

“This whole island has only two thousand residents. If we had a couple of days, we could knock on every door in the place until we found her.”

"Yeah, but we don't have a couple of days." Drake checked his watch. "We've got a couple of hours before we confront Brand at the hospital."

"How about lunch? I noticed a couple of busy restaurants near the main drag. Local hangouts. Someone will know who's been spending time with Dr. Stephen Brand," Flint said. "Small towns are the same everywhere. They all know each other. And they're all up in each other's business."

"Okay."

"Follow my lead," Flint said as he opened Brand's front door and waved Drake onto the porch.

He followed Drake outside. He turned toward the doorway, pretending to talk to someone inside as he pulled the door closed. "Thanks for the coffee. See you again soon."

Flint donned his sunglasses. Drake shoved his hands into his pockets, and they walked along the sidewalk toward the street. A group of laughing women was passing. Two were dressed in pink hospital scrubs. Drake gave them a friendly wave, but they barely noticed.

Flint and Drake sauntered along the sidewalk across the street. "As long as we stay visible among the citizens, Hedinger won't come after us."

“You hope,” Drake replied flatly.

“More to the point, that guy’s partners haven’t moved in yet,” Flint said casually, as if eavesdroppers might believe the topic of conversation was innocuous. Like last night’s Marlins game or the one scheduled for tonight.

They continued along the sidewalk to the crosswalk. When the light changed, they crossed the street. Flint kept his hands in position to reach his weapon as his eyes scanned the area and the people around them.

When they reached a quaint wooden building on a side street boasting “the best conch chowder in Atabei,”

Flint walked toward the restaurant's entrance. Drake followed.

Breeze In was a casual restaurant. The square building was constructed with wooden clapboards and a metal roof. The walls were hinged shutters that stood wide open extending the look and feel of the tropical paradise outdoors.

Inside, the breezy, open interior was equally inviting. The floors were wide mahogany planks worn smooth by hundreds of feet shuffling along the wood's surface over time.

The center of the square building was occupied by an inviting bar, also square shaped. The casually dressed bartender and all his supplies rested inside the square.

Wicker stools painted in tropical colors and sporting comfortable floral cushions were arranged around the perimeter of the bar were. Guests leaned on the carved wooden bar top where hundreds of others had polished the mahogany to a high gloss.

The remainder of the Breeze In was furnished with square tables and ladder-backed chairs, also painted in bright tropical orange, pink, green, blue, and yellow. Floral cushions perched on the seats. Tabletops matched the mahogany of the bar and the floor.

Cheerful calypso music played through the sound system speakers mounted in the corners.

Overall, the Breeze In's ambience was relaxed and pleasant. Comfortable. The kind of place tourists, if there had been any allowed on Atabei, might have spent happy days and nights mingling in a relaxing tropical vacation paradise with Atabei locals.

It was still early for lunch, but a couple of two-tops and a four-top were occupied. A few singles gathered around the bar dressed in brightly colored hospital scrubs.

Strangers were unusual here. Patrons noticed when Flint and Drake moved past. Flint felt their eyes following him and pretended he didn't.

They approached the bar and climbed onto barstools offering a clear view of the main entrance and the doorway in the back that led to the kitchen. If the dead guy at Brand's house had called for backup, Flint hadn't seen anyone. But smarter to keep his guard up.

The bartender was a dark-skinned man with a snake tattoo winding around his shaved head and an easy smile.

Along with water glasses, he offered suggestions in the friendly way of bartenders everywhere. "The luncheon special is our conch chowder. Fresh bread baked in the kitchen every day. If you're hungrier, add the grouper sandwich and plantains."

“Sounds good,” Drake said.

“Make it two,” Flint replied.

“Rum runners? Rum punch? Red Stripe?” the bartender asked, naming a few local favorites.

“Too early in the day.” Flint shook his head sadly. “Iced tea, please.”

Drake held up two fingers.

“Two iced teas coming up. I’m Sammy. Let me know if you need anything else.” The bartender grinned and left to put their orders in.

Flint glanced around the room. Two strangers sitting at the bar seemed to have lost its curiosity factor for the other patrons. They’d returned to their private conversations.

“Looks like a few of these folks work at the hospital,” Flint said quietly.

Drake cocked his head toward two men seated halfway down on his right. They were engaged in a quiet but serious conversation.

The men looked similar enough to be brothers. One was slightly older than the other. A year or two, at most. Both had brown eyes, close-cropped hair, and dark skin.

One was wearing green surgical scrubs and running shoes. The other was dressed in a khaki uniform and boots. On his breast pocket was a logo patch.

When the older one turned his torso toward Flint, he could read the patch.

ATABEI CREMATORIUM

“That’s curious,” Flint said quietly, tilting his head toward the two men. “Why does Atabei need a crematorium?”

“What do you mean?” Drake asked.

“Population here is only two thousand full-time residents. Death and cremation rates being what they are, how can he run an expensive operation like that with only ten cases a year?”

“Good question.” Drake shrugged. “So what are they really doing, then?”

“Only one way to find out. Sammy asks, I went to the men’s room,” Flint told Drake quietly. Truthfully, he added, “I’m not feeling well. Damned concussion.”

“Where are you really going?” Drake asked.

# Chapter 43

Otis Jarsdel kept an open mind, and he believed in serendipity. Dogged determination took him only so far. He solved cases by employing a combination of hard work and following his whims.

His process was far from scientific.

Which was why, this afternoon, he'd stood on the street at the exact location where the balloon video had been recorded before the royal wedding.

The video itself was serendipity, wasn't it? The balloon, the boy, the horseman. Hollywood directors with unlimited budgets couldn't have choreographed that scene as perfectly.

Add into the mix that the woman had been standing just there, near that streetlight pole, when the balloon escaped from the boy's grubby fingers.

And the entire scene had been captured by the BBC's news coverage of the royal wedding.

The balloon scene had delighted the crowd on the day of the wedding. Which was good enough. But later, the video aired on the news coverage of the day's events. Still later, it captured imaginations online as the short clip went viral on social media.

Overall, countless millions had watched the boy, the balloon, and the horseman.

More importantly for Jarsdel's purposes, they'd seen the woman.

Serendipity had provided millions of witnesses.

At least one of those witnesses had to know this woman and what he'd come to believe was her little family.

If he had the time and the manpower, he could ask around and eventually he'd find her. He knew he would.

But his resources were limited.

He had neither time nor manpower.

So he improvised.

He'd called in a favor to get a good copy of the video from one of his contacts at the BBC. From the video, he'd isolated two high-resolution images of the woman.

The angles and the lighting were far from perfect. He refused to let perfect be the enemy of the good here.

So he cheated a bit.

He used sophisticated facial recognition software to compare the video images to Greta Campbell Reed's US passport photo.

The software wasn't perfect either. Not even close.

But it could narrow the margin of error and reduce the resources he'd need to find Greta.

While Jarsdel brewed a cup of tea, the software finished its work. He studied the results and frowned. Not as good as he'd hoped.

The confidence score was low. Which meant there was a chance of a false positive result.

But to his eye, there was a match between the image of the woman on the street and Reed's passport photo. It was at least worth exploring.

Next he compared the two video images with Greta Reed's Florida driver's license photo.

This time the confidence score was slightly higher. But not as high as it should have been if the same woman was the subject in all four images.

Jarsdel had found a few old candid snaps of Greta Reed on social media. He fed those into the software, too.

Perhaps because of the lighting conditions and facial expressions, the final confidence score was more ambiguous than the first one.

Not the result he was hoping for.

After all the effort, the original question remained.

Was the woman at the wedding in the balloon video Greta Campbell Reed or not?

The short answer was maybe.

For Jarsdel's purposes, assuming that the woman **was** Greta Reed was the way to go. Much more likely to keep Hedinger off his back than assuming they were **not** the same person.

Hedinger wanted the woman to be Greta and he wanted her found and eliminated. Quickly.

"As quickly as possible" was Hedinger's answer when Jarsdel had asked when the job should be completed.

Eliminating Greta now had been his second choice.

Jarsdel reset the software with new parameters. This time he ignored the woman and focused on the man standing with her.

He ran the man's image through the US passport database.

The assumption he wanted to confirm was that they'd known each other before the balloon video. If he could identify the man, that might help to find the woman.

Allowing Hedinger into Jarsdel's thought process was a mistake. Serendipitously, the phone Hedinger used exclusively to contact him rang.

He picked up the call. "Yes."

"What's the status of my project?" Hedinger demanded.

"Nothing to report yet," Jarsdel said, sipping tea and watching the images flash across the screen.

The passport databases contained standardized images and biometrics, which was good. But it was a large database. Could take a while to get all the way through it.

“Keep me posted,” Hedinger demanded before he hung up.

Jarsdel smirked and shook his head as he slipped the phone into his pocket.

Patience was a virtue and Hedinger had precious little of it. Good thing the man was rich. Money was the only virtue he possessed.

Jarsdel accessed the software again and set it to compare the woman’s video image with the UK passport database. He had no reason to believe she owned a UK passport. But it was an easy thing to check, so why not?

And having gone that far, why not check the man and the kid, too? Why not check all the UK databases at once?

Jarsdel fed all the images into the software and set them to run against UK databases.

His tea had grown cold. He carried the mug into the kitchen to warm it up.

When he came back with the hot tea and a couple of cookies, one of the searches had found a match. Confidence level was one hundred percent.

Jarsdel dry swallowed the shortbread, swigged tea to wash it down, and stared at the screen. The man's video image was a match to the UK passport photo for Avery Tumbler.

"Mr. Tumbler. Nice to meet ya," Jarsdel mumbled toward the screen.

The other two searches were still running, so Jarsdel pulled up a background check on Tumbler. A few short queries later and Jarsdel had a complete history.

None of it reported that Tumbler was married or that he had a son.

Meanwhile, the images of the woman and the boy failed to match anything in the UK passport databases, which Jarsdel had been expecting.

He watched the balloon video again. The boy sat easily on Tumbler's shoulders. The woman grasped his arm the way a girlfriend would.

"Maybe they're not married. But they know each other. For sure," Jarsdel said aloud.

He checked Scotland's tax rolls. Tumbler owned a home. He found Tumbler's address on a map of Scotland.

The village, called Portmahomack, was in the Scottish Highlands on the northeast coast. According to the internet, the total population of the village was a mere seven hundred souls.

Tumbler lived outside the village on a small farm he'd inherited from his father. The farm had been in the Tumbler family for generations.

Jarsdel could take a flight up to Inverness, rent a car to drive farther north, look around. But it was a long way to go on a hunch. He'd lose a whole day. Maybe more.

With Hedinger already on his ass about results, he was reluctant to waste resources.

He needed confirmation. Or at least a reason to believe the woman might be living in Portmahomack.

How could he get confirmation?

He'd already tried all the available databases. Perhaps the human approach would yield results.

Jarsdel pulled up a list of pubs in Portmahomack. Pubs served as gathering places for locals in rural communities everywhere across the UK. If Tumbler had a woman and a kid, folks at his local pub would know about them.

He located the pub closest to Tumbler's address, opened a fresh burner phone, and dialed.

The call clicked several times while the cell towers connected. Eventually, it rang on the other end. After ten rings with no answer, Jarsdel gave up and tried the second pub on the list.

# Chapter 44

**Atabei**

Flint walked slowly past the two men still deep in quiet conversation. He glanced back toward Drake and ducked into the hallway.

On the right were the restrooms. At the end of the hallway was the exit to the parking lot.

Flint walked through and squinted against the bright sunshine which exacerbated the constant headache he'd been living with for days.

He slid his sunglasses on and propped the exit door open with a rock.

Half a dozen vehicles were parked in the flat gravel lot. Mostly small SUVs. A khaki panel van sporting the Atabei Crematorium logo rested in the shade at the end of the first row.

Flint fished his phone from his pocket and snapped photos of the van, the logo, and the Atabei plate on the back bumper.

He also took quick shots of the other parked vehicles and their license plates.

When he'd finished with the snaps, he dropped the phone into his pocket and walked around to the back of the panel van again. The doors were locked, as expected.

Flint removed his sunglasses and peered into the windows.

Inside the panel van were four long mortuary trays, two mounted on each side panel and two on the floor beneath. The shelves were shiny steel. The kind that could be washed down with a hose.

All four trays were occupied by black plastic body bags.

Flint couldn't see the contents without opening the zippers, but from the shape of the bags it was obvious there were four bodies, one in each bag.

He gloved up and retrieved his knife from his pocket and went to work on the rear door lock. He manipulated the blade, popped the lock, and climbed inside. He pulled the doors closed but left a crack between them.

Flint's head swam and his gag reflex choked on the hot, stale air inside the box. He folded his elbow across his nose and ignored the urge to retch as he approached the first body bag.

He tugged hard to open the zipper all the way.

"What the hell?" Flint murmured as he stared at the body.

The man was cold to the touch. The body had been stored long enough to freeze all the way through to the bones. More than a couple of days, for sure.

Even so, the body had begun to thaw. The skin was slimy and discolored, like a spoiled Thanksgiving turkey.

The most revolting aspect was the man's gaping torso. The body had been opened by a sharp scalpel with the familiar pathologist's wide and deep Y incision. Organs had been removed and the skin flopped down into the empty cavity.

Flint's stomach heaved at the sight.

He clamped his jaw shut, grabbed shallow breaths, and kept going.

He opened all four bags and snapped photos of each body. Three men and one woman. All gutted in the same way. Two of the bodies were less decomposed. Maybe they'd died more recently.

Working as quickly as he could manage, Flint used the app on his phone to take fingerprints from each body. The prints were far from perfect. With luck, they could get partials.

Barely controlling the nausea overwhelming him from the stench and heat, he searched the interior of the van for a first aid kit.

He swabbed the open torso of each body with gauze and wrapped the gauze with tape.

Not as good as a DNA swab kit, but the best he could do at the moment.

His intense dizziness, headache, and nausea were overwhelming. He could stay inside the hot box no longer.

Flint zipped the body bags and climbed out of the van. Quickly, he closed and locked the back doors. Maybe the body removal technician wouldn't notice he'd tampered with the lock.

He gave the back of the van one last glance. It seemed okay. Flint hurried back to the door. He took several gulps of cool air into his lungs on the way, attempting to control the dizziness and nausea.

Flint sent the photos and prints to Gaspar's server. Then he kicked the rock away from the exit door and went inside.

He slipped into the men's room and washed the grime and stench from his face and hands. As soon as he felt well enough, he made his way to the bar.

The two brothers were still talking quietly. The dining room had filled with more locals. Flint resumed his place and swigged the iced tea, hoping the caffeine would steady his shaking muscles.

Sammy returned with a fresh glass of iced tea for both of them. “You okay, man? You look peaked.”

“Fine. Really. Just low blood sugar,” Flint replied, reaching for a pack of saltines and popping one into his mouth. He took a long swig of the cold tea.

“Yeah, that’s rough. Sorry the food is taking so long. Want me to bring your chowder?" Sammy asked. "The folks at the hospital have their lunch break about now. The kitchen always gets a little backed up."

"I can wait, Sammy. Thanks," Flint said, sipping the tea to calm his queasy stomach. "Looks like you do get quite a few hospital employees in here at lunch. Do you know them all?"

"Pretty much. Atabei is a small community. Not many of us. We can spot outsiders pretty quickly." Sammy smiled.

Drake grinned. "So you mean you didn't think we were locals?"

"Not hardly," Sammy replied good-naturedly.

Flint pointed his chin toward the two brothers. “What about those two? Visitors?”

“Not even close. I’ll save you the trouble of asking about everyone here. You’re the only two visitors in the place,” Sammy said. “So who are you looking for? Happy to help.”

Drake glanced around the room. “Because they all want to know, right?”

Sammy shrugged.

“It’s a reasonable question. Strangers come into town. Folks want to know why we’re here.” Flint cocked his head. “Truth is we’re looking for our sister. She disappeared a while back. She told us she was coming here because of Stephen Brand. You know him?"

"Sure. Everybody knows Dr. Brand," Sammy replied easily. "Did your sister need a heart transplant?"

Drake said, "Actually, we thought she was romantically involved with him. She told us they were dating. We thought they were living here together."

"That can't be right." Sammy frowned. "Dr. Brand has a girlfriend. They have been together quite a while now. You might ask her, though. Genevieve Sweeting, the hospital CEO."

A young woman brought their food from the kitchen and Sammy left them alone to eat. Sammy came back with fresh iced tea shortly after the two brothers paid their bill and left.

“Those two guys who were sitting over there,” Flint said, tilting his head toward their now abandoned seats. “Who are they?”

Sammy smiled. “Jimmy and Joey. Twins, don’tcha know. Lived here forever.”

“Which one works for the crematorium? Jimmy or Joey?” Flint asked.

“They kinda both do, I guess. Joey’s the one that moves the bodies to be cremated. Jimmy’s an orderly at the hospital morgue,” Sammy explained, cleaning up the plates as his customers finished their lunch breaks and left.

"Hard to believe you have a need for a crematorium here, isn't it? I mean, this is a small place. Guy can't have that much business, right?" Drake said.

"It's not just Atabei residents, though." Sadness settled across Sammy's normally pleasant face. "Often, the organ donors don't make it. Shipping bodies home for burial is expensive and troublesome. The hospital provides the cremation services to the families as a courtesy."

"A courtesy? You mean they don't charge anything at all?" Flint asked.

"The families are already grieving. No reason they should be worried about money, too, you know?" Sammy replied as he picked up a big plastic bin filled with dirty dishes and lugged it toward the kitchen.

Drake finished his sandwich and pushed the plate away. "Now what? Back to the hospital?"

"Yeah. Greta's not here."

"How do you know?"

"Sammy would have reacted differently if he'd ever seen Greta or heard anything about her. And Brand wouldn't be with another woman if Greta were living with him," Flint replied, draining the last of the tea. "This town's too small for secrets like that."

"Agreed. What about the crematorium? How's that fit in?" Drake asked.

"The only answer that fits the known facts is too heinous to believe. Greta Campbell might have taken her own life if she'd found out," Flint replied stone-faced. "Unless Brand killed her before she had the chance."

"That can't be true. Because Hanna saw Greta on that video," Drake said like a petulant bulldog refusing to accept defeat.

"Did she actually see Greta, though? She can't prove it. Neither can we." Flint tossed a few bills on the bar. "Let's find the bastard, get what we came for, and get the hell out of here."

# Chapter 45

Flint led the way to the gravel parking lot at Breeze In's back exit. The crematorium van was gone, and the parking lot was almost deserted.

"Brand is expecting us to show up at the hospital. He's a coward. He'll leave early if Genevieve delivered our message," Drake said, taking long strides to keep up with Flint.

"That's why we're getting there before he can hightail it off the island."

"You're planning to stop him?" Drake said. "I'm up for that."

Flint grinned. "Thought you might be."

"What did you find in that van that's got you so riled up anyway?" Drake asked as they rounded the corner.

Flint took a deep breath to steady his queasy stomach. "Looks like Brand may be selling organs to wealthy patients and killing the donors to get their hearts and complete the deal. Just like he did to Ella Belle."

Drake turned green. "Was he planning to do the same thing to Greta?"

"I wouldn't put it past the bastard," Flint replied without pausing.

They retraced their route to the parked Vespas, fired them up, and rolled past the country club toward Atabei Hospital.

The tropical community was still pristine and beautiful.

Yet, after finding the desecrated bodies in the van, the inviting paradise made Flint's skin crawl. Deep malevolence was thriving here. Hedinger and Brand were to blame.

Ernst Hedinger was the furthest thing from a Boy Scout, but this was a new level of depraved, even for him.

They pulled the Vespas around to the hospital's back parking lot. Flint rolled along slowly until he found a parking place reserved for Dr. Stephen Brand. He parked the Vespa behind Brand's luxury sedan and dismounted.

"Wait here," he said as he removed his helmet and hung it on the Vespa. "Keep a lookout for Brand."

"You're going inside alone?" Drake asked. "Are you sure you're up for this?"

Flint ignored the question. "I'll flush him out. If we're lucky, he'll come back here for his car."

"And if he does?"

"Hold him. We need to know about Greta. He might know where she is," Flint said. "But if he strikes, take him out. We'll find her without him if we need to."

Flint hurried past Brand's car and headed toward the hospital's back entrance.

Flint's strategy relied on his knowledge of Hedinger's methods. Hedinger was an extremely wealthy, powerful, and influential man. Which meant he could hire the best security money could buy. Which he did.

Employing an excellent security staff on a private island was okay. But Hedinger's combination of ruthless enforcement and top performing security officers could also create a false sense of safety, which wasn't even remotely okay.

Hedinger's private island security was no doubt diligent as well as ruthless at first. Infractions of the rules would have been discovered promptly and punishment dealt swiftly. With extreme prejudice.

Hedinger despised thieves. He handled them personally. Punishment was swift, ruthless, and public. He believed in deterrence, not redemption. A thief who dared to steal so much as a piece of fruit lost the hand that dared to rob Hedinger. No exceptions.

Similarly, no citizen was permitted to carry weapons of any kind. Illegal weapons were confiscated and used to inflict bodily harm on the violators.

Over time, the population became aware of Hedinger's rules and were desperate to avoid his retribution.

Flint believed rebelliousness and bad behavior would have been eradicated among Atabei's easygoing citizens within the first month.

Which inevitably made Hedinger's security team cocky and lazy and in no hurry to hunt down what few criminal elements might exist. No need to rush and no desire to.

After all, no one could escape Atabei Island. Only approved persons were allowed to enter or leave.

Agents would discover any infractions and locate the perpetrators all in good time.

If Flint's assumptions were correct, and he was willing to bet they were, Hedinger's skeleton crew of agents had developed insufferable hubris.

The agents were highly trained, ruthless, and they believed they had total control of the entire island population's behavior. Most of the time, they probably did.

Simply put, today they were wrong.

Flint had already proven the folly several times just in the last few hours.

And he wasn't finished.

He hustled through the back entrance. Like the front, he spied no obvious surveillance. No posted security. No desk for visitor check-in. Nothing.

Flint pulled up the diagram of the hospital's layout on his phone as he strode deeper into the building. He'd paid handsomely for the diagram, and he hoped it was accurate.

Another truism. A corrupt boss encouraged corrupt personnel. Hedinger was a fool to trust them.

Brand was the obvious example. He was an exceptionally competent surgeon who thought he was God. Hedinger tolerated his ego because his skill and competence increased Hedinger's wealth and influence.

The relationship was forged and strengthened by uninhibited success. Simply put, neither had any reason to be dissatisfied.

Until now.

Like all despots everywhere, Hedinger was a psycho. That unpredictability could be exploited. If Flint could only get past the effects of that damned concussion.

The Chief of Surgery's spacious office faced the luxurious courtyard in the wing opposite the operating rooms. Next to the Chief of Surgery's office was the CEO's office.

There was a connecting door between them. How cozy.

Flint heard raised voices inside Brand's office. A man and a woman. Probably Brand and his mistress. Flint paused to listen.

"**Where** is my cell phone, Genevieve?" Brand demanded angrily, tossing objects to the floor.

"It's not my job to inventory your possessions," she responded with an equal amount of anger. "Did you leave it at my place? You were on a call last night in bed."

"Who do you think you're talking to?" Brand demanded.

The crack of a loud slap and then a heavy thump.

Flint suffered another wave of dizziness and nausea and waited briefly until it receded. Then he pulled his gun, opened the door, and stepped inside Brand's office.

Brand and Genevieve were standing close together near his sofa. She held one palm to her cheek, eyes blazing. His arm was raised, prepared to strike her again.

Genevieve's back was to the doorway. Brand would have seen Flint enter the room if he weren't so furiously engaged with his mistress.

"When you have a minute," Flint pointed the pistol.

If they heard him, they didn't act like it.

A single shot from the Glock could have entered Genevieve's back and traveled all the way through to embed itself in Brand's torso.

Flint considered the idea briefly.

But he didn't want to kill her.

Not yet anyway.

He moved slightly to improve his shooting angle. He elbowed a large ceramic table lamp and sent it crashing to the marble floor.

The noise produced the desired reaction.

Genevieve turned abruptly.

Brand's line of sight was wide open.

He saw Flint standing six feet away with the business end of the Glock pointed directly at him.

Brand gave Genevieve a hard push and she took the hint. She stepped aside, out of the line of fire.

Brand stood facing Flint's weapon.

"Stay put," Flint said harshly. "You make a better target there."

Genevieve replied, "This is one of the men I told you about. John Campbell. He was here earlier with his brother, James. They say you knew his missing sister, Greta Campbell."

Brand’s eyes narrowed. “That’s a ridiculous lie.”

“Why don’t you tell her how you know I lied, Phillip,” Flint replied.

Genevieve gasped. “What the hell are you talking about?”

“He told you he didn’t know Greta Campbell, didn’t he?” Flint asked.

Genevieve nodded. Brand’s nostrils flared as he set his lips into a hard line.

Flint said, “Did he say that he didn’t kill Greta, too?”

Genevieve gasped again. “Stephen hasn’t killed anyone. That’s preposterous.”

"Shut up." Brand doubled his fist and punched her in the face.

Shock stopped her breathing momentarily before she screamed loudly enough to halt traffic. Her hands flew to her nose, which was bleeding like a running faucet. Blood covered her chin and fell to mingle with the pattern of her floral dress.

She lost consciousness and crumpled onto the sofa.

"Who the hell are you and what do you want?" Brand demanded, feet apart, both hands clenched at his sides, chin jutting forward.

"Let's talk about you, Phillip. Your name is Phillip Reed. You were married to Ella Belle Reed until you had her killed because you'd sold her organs to wealthy buyers," Flint said. "Was she your first, Phillip? Or had you killed to provide donor organs before?"

"You're insane," Brand replied. "My security team is on the way. Get out of here before they arrive. They might let you live if you get off the island before they find you."

"What about Greta Campbell? Did you kill her so you could sell her organs, too?" Flint pushed, seeking to provoke Brand.

"Why do you think Greta's dead?" Brand said easily, a knowing smirk on his face. "They never found her body, did they? No body, no murder."

Flint raised the Glock and held it steady. “You’re right, Phillip. Greta’s not dead. We thought she might be living here with you. But of course she knows what a monster you are now. She’d never live with you again.”

Brand shrugged, but he’d gone pale when Flint confirmed Greta was alive. His voice was weak and breathy when he croaked, “I have no idea what you’re talking about.”

“Nice try,” Flint replied, shaking his head. “You staged the boating accident. You left Greta in the water. You believed she’d drowned. But like you, she survived.”

Brand shook his head slowly, denying Flint’s accusations.

"You came here. You started up your depraved organ-selling business. You thought you were safe. Because you thought Greta had drowned," Flint pressed on. "But she didn't. Greta's alive. And she'll testify against you."

"What do you mean?" Brand asked, astonished.

"Shut up. I can't stand to listen to you." Flint reached into his pocket for the handcuffs he'd brought along. He moved toward Brand to lock his wrists in the cuffs when another bout of dizziness overwhelmed him. He staggered slightly.

Brand saw his chance.

Quickly, he stepped forward and jammed his shoulder into Flint's sternum, putting all his weight behind the maneuver.

Flint attempted to balance on one foot, both hands occupied, overwhelmed by dizziness.

Brand's hard shove took Flint down and stole his breath away. He hit the floor. Blackness circled his vision. He struggled to remain conscious.

Brand grabbed the Glock and jumped across Flint's body. He pointed the pistol at Genevieve and fired a quick round into her head.

Flint scrambled behind a chair.

Brand pivoted toward Flint, moving the gun as he tried to aim.

He couldn't get a clean shot.

He fired twice but managed only to hit the furniture before he gave up.

A few quick strides to the door and Brand ran out into the corridor. Flint could hear his footsteps pounding on the marble floors.

Flint struggled to stand. His sternum felt like he'd been head-butted by a bull. He'd have a bruise blacker than a bowling ball tomorrow.

But he could breathe.

Once he was able to draw air into his lungs, he overcame the nausea.

And quelled the dizziness.

He scrambled to put one foot in front of the other, loping to the cadence of his pounding head.

He picked up the pace after a few steps and ran toward the rear exit, in hot pursuit of Stephen Brand or Phillip Reed or whoever the hell he really was.

Two good thoughts battled in his mind.

First, Greta Campbell was not dead.

If she were, Brand wouldn't have been so spooked by Flint's flat certainty.

Brand would have laughed it off. Boldly maintained his innocence.

Which he didn't.

And second, a totally pissed-off Alonzo Drake would be waiting for Brand when he came through the back door to the parking lot.

Brand wouldn't know what hit him.

Flint trotted as rapidly as he dared, weaving through patients and workers and around various equipment obstacles toward Drake and Brand outside.

About halfway to the exit door, he heard pounding footsteps and shouted orders coming from behind him. He glanced over his shoulder.

Two armed goons, one short and heavy, one lanky and awkward, coming up fast.

# Chapter 46

Flint picked up his pace. He could hear their hard-soled shoes slipping on the marble behind him but gaining ground. What he'd remembered as a short hallway now seemed longer than a football field.

Hoping to slow his pursuers down, Flint pushed a trash barrel to the floor behind him, strewing garbage in his wake.

The short one slipped and fell, cursing when he landed on his ass. The lanky one paused to offer a hand.

Flint struggled to increase his speed and put more distance between himself and the armed guards.

When the two guards were vertical and moving again, they came after him with a vengeance. They'd been doing the job before. Now they were angry.

"Stop! Stop or we'll shoot!" one of them yelled like dialogue from a bad movie.

Laughable words but the threats were dead serious.

A moment later, they fired two shots to prove how serious they were.

The deafening blast and acrid stench of gunshots in the enclosed corridor were unmistakable.

When the shots rang out, hospital personnel screamed and moved aside, crouching low near the walls, clearing a path.

Flint ducked instinctively and covered his head with both arms as he ran.

Both shots went wild.

One hit the wall near Flint, sending a mini spray of drywall dust over the floor.

The second bullet penetrated the ceiling on his left.

Flint zigzagged and bobbed and weaved, taking quick looks over his shoulder for brief risk assessments.

Only short glances were required to prove he was losing the battle.

Never a fast runner even when he wasn't nursing a concussion, Flint took a deep breath and poured on as much speed as he dared, running full out toward the exit.

The door was only twenty feet of unobstructed corridor ahead now.

He could make it before they killed him.

Possibly.

If he kept going.

The goons shot and missed again. But they ramped up their running speed at the same time.

He could hear them. They were close now.

Too close.

He lunged forward to cover the last three feet of distance and landed with all his weight on the exit bar that crossed the glass door.

The entire heavy framed door pushed open.

Flint inhaled fresh air deep into his gasping lungs and kept moving, scanning the lot.

He spotted Drake off to the right near a palm tree.

Drake stood holding Brand's head against the hot steel of the sedan's trunk, arms pinned behind his back. Brand had stopped struggling. He must have realized he was no match for Drake in size or skill set.

If the guards kept coming, they'd be closing in fast behind Flint. He had a short hot moment to act.

He dashed to Drake's side, still gasping for air.

"Glock," he demanded breathily.

Drake turned his body to reveal Flint's pistol poking out of the back pocket of his jeans. Flint grabbed the pistol and turned toward the exit door, setting his shooter's stance and taking aim.

When the glass door flew open, Flint steadied his weapon and fired.

Two shots.

Two more.

Center mass.

Hedinger's two goons dropped like heavy punching bags that had been cut loose from the rope holding them up from the top. The short one hit the ground first. The lanky one landed on top of him.

Neither guard had been wearing body armor.

They were making no effort to get up. No moaning, either. No breathing.

They were both dead.

Hubris. Just like he'd thought.

Both bodies blocked the doorway exit.

No one else could come through the door.

He didn't pause to gloat.

"Throw Brand in the trunk. I'll clean out the Vespas." Flint rapid-fired the instructions and Drake followed through.

Flint emptied the Vespas' storage of the evidence they'd gathered so far and the equipment they'd need to escape Atabei.

Before they left Houston, Scarlett had insisted they make a plan B. Flint had had no desire to argue, so they'd done as she demanded.

Which was a good thing.

Not that he'd ever let her know it.

The original plan—to take the construction crew transport flight back to Miami—would have worked if things had unfolded differently.

Now that shots had been fired and three of Hedinger's goons plus the hospital CEO were dead, flying back to Miami with the construction crew at the end of the workday was no longer a viable option.

Hedinger was three men down. Plus Brand and the woman. With any luck, he wouldn't be able to replenish his team quickly enough.

Drake popped the trunk and patted Brand down. He found and removed the key fob for the sedan, a pocketknife, and a cigarette case. He shoved Brand inside, and he was none too careful about it, either.

"Don't panic, Brand. No whining. You've got plenty of room and plenty of air," Drake said before he slammed the trunk lid down and made his way to the driver's seat.

Flint was already seated in the passenger's seat. The engine was running with the air-conditioning on to cool down the cabin's interior.

"Push-button start?" Drake arched his eyebrows and flashed a grin. "How convenient."

"Let's go before we have more of Hedinger's goons to deal with. Head southwest. There's an undeveloped cove over there. A place to interrogate Brand before we get the hell off this island."

Flint gestured in the general direction of the abandoned road he'd found while studying Gaspar's maps.

Drake turned the big sedan and headed in the right direction. “What are we going to do with Brand?”

“Let’s cross that bridge when we come to it.” Flint shrugged and ran a flat palm across his weary face. He pointed. “Take a left turn up ahead.”

Atabei was the characteristic shape of a volcanic Caribbean Island. The cone-shaped mountain was surrounded by sloping land leading down to the sea.

The island’s crescent perimeter had been partially developed to showcase its beautiful beaches. But the western side of the island was steep and rocky.

The abandoned road ran along a cliff on the western side. Below the cliff's edge was a large section of protruding black limestone formations, giving it an eerie and sinister feel. The limestone was sharp and dangerous.

"Are you sure?" Drake asked.

"Yeah. It's a defensible location. Anybody tries to come in, we'll know it," Flint replied.

There was only one good road from Atabei Town which encircled the volcanic island. It was a twisty two-lane road. They'd traveled it that morning on the bus from the airport.

The abandoned road had been built long before Hedinger bought the island. It had crested the big hill at the top of the inactive volcano and then wound its way down the other side of the hill. Hedinger had cut off the road when repairing and maintaining it was no longer necessary.

Drake slowed the big sedan over the potholes as the road wound around and up the hillside.

When the sedan rounded the back of the volcano, Flint gestured toward the soft, crumbling shoulder.

“Pull off here. We’ll be out of sight from ground surveillance. Don’t get too close to the cliff,” Flint said, opening his door to step outside. “Let’s drag Brand out of the trunk and find out what he knows about Greta.”

“Works for me.” Drake walked around to the rear of the sedan and pressed the trunk release.

The trunk lid popped open like a child’s toy. Brand sat up, shielding his eyes from the bright sunlight.

Drake reached over, grabbed his arm, and jerked him out of the trunk. Brand went limp, his knees buckled, and he sat on the ground.

“Stand up.” Drake yanked him up and then shoved him against the sedan.

“What do you want?” Brand demanded.

“You’re Phillip Reed. You were married to Ella Belle Reed and then to Greta Campbell Reed,” Flint said.

Brand shook his head slowly.

Flint said, "You had Ella Belle killed so you could transplant her heart into the man who paid you a fortune for it."

"You're crazy. Nobody will believe that," Brand stated flatly, still holding his hands up to shield his face from the glaring sun. "You killed Genevieve just now. You shot my security team. You broke into my home. You're the killer, not me."

"You can tell that to the prosecutors in Atlanta." Flint's tone was harder than steel. "What about Greta Campbell? Did you kill her and sell her heart, too?"

"I have no idea what you're talking about," Brand said flatly.

"See, I don't think you killed Greta. You probably tried. But you failed. Greta's alive. We will find her," Flint declared with hard certainty. "And when we do, you'll spend the rest of your miserable life in prison, waiting years to be executed."

"You're insane!" Brand roared like an outraged lion as he lunged forward and shoved Flint forcefully toward the cliff's edge.

Off balance, dizzy, head pounding, Flint scrambled to keep his footing on the slippery gravel.

# Chapter 47

Drake grabbed Brand, trying to hold him back.

Frenzied, Brand whipped around faster than a dive-bombing falcon and pounded Drake's temple with the flat of his fist in an explosive full-force strike.

The blow dropped Drake to his knees, leaving him dazed.

While he struggled to get back on his feet, Brand delivered a swift, solid kick to his chin. Drake fell backward, hitting the back of his head on a boulder, and slumped to the ground.

With Drake down and unconscious, Brand returned his frenzied rage to Flint.

Flint's headache pounded in tempo with his pulse. He was dizzy and nauseous.

He gathered his focus, attempting to control the lingering concussion symptoms while defending against Brand's furious attack.

Flint's reaction time proved too slow.

Brand gave Flint one final heave, shoving him sideways while he was standing awkwardly on the uneven gravel. Gravity did the rest.

Flint felt himself falling down and over the edge of the cliff.

He windmilled his arms, attempting to stay upright.

At the same time, he tried to bend forward and change his center of gravity, seeking to avoid tumbling down the mountainside and becoming impaled on the sharp limestone pillars below.

Brand was a raging bull. He bellowed as his footing floundered and advanced once more, determined to force Flint to his death.

Flint managed to bend forward at the waist and grasp a small bush growing on the cliffside. He held the bush in his right hand as he pressed the soles of his boots into the gravel slope to stop his downward slide.

It worked. He slowed his momentum and stopped falling.

Barely hanging on, Flint paused for a steadying breath.

Once again he heard Brand's enraged bellowing ten feet above.

He glanced upward.

Brand was balancing on his heels, descending rapidly, intending to kick away Flint's tenuous hold on the shrub.

Flint saw the strategy developing but was powerless to stop it.

He set his feet as firmly as possible into the loose gravel on the cliff side, prepared to block Brand's full-frontal attack.

Loose gravel flew in every direction as Brand continued his rush toward Flint, picking up speed.

Flint closed his eyes briefly to avoid the blinding sun and spewing gravel as Brand attacked from above.

Flint had been in tough spots before. Many times. He'd been trained by Uncle Sam to be the best he could possibly be. He knew what he had to do to save Drake and himself.

When the options were kill or be killed, he had only one choice.

He blocked every distraction from his mind as he slowed his sense of time to a manageable speed.

He ignored the headache, dizziness, nausea, and blinding sunlight.

He gathered the few tools at hand to prepare his defense.

Rage. Momentum. Gravity. Timing.

All four were working against Brand and he didn't seem to notice.

Brand's overwhelming desire was to kill Flint and do it now. That desire drove him to make foolish mistakes.

Flint forced himself to wait for his chance.

He was in that place where things move fast but his mind seemed slow. There was a name for that state of consciousness, but he couldn't remember it at the moment. He experienced the action like watching an old film, one frame at a time.

Brand was ten feet above Flint now, coming down fast, screaming all the way.

Each footfall landed on the cliffside and held for half a moment before Brand was forced to keep going, like fast pedaling a racing bicycle downhill to avoid taking a serious ass-over-head tumble.

Rage pushed Brand while momentum and gravity pulled him down too fast to manage.

Flint squeezed his eyes closed against the falling debris and the brilliant sunshine splitting his head like a swift cleaver.

Timing.

If Flint could throw him off stride, momentum and gravity would do the rest.

With luck.

Brand was coming down more swiftly than a rushing waterfall.

Only five feet above Flint's head now.

Four.

Three.

Two.

Flint reached out and lunged at Brand's right ankle.

Momentum pitched him forward.

His arms flailed as he tried to regain his balance while his feet scrambled on the slippery slope.

## 667 Ground Truth

Gravity pulled Brand downward ever faster.

On the way past, he bent his right knee and kicked toward Flint's head.

Brand was heavy and moving too fast.

Weight and velocity forced Flint to release his grip on Brand's ankle. He let go.

But he'd held on long enough.

Brand's gait was broken, and he was floundering.

He couldn't get his legs under control.

Brand fell forward, hitting the gravel cliffside with his face. Skin scraped off from his chin to his forehead. He howled with pain.

His body tumbled backward over itself. He was suddenly sliding down the cliffside on his back.

Flint heard a loud and sickening crack as Brand's bag of bones passed him on the slope, bouncing against the rocks.

In the struggle with Brand, Flint had lost his grip on the shrub. He quickly grabbed another bush and held on to the undergrowth now for dear life.

Brand continued rolling down the side of the cliff for what seemed like an unnaturally long time. As if time had slowed to a crawl.

When he finally hit the sharp rocks at the bottom of the hill, there was no shriek at all.

He'd stopped howling long before he reached the serrated peaks.

Brand, as a threat, was done.

But Flint was still in trouble.

He closed his eyes against the grit and the sun and drew deep breaths into his lungs to control his nausea.

Didn't work.

He leaned over and retched in the dirt. He barely managed not to fall into the mess when he rolled to one side and lay flat on the ground in the beating sun.

Flint had no idea how long he lay in the dirt below the cliff. He might have passed out for a while.

When he regained his senses, he looked up to the rim of the cliffside.

There were only two ways to go. Up or down.

At the bottom were the piercing rocks where Brand's body lay impaled.

Which meant there was, once again, only one choice.

Like his friend Kim Otto had said many times, when there's only one choice, it's the right choice.

Slowly and carefully, Flint began to crawl up the steep side of the cliff, keeping his belly flat on the sloping ground.

There were small bushes and protruding rocks he managed to hold on to as he made his way up. Every few minutes, his pounding headache and dizziness required him to stop for rest.

He tried not to focus on how little progress he was making and instead concentrated on the slowly approaching horizon at the summit above.

Finally, dehydrated and weak and filthy with dirt and sweat and vomit, he reached the crest and pulled himself up over the cliff and onto the narrow shoulder.

Where he slumped onto flat ground.

The next time he opened his eyes, he saw Drake lying inert behind the sedan. Flint struggled to his feet and stumbled to his friend.

He put two fingers on Drake’s neck to check his carotid pulse. He was breathing erratically. But he was alive.

Flint searched Drake's pockets until he found the satellite phone.

He fired up the phone and pressed the redial. Gaspar answered immediately.

"Need extraction," Flint rasped in two-word bursts. "Drake's hurt. Need medic. Send helo."

"They'll see us incoming if we do that," Gaspar said. "You prepared for the pushback?"

"No."

"How many armed men does Hedinger have available to attack us?" Gaspar asked.

"Unknown," Flint replied, breathing deeply to stay alert and power longer sentences. “Good guess, fewer than a dozen. This is a small place. He’s lost at least three of them today.”

“Have you seen any artillery?”

“Sidearms only.” Flint kneaded the piercing headache between his eyebrows. “We don’t have any other options. Can you handle it?”

“Where are you, exactly?” Gaspar asked.

Flint could hear him clacking the keyboard keys, probably trying to triangulate the satellite phone.

“On the back of the island. An old road that runs along the cliff. Black Mercedes sedan.”

A few seconds later, Gaspar said, "Got it. I see you. How long can you hold out?"

"As long as it takes," Flint replied. "But don't dawdle."

"Looks like we can set a helo down on that road. No civilians in the area. We can lay down suppressive fire if needed. Take us twenty minutes to get there. Tops," Gaspar promised. "But they're gonna know we're coming."

"Yeah, well, we blew our cover a while ago," Flint replied.

"Copy that," Gaspar said. "Looking along that road, nobody else is on the way toward you at the moment."

“Doesn’t mean they aren’t coming,” Flint said wearily. “Fly low. Come in behind the cover of the old volcano. Do whatever you need to do to confuse their detection systems.”

“Depending on what kind of antiaircraft weapons they have, we could get in and get out without taking fire.”

“If we’re very lucky, they don’t have any,” Flint said.

The sun and the heat and the exertion had ganged up on him. He was dizzy. Dehydrated. Exhausted.

“Copy that. We’re in the air. Not long now,” Gaspar replied, talking now simply to keep Flint awake and aware. “How’s your concussion?”

"Been worse."

"How's Drake?"

"Not good."

A few moments of silence passed between them. Flint felt his eyelids closing and forced them wide again.

"Want some good news?" Gaspar asked, probably trying to keep him alert by talking.

"Desperate for it."

"Scarlett says she found a dog sitter for Whiskers. She suggested you're unreliable with kids." Gaspar chuckled.

Flint said nothing.

# Chapter 48

Flint was conserving his limited resources. Seated on the ground near Drake, he leaned against the big sedan, listening for Gaspar's helo and hoping to hear it before any other approaching vehicles.

He took a quick inventory. His body was aching and battered, and his headache simply wouldn't quit, but he'd endured worse.

Nausea and dizziness were the most dangerous of his remaining symptoms, mainly because he couldn't control them.

Nausea was messy but not fatal. Dizziness could be.

Hedinger's security squad should be coming soon.

Hell, they should have arrived a while ago. Why weren't they already here?

He shrugged. Totally fine with him if they wanted to procrastinate. They could take all week if they wanted.

He had three pistols, including the one Drake took off the guy back in Brand's house, limited ammo, and no backup. He was in no hurry to go another round with those goons.

Almost as soon as he finished the thought, the breeze carried the sound of Gaspar's helo in the distance. He'd lost his sunglasses during the fight with Brand, so he shielded his eyes with his palm and squinted toward the sea.

He didn't see it. The helo must have been too far out.

Dust and pollution and the curvature of the earth limit normal human vision to about three miles on the sea.

Out here where the sky was clear and he was elevated from the sea, he should be able to see a helo in the air much farther away.

But the sound alone was reassuring.

Until he heard the growling noise of a diesel-powered truck engine speeding toward him along the old road. The truck was rolling fast, closing the distance.

Flint remembered an SUV parked at the airport. But this sounded more like a rugged full-size pickup truck, the kind with a powerful engine and an impressive payload from its high-strength, military-grade aluminum alloy body.

Meaning, a vehicle that could carry six men with weapons. Maybe more.

Flint glanced at Drake, who was still out cold on the ground. He pulled Drake's pistol and extra magazine as well as the dead security guy's weapon from Drake's pocket.

Flint put the sedan between them and the approaching truck. He crouched on the passenger side, behind the sedan's engine block, with his weapon ready.

The truck's engine was coming closer by the second. The noise was loud enough to drown the faint **whop-whop** of the helo farther out.

Shooting at the truck was a waste of good bullets. Even if he hit the target, the truck would keep coming. And if he managed to stop the truck, the guards would keep coming.

His best chance was to shoot first.

But only if he managed to neutralize the targets.

He wiped perspiration from his brow, ignored the headache, and squinted toward the approaching enemy. His sight line was blocked by a turn in the road. He couldn't see the truck or its passengers until it rounded the bend.

When the truck came into view, his aim would be hampered by geography. The truck was climbing uphill. Which meant that his view of the guards in the bed of the truck would be blocked by the cab. He couldn't pick them off while they were in the truck until they came much too close.

He expected them to have automatic weapons. They could fire exponentially more rounds than he could.

All of which meant his chances of success here were slim. He was outnumbered and outgunned.

He'd hit some of them, but not all.

The scent of dirt and sweat mixed with heart-pounding nausea swamped his senses. The truck came over the hill, throwing gravel as it approached and skidded to a stop. Flint knew he had to act fast. His narrow window of opportunity was rapidly closing.

The enemy had every advantage. But they were all bunched up. He had a chance if he could pick them off now.

Flint rose up over the hood of the sedan and fired off four shots, aiming for the first two men in the truck. His aim was true. The two screamed and fell.

The others immediately returned fire, taking aim at Flint's position.

The sound of gunfire was deafening, and the smell filled the air. Flint managed to duck behind the engine block before they riddled the sedan with bullets.

He peeked out and fired again, taking down another man. He counted three enemy combatants left. One of them lobbed a grenade toward the sedan. The grenade fell short.

Flint hit the ground and covered his head.

The grenade exploded, sending dirt and gravel everywhere. He felt two small stones slice his cheek. Blood trickled into his mouth.

He glanced toward Drake, who hadn't moved. Dust and stones covered Drake's still body.

Flint's vision blurred and his ears rang, but he couldn't stop. Quitting now meant certain death for him and Drake.

Drake had pulled Flint from too many tough circumstances. Flint couldn't give up. Not when Drake couldn't defend himself.

He might lose, but he'd go down fighting.

How many of the guards were still alive? Impossible to say for sure.

Flint rolled onto his side and peered under the sedan through the dust.

He counted six booted feet headed his way.

They split up, two headed toward the back of the sedan and one rounding the front. They made no attempt to seek cover.

Perhaps they thought the grenade had done its job. They were coming to confirm the kill.

They might be wearing full body armor beneath their uniforms.

More likely, they'd be wearing only partial armor. They probably didn't think Flint and Drake presented a serious threat, given their two previous engagements today when Flint and Drake had barely managed to stay alive.

And partial body armor was vulnerable. Flint knew the failure points.

He bent at the waist and swept both pistols around toward the sedan's trunk. When the two men rounded the vehicle, Flint was crouched low, pistols ready.

He shot the first man in the face with two bullets.

The second man raised his gun to return fire, but Flint fired first.

Flint swept around to confront the last of the armed guards rounding the front of the sedan. The shooter had his weapon leveled and Flint in his sights, ready to take the final shot.

Just then, the helicopter arrived overhead, rotor blades beating the air, pushing a gusty windstorm. The shooter looked up, distracted, taking his eye off Flint.

Which was all the time Flint needed.

He fired off three rounds. One bullet hit the shooter in the neck. Blood spurted from his wound. He dropped his weapon and slapped both hands over the flowing blood streaming between his fingers and down the front of his body.

The helo landed. Two paramedics jumped out with a gurney, keeping low under the rotor wash. One man ran to the wounded shooter. The other ran toward Drake.

Flint's quick gymnastics during the firefight had increased his dizziness and nausea to undeniable levels. He stumbled and fell. As soon as his ass hit the ground, he leaned over and began to retch.

They put Drake on the gurney and wheeled him to the helo. One of the paramedics came back for Flint.

"Can you walk?" he yelled over the noise of the helo, offering Flint a hand up. "We don't have another gurney."

"Yeah," Flint said, managing to pull himself up on shaky legs. He pointed to the last guard. "What about that guy?"

"He didn't make it."

"Grab my stuff from the trunk of the sedan. We've got evidence in there. Can't leave it behind," he shouted.

The paramedic replied, "Will do."

Flint walked on his own to the helo.

The paramedic returned with the contents of the trunk. He held up the armful. "This all of it?"

"Yeah. Thanks."

He helped Flint climb aboard and fasten his harness.

As the helo lifted off, the worst of the tension drained from Flint's body. He donned headphones to exclude the noise and closed his eyes.

The paramedics were working on Drake. They had an IV in him and were feeding him fluids. Which reminded Flint that his mouth tasted like he'd been on a two-day bender. He opened a bottle of water, swished it around in his mouth, and swallowed.

Not great. But the best he could do at the moment.

He and Drake were both alive, but barely.

Which was a damn sighted better than those other guys.

# Chapter 49

**Three days later**
**Switzerland**

"Let me be certain I understand," Ernst Hedinger said through gritted teeth. He was furious and he felt no need to conceal his anger. "Dr. Brand and ten members of your security team are dead. Ten. Atabei Hospital's CEO is also dead. That's eleven of my employees. **Eleven**. And the **two** men responsible are not only still alive, they've escaped. And you have no idea where they are."

Bauer stood beside the breakfast table, feet shoulder-width apart, hands clasped behind his back. Hedinger had sent his private jet to fly Bauer from Atabei first thing that morning.

He didn't point out that Hedinger himself had killed one of the eleven employees. And two others. For a total of thirteen dead.

Instead, he soaked up Hedinger's rage like a sponge.

Because it was his job to do so.

And because Bauer failed. Hedinger's anger was justified.

Bauer shouldn't expect to live out the day.

"**How** did this happen?" Hedinger demanded, slamming his coffee cup hard against the table. It shattered, sending coffee and shards of fine bone china across the room.

“We became complacent, Herr Hedinger. Atabei was too perfect. Too quiet. We had no crime. No reason to believe crime could happen.” Bauer cleared his throat and lowered his voice. “We weren’t prepared. One hundred percent my fault, sir. I take full responsibility.”

His words only increased Hedinger’s seething rage.

He lowered the volume of his voice and spoke in clipped, steely words. “You are responsible. Your actions have cost me millions. An excellent surgeon is dead. The thriving business he ran has vanished. How do you propose to fix that?"

"I don't believe I can, sir," Bauer replied.

Hedinger's fury pounded in his body from his toes to the tips of his ears. **The insolence**.

He wanted Bauer dead. But not instantly. A long, painful death.

Hedinger owned a collection of bayonets. He imagined driving a bayonet through Bauer's stomach as the man screamed, twisting his guts with the sharp steel blade.

The only thing that stopped him was the stains Bauer's blood would leave on his beautiful rugs.

Hedinger returned attention to his breakfast, leaving Bauer standing.

He pushed the call button for his maid.

“Let me clear this mess, sir, and bring another cup,” she said obsequiously as she proceeded to do exactly that.

Moments later, she’d replaced his coffee and retreated with the trash, and he’d returned to his meal.

When he finished, Hedinger said, “Have you identified the men responsible?”

“Yes, sir. As you said, two men. Michael Flint and Alonzo Drake. Residents of Houston, Texas.”

“Where are they now?”

“Flint has returned to Houston. Drake

suffered a hematoma in his skull during the fight with Dr. Brand. He's had surgery to remove it. I'm told he's currently resting in a medically induced coma."

"Is he expected to recover?"

"According to our sources, they believe he will recover eventually."

Hedinger paused to absorb the intel. "What were they after?"

"They seemed to believe that Dr. Brand was someone else, sir. A man named Phillip Reed. They were seeking information about his dead wife."

"So you're saying they breached your security to gain admittance to Atabei. They killed eleven people.

And they escaped capture. All simply to get information about a man's dead wife? Information Brand didn't possess?" Hedinger said, barely controlling his anger. "Does that sound remotely reasonable to you, Bauer?"

"No, sir." Bauer swallowed. "But it seems to be true, nonetheless."

The house phone resting on the breakfast table rang. Hedinger picked up.

"Otis Jarsdel is here, sir," the maid said.

"Send him in," Hedinger replied before replacing the receiver in its cradle.

Jarsdel entered moments later. "Good morning, Herr Hedinger."

"Jarsdel." Hedinger was in no mood for nonsense. He offered one quick nod in greeting. "Report."

Jarsdel gave a quick glance toward Bauer.

"I've found Greta Campbell, sir. She's living in a small village in Scotland with a man. They have a child," Jarsdel reported quickly and to the point.

Hedinger set his coffee cup on the table and waved Jarsdel to a chair. "How did you find her?"

"I'm sorry it took so long, but it wasn't easy. She's living under an assumed name. She has no official papers of any kind," Jarsdel said as if he'd rehearsed his speech. Which he probably had.

"How do you know it's her?" Hedinger asked.

"Technology, chronology, eyewitnesses," Jarsdel replied. "We started with facial recognition. Moved through immigration records around the time she supposedly died. Birth records for the boy. The final piece was local eyewitnesses."

"You've seen her? Yourself, I mean. Not one of your operatives," Hedinger asked.

Jarsdel nodded. "I have. I have acquired a DNA sample we can test to be sure. But we need a known sample to match for total certainty. We're searching for that now."

Hedinger pressed his lips into a pout. "Excellent work, Jarsdel."

"Thank you, sir."

After waiting a few minutes for further instructions that never came, Jarsdel said, "What should we do now, sir?"

"Bauer, sit down," Hedinger said. "Jarsdel, take us through this step by step. After that, Bauer will get the comparison DNA sample you need for certainty."

"It shouldn't be too difficult, sir. Greta Campbell has a sister," Jarsdel replied before he began to explain exactly how he'd found Greta Campbell.

Something like a smile lifted the corner of Hedinger's mouth as he listened. He would have revenge on Greta Campbell. Flint and Drake, too. A plan was unfolding in his mind.

# Chapter 50

**Four days later**
**Houston**

Scarlett Investigations occupied the fourth floor of an historic downtown Houston office building. Flint thanked his driver, left the car at the curb, and hustled up the front stairs.
His concussion had healed itself, apparently. He felt better than he'd felt in days.

As he approached the entrance his face triggered security cameras which quickly compared his image to approved visitors and unlocked the door. He slipped inside and the door locked automatically behind him.

He took the stairs to the fourth floor two at a time, his boots pounding the marble floors like John Bonham played drums. When he reached Scarlett's office, he stepped through the open doorway without knocking.

She was waiting. Curly black hair swirled wildly around her shoulders. Reading glasses perched on her nose magnified her eyes to the size of the boulder marbles he'd owned as a kid.

The marbles she'd stolen from him because she liked them. The ones he'd fought to get back and still had the scars to prove she'd won.

He grinned and plopped down in one of her client chairs and picked up the square paperweight of those same cat's eye marbles encased in glass from her desk.

"Well?" he asked. "What have you got?"

She gave him a once-over and didn't much like what she saw. "You look like hell."

He didn't argue with her. The last symptoms of his concussion had resolved, but he still felt wrung out. Instead, he grinned. "You're too kind to me."

Without another word, she strode toward her conference room. He followed and closed the door and stood in front of the big display screens.

"Thanks for all your help, Gaspar," Flint said when he saw Gaspar's image on one of the screens, waiting.

Gaspar grinned and shrugged off the gratitude. "Hey, it's what I do."

"Seriously, man. I owe you." Flint cleared his throat. "We'd have died without you. More than once."

"One day I'm sure I'll need to call in that favor," Gaspar replied lightheartedly, although neither of them was joking. "How's Drake?"

"They removed the hematoma inside his skull and stopped the brain bleed," Flint replied. "They think he'll fully recover, but it may take longer than we all hope."

“We’ve got around-the-clock security at the hospital,” Scarlett said. “Just in case Hedinger decides to try anything.”

“And Hedinger?” Gaspar asked. “He’s not the kind of man who gives up gracefully.”

Flint shrugged. “Like she said, Drake’s got around-the-clock protection. I can take care of myself.”

Silence settled on the conversation until Scarlett pushed a couple of buttons to wake up two more big screens. “Let’s see what you’ve got, Gaspar.”

One screen showed an idyllic fishing village perched along a verdant coastline abutting the ocean. The homes overlooking the beach were definitely not new construction.

"This is the village of Portmahomack. Population about seven hundred. It sits on the north coast of Scotland. That's the North Sea," Gaspar explained. "You can see the Tarbat Ness Lighthouse there. It's about three miles from the village at the end of the headland. Ballone Castle is a mile or so away. Portmahomack's been there for centuries, but lately it's become a tourist destination. Swimming, golf, dolphins, and whales. The usual seaside stuff tourists like."

After watching the short tourism video on the screen, Scarlett said, "It's lovely but very remote."

"Extremely remote." Gaspar put another image on the third screen. A whitewashed farmhouse surrounded by a lovely garden. "This home is a small farm about two miles from the village itself. It's owned by a man named Avery Tumbler. He inherited the house from his father, who inherited from his father, and so on."

Gaspar had pulled several images and satellite videos of the house and the people who lived in it. He displayed the first image.

"This is Avery Tumbler. A man we've all seen before. On the video of the royal wedding that brought Hanna Campbell to Drake," Gaspar said. "Here's a video from last week."

Tumbler stood in the garden of the farmhouse playing with a child.

“That’s the boy with the balloon?” Scarlett asked, leaning closer to the screen.

“Yes,” Gaspar said. The next image added a woman to the pair in the garden, followed by another video.

“Hello, Greta Campbell,” Flint said quietly.

“She doesn’t look much like Hanna, does she?” Scarlett asked.

Gaspar played two more videos of the young family coming and going from the farmhouse. In one of the videos, they walked into a village pub.

"How certain are you that this woman is Greta Campbell?" Flint asked.

Gaspar shrugged. "As certain as I can be without DNA or a confession. Not quite as high a confidence score as the facial recognition match for Phillip Reed and Stephen Brand."

"Walk me through it." Scarlett settled into one of the client chairs. She folded her hands together and waited.

"According to a chat I had with one of the local bartenders, between four and five years ago, Avery Tumbler returned from his vacation in Mexico with a new girlfriend. Claimed he'd met her there and fell in love. Not long after they met, she turned up pregnant," Gaspar explained.

"So the timing fits," Flint said. "Was Tumbler actually in Mexico?"

"According to his passport, he was. Cancun, specifically. On the coast of the Gulf of Mexico. Where the currents tend to push debris of all sorts onto the beaches," Gaspar replied. "Sometimes boats with undocumented passengers, too."

"How about Tumbler's girlfriend? What's her passport say?" Scarlett wanted to know.

"She doesn't seem to have a UK passport. Nor does she have a Mexican passport," Gaspar said. "Her name is Gretchen Tumbler now. And I couldn't find a passport to match her in that name anywhere."

“Is the name uncommon?”

“Extinct, actually, according to my research of ancestry records,” Gaspar replied. “The last name, anyway. There aren’t that many Tumblers out there in the world.”

“I suppose it’s not all that difficult to enter the UK illegally, either,” Scarlett said.

“Slightly more difficult than entering the US, since she couldn’t just walk in from an adjoining country,” Flint said. “But there are ways to make it happen. With the right resources. And Tumbler seems like a guy who could have those resources.”

“So to recap,” Scarlett said, “we think Greta came ashore in Mexico. Either washed up on her own or more likely picked up out of the Gulf by some motorist or boat of illegals or something. She was dropped off in Mexico, where she met Tumbler. She traveled with him to Scotland, where they've lived quietly for the past four years. That about it?"

Scarlett paused to lock gazes with each of them in turn.

"Sounds unlikely, doesn't it?" Drake replied wearily.

Flint shrugged. "Stranger things have happened."

Scarlett mused, "Wouldn't someone have noticed that she was in the country illegally after all this time?"

Flint shook his head and smiled. “How often do you ask your neighbors to prove they’re living in Houston legally? It’s not what people do, is it?”

“Although we might be more inclined to ask here in Texas than they do in the north of Scotland,” Scarlett replied. “But doesn’t she work? Have a bank account? A driver’s license? Need health care? Send her kid to school? She’d need government-issued identification for any of that.”

“All good questions. For which we have no answers. Guess I’m making a trip to Portmahomack,” Flint said with a sigh. “Question is, should I take Hanna with me?”

"That's her call, isn't it?" Scarlett said. "She'll want to go. And she's better off going with you than traveling alone. Which she'll do if you don't take her. When are you leaving?"

"No time like the present. I've got a few things to do first. After that, I guess we'll go as soon as Hanna can pack a bag," Flint replied. "We'll fly commercial. It's faster."

Gaspar cocked his head. "And you have passports."

"Meaning what?"

"Meaning you can use standard international transportation and any halfway decent hacker paying attention will know about it," Gaspar replied.

“If we’re lucky,” Flint replied. Gaspar frowned and Flint shrugged him off. “I prefer to choose my battles.”

Gaspar said, “So your plan is to lure Hedinger to Scotland? While you have civilians in play? Sounds dangerous to me.”

“Dangerous to Hedinger and only if he shows up.” Flint said. “Don’t worry. I don’t have a death wish. But I’ve gotta go. There’s a lot to do before we fly out.”

“Hurry back,” Scarlett said with a smile. “I need you to watch the shop while Maddy and I are at Disney World. We leave next week.”

# Chapter 51

**Six days later**
**Portmahomack**

An observer would believe Otis Jarsdel's last morning in Portmahomack had begun like all the others. He'd planned his days to reveal a comfortable sameness for anyone who might be watching. Soon they'd stop watching him from sheer boredom.

It had occurred to Jarsdel that a man could relax in a place like this. Maybe live out his days in peace by the stormy sea. Which once would have bored Jarsdel to the point of madness. He was surprised by how inviting it seemed now.

He rose every day at six o'clock and walked down the sidewalk from the hotel to the Stag and Hounds pub on Main Street for breakfast. Along the way, he observed the village as it came alive.

Regardless of the weather, locals drove out for work in Inverness or Tain. After breakfast, the shops began to open. The chemist, the post office, the grocery.

Tourists laced their trainers and jogged along the beach. Jarsdel dressed like them, too. Villagers assumed he was one of the tourists and, in a sense, he was.

He'd found Portmahomack residents welcoming but not nosy. After a couple of days, it was easy to understand both why and how Greta Campbell had settled down in this particular village with her boy.

Jarsdel had tried interviewing the villagers, but Campbell had revealed almost nothing of her previous life to her friends and neighbors. Which would not have been possible in some small villages. Here, people minded their own business.

He'd been here a short time, watching the farmhouse around the clock, preparing for the upcoming mission. Yet he knew more about the pair who called themselves Mr. and Mrs. Tumbler than anyone else in the village, even with years of exposure to the family, seemed to know.

Avery Tumbler was a dull man. Nothing like Campbell's prior husband. If Tumbler **was** her husband, which Jarsdel doubted. They were living as husband and wife, but Jarsdel suspected that was a lie. He could find no documents in the databases reflecting a marriage. Nor the birth records for the boy.

The absence of records was solid proof that Gretchen Tumbler was not who she claimed to be, as far as Jarsdel was concerned.

In fact, he believed Gretchen Tumbler was a total fiction. If she were a legitimate resident, she'd have been documented up the wazoo, like every other legal resident.

The only reasonable conclusion? Gretchen Tumbler was an alias. The woman was Greta Campbell Reed. No doubt in Jarsdel's mind. Even if he couldn't prove it.

Yet.

Jarsdel waited outside the newsstand in the pouring rain, holding the newspaper to conceal his face until Avery Tumbler's decrepit Range Rover drove past.

He glanced at his watch. Tumbler was right on time.

Some Portmahomack folks went home or to the pubs for lunch, but Avery Tumbler never did. He brought his lunch from home and ate alone at his desk in Tain. Every day. Without fail.

He wouldn't return home from work at the pottery factory until after six o'clock tonight. By then the mission would be accomplished, and Tumbler's life would never be the same.

The mission was on schedule and Tumbler was now out of the way. He sent a text to Hedinger to confirm.

After Tumbler passed, Jarsdel walked along the soggy shoulder of the road toward the outskirts of the village through fog so thick he could barely see his own feet. The farmhouse was a two-mile walk from the village. He'd be there in twenty minutes.

Jarsdel's observation point was on a hill in the woods opposite the farmhouse. Hedinger and Bauer were waiting there now.

They wouldn't be able to see much from that vantage point in this weather. They'd be forced to move closer to the house.

The plan had fallen into place more quickly than Jarsdel expected.

One of Hedinger's automatic alerts had been triggered when Flint purchased two plane tickets for travel from Houston to Inverness.

Hedinger's London mansion was within easy reach, and he'd arrived with Bauer several hours ago. They were now in place.

When Jarsdel rounded the last curve in the road before the farmhouse, he saw headlights on an SUV approach from the opposite direction and turn into the driveway. The SUV parked near the front of the house.

Bauer and Hedinger would also be watching from two observation points nearby.

After a couple of minutes, a man and a woman stepped out of the SUV's front doors. Jarsdel could barely make out their shapes in the fog. Which meant he couldn't confirm their identity.

But he knew who they were.

Michael Flint and Hanna Campbell had been observed from the moment they arrived at the airport in Houston until they deplaned in Inverness and acquired the SUV.

Hedinger's hacker was a genius. He'd accessed the rental SUV's dashcam, which enabled him to monitor not only their travel but also their conversations inside the vehicle.

Only after they left the SUV did Hedinger's crew no longer have access to their conversations.

Flint and Campbell walked together to the front door, not bothering to hurry through the rain. Flint raised the brass knocker and let it fall.

A few seconds later, Gretchen Tumbler opened the front door. After a brief conversation, she invited Flint and Campbell inside and closed the door.

Three people were together in the small farmhouse now, Flint and the Campbell sisters. Four if the child was present. Which Jarsdel hoped he wasn't.

Hedinger wouldn't spare the boy's life, even though he was the only reason they'd found Greta Campbell. Had the boy only managed to hold onto his balloon, Hedinger might never have known Greta Campbell survived his attempt to murder her.

Hedinger wasn't the least bit grateful. He'd kill the boy without a moment's hesitation.

Jarsdel shook his head. Just like shooting fish in a barrel.

He veered off the road behind the next stand of trees. Crouched low, weapon in hand, he dashed from one bit of cover to the next, toward the back of the farmhouse.

Although he couldn't see Bauer, Jarsdel knew he was approaching the house from the opposite direction at the same time. That was the plan and Bauer wouldn't dare deviate from it.

# Chapter 52

“Looks like we’re here.” Flint parked the SUV in the front driveway, killed the engine, and turned off the windshield wipers.

The steady rain they’d battled all the way from Inverness continued to fall in the thick fog, like a miles-wide cloud had settled down on the road and refused to move.

“Are you ready?” He glanced across the cabin.

Hanna’s thin body was held taut against the bucket seat by the shoulder harness. She was dressed in dark jeans and a white T-shirt, camel blazer, and sneakers. She looked like a frail, undernourished teenager.

She cleared her throat. “As ready as I’m going to get, I guess.”

Flint placed a calming hand on her bony arm. “We talked about this. She knows you’re coming. She’s excited to see you. There’s nothing to be nervous about.”

“She’s not worried about being found?”

“Not after I told her Phillip Reed was dead.”

“She believed you?”

“We’ve been over this, Hanna. I talked to her myself. I sent her photos to prove everything," Flint said, trying to reassure the nervous young woman. "You can wait in the car if you want. But we've come such a long way."

Hanna clasped her hands in her lap, looking down, eyes closed.

"I have to go in. I need her DNA. And I want to tell her about Brand in person. She deserves to have all her questions answered."

Hanna didn't speak.

"You don't have to come with me. But let's at least try, okay?"

Hanna remained mute.

Flint said, "If it doesn't work out, we'll leave. I'll take you back to Houston."

Hanna tipped her head almost imperceptibly in reply. As if she didn't trust her voice.

He waited a couple of moments.

She coughed into a handkerchief and then stuffed it into her jacket pocket.

"Let's do this," she whispered. "But leave the doors unlocked in case I have to come out alone before you're ready."

"Okay." Flint pressed the button to unlock the doors and they stepped out into the rainy morning.

The wind had whipped up. Sharp salty air blew in from the North Sea, stinging his eyes.

## 733 Ground Truth

Hanna leaned her head forward against the rain and stepped quickly across the gravel through the soupy fog.

Flint draped his arm around her slight shoulders. He scanned the area surrounding the farmhouse. There were trees and verdant grass and colorful flowers in the garden.

He saw nothing alarming. Yet.

Hanna stepped onto the stoop under the overhang and used her hands to wipe the water from her face.

Flint reached for the door knocker and dropped the heavy brass twice against the thick wooden door.

After a brief wait, the heavy door creaked as it was pulled open. A woman stood deep in the shadows.

"Come in, come in. The weather's horrible out there," she said, gesturing as if they might not grasp the meaning of her Americanized language. She lacked the heavy Scottish accent they'd been hearing since they landed in Inverness.

For a brief moment, their little tableau froze in place.

She was older and plainer than her publicity photos from the Orlando television station four years ago. But her expressive blue eyes were the same. Tears leaked from the corners of her eyes as she gently raised her fist to her mouth.

Hanna hesitated at the threshold staring at the woman. Neither seemed capable of making the next move.

Flint gave Hanna a little push on the small of her back, but she didn't budge. The howling wind and blowing rain whipped around them as they stood, waiting for Hanna.

Finally, Flint reached across her back and grasped her shoulder. He gave her a reassuring squeeze and guided her across the threshold. He followed her inside her sister's warm, welcoming home.

"Mrs. Tumbler," he said, extending his hand. "I'm Michael Flint. We talked on the phone."

"Call me Gretchen." She shook hands with him naturally enough, but her attention was glued to Hanna.

After a few moments of awkwardness, she tossed her concerns aside and embraced Hanna in a hearty hug.

Soon both women were crying. They moved to a sofa, where they hugged and cried and talked quietly for a good long time.

Flint wandered around the great room and into the kitchen. He saw no sign of the boy. Knowing Flint and Hanna were coming, the boy's father must have taken him out this morning.

Flint noticed the teakettle was still warm. He refilled it, turned the burner on, and rummaged through the cabinets for tea.

## 737 Ground Truth

When he glanced through the large window over the sink, he caught a flash of movement in the side yard in his periphery.

He took three strides to the back door and stood alongside the window where he'd have a better view.

The fog was thick and heavy, but Flint glimpsed a man dressed in black not far from the house.

He held a gun in one hand. Crouched low, he ran behind the outbuildings and across the dirt path leading to the pasture out back of the farmhouse.

Flint didn't see anyone else. A lone assassin? Not likely.

Two or three men working together made more sense. The house had more than one exit. One man out back and a second man covering the front entrance was a solid plan.

Flint moved quickly to the front of the house, carefully peering through the front windows. The fog blanketed everything out front in thick mist. The rented SUV was barely visible from his position.

The two women were still crying and whispering together on the sofa. Across the room from where they sat was another large window offering a more expansive view of the garden.

Greta glanced up when she noticed Flint was in the room. She gasped.

Flint turned. “What?”

“Out there. I saw someone,” she said, pointing through the large window. “He ducked behind those trees.”

“Okay. Greta, is there a room in the house with no windows?” He realized he’d slipped into using her real name. Hearing it startled her, but she nodded. “Take Hanna there. Lock the door. Don’t come out until I say it’s safe.”

She ran to the window and peered into the fog. “My husband’s a hunter. We have to be, living out here on the farm. We’ve got shotguns and rifles. I’m a good shot.”

Hanna was shaking her head violently, a terrified look on her face. She whispered as if she could barely breathe, "Don't lock me in a room by myself. Please."

Greta's indecision was palpable. She glanced outside and then quickly returned to her sister's heart-wrenching pleas.

"You wait here with Hanna," Greta said. "I'll bring the guns."

Before Flint could hold her back, Greta took off running toward the south wing of the house.

A moment later, the first gunshot blasted through the kitchen window sending glass everywhere.

## Chapter 53

When a second shot followed the first, Flint dashed across the room and pulled Hanna to the floor behind the large sofa. Her eyes were the size of saucers, and she was shaking like a petrified animal.

Greta returned from the back of the house with two long guns and two boxes of ammunition. She hurried to Flint, offering the weapons, and lowered her head near Hanna to whisper reassurances that didn't carry to his ears.

Two more shots shattered windows in the back of the house. Gusty winds carried dampness along the floor.

Flint guessed they were trying to blast the back door open, allowing them to rush inside.

He grabbed one of the shotguns and a box of shells. He touched Greta's arm to get her attention and leaned in so that only she could hear his words.

"Sounds like there's two of them," Flint said. "I'm going out the front. I'll circle around to the backyard."

"With the fog, they can't see the house well. They'll come closer," Greta warned.

"Which makes my job easier," Flint said with a nod.

“What if they get past you? Come in here?” Greta asked. “Should I shoot them?”

“That won’t happen,” Flint said firmly.

“But what if it does? Shoot to kill?” Greta asked.

“You ever shoot a man before?”

Greta shook her head.

“It’s harder than you think,” Flint said.

“He comes in my house, he gets what he gets,” she said flatly.

“Don’t wait. Fire immediately. All you need to do is hit close enough. He’ll retreat and I’ll handle it.” He watched her absorb his words.

Greta gave Hanna a meaningful look. "We'll be fine right here until you get back."

Flint intended to reassure Hanna. Her hyperventilating had stopped. But she stared straight ahead as if her mind had traveled somewhere else entirely. She was almost catatonic.

"Stay low. Don't go outside. No matter what. Understand?" Flint said, as if Hanna could be persuaded to go anywhere at all.

Which he seriously doubted.

She'd backed as close to the corner as she could possibly get without actually blending into the plaster.

"Yeah. We'll wait here. I promise," Greta said, holding her shotgun ready and giving him a little push. "Go."

Another gunshot came through the back door. They'd had plenty of chances to knock the damned door down by now. Either they were lousy shots or the soupy fog was thick enough to interfere.

Flint crouched low, staying out of the line of fire, and rushed into the kitchen. The kettle was still on the stove. Any minute now, it would start shrieking.

He stuffed the Glock into his belt and readied the shotgun. He moved to the window, back flat against the wall, and looked out into fog so thick he couldn't see more than twenty yards ahead. It was as if the cloud had landed directly on the house.

The gunmen had the advantage, though.

They knew where he was.

They'd seen him enter the house.

And they were probably equipped with thermal vision.

Which is what he'd have done if their roles were reversed and he'd come here to hunt them down.

He had no idea where they were hiding and no high-tech equipment. The odds were heavily against him.

"When in doubt, send a scout," he murmured under his breath.

He studied the broken glass on the floor and the holes in the windows and made an educated guess. He raised the Glock and fired twice toward the old wagon parked near the tool shed where the Tumblers kept the lawn mower.

As he'd hoped, the shots drew return fire from one of the shooters.

A moment later, the tea kettle began its ear-splitting squeal. Which didn't sound like an injured man. But it was the best diversion he could come up with under the circumstances.

It worked. The noise drew more return fire. This time both shooters let several rounds fly.

Flint judged the shots to be coming from only two shooters and two different directions. Which made things somewhat easier.

He crept quickly through the kitchen, returning to the front room. He waved to Greta as he went, gesturing that he'd be leaving through the front door.

Like a small child, Hanna had covered her ears against the teakettle's continued screeching. He had no time to comfort her.

When he reached the heavy front door, he stopped for a steadying breath. Then he unlocked the door, pulled it open quickly, and slipped out into the dense fog, closing the door behind him.

With luck, he'd placed the thick walls of the house between his heat signature and the thermal scopes the shooters were most likely using.

The house and the dense fog should partially obscure his images on their equipment.

But if they were close enough, or their equipment good enough, they'd be able to see him when he left the shelter of the block building to close the distance between them.

Outside, the first thing he noticed was the bone-chillingly wet cold.

Heavy water droplets settled on his hair and eyebrows and eyelashes. Drops trickled down his face.

The dampness settled into his clothes and chilled his skin. His teeth began to chatter. He clamped his jaw shut to reduce the noise.

The wind had died down, allowing more fog to roll in.

Visibility was almost nil.

He could see his shoes but no more than twenty feet ahead when looking in any direction with the naked eye.

The fog had blanketed the countryside as if covering it with cotton.

Fog severely restricted vision, even high-tech vision.

Planes were grounded or prevented from landing by fog every day.

Technology hadn't been able to conquer fog. It impacted radar, night vision, infrared. Everything.

In short, fog was dangerous. No question.

But the fog didn't inhibit sound.

Nor did fog change basic ballistics.

Which meant Flint's ability to hear the shooters and judge their positions and their weapons should not be hindered by the foggy weather.

Still, if he came close enough to see the enemy, they'd definitely see him first. They had equipment and he didn't. Which gave them the advantage, even in less than perfect conditions.

He had to assume the shooters came prepared. They'd have infrared, night vision, and other tools Flint didn't bring along.

He could use the dense fog to level the playing field somewhat. Otherwise, he'd have to rely on his experience and instinct.

He crawled close to the exterior masonry wall, crouched behind the bushes, rounding the first corner of the house toward the back yard. He used the same technique to move along the north wall.

When he reached the northeast corner, he visualized the exact location of the shed in the backyard.

It was thirty yards from the back entrance, which meant he couldn't see it well from his vantage point.

He visualized the shed. It was constructed of the same whitewashed masonry as the house and looked to be about the same vintage. The roof was thatched. There were no windows and only one double door facing in his direction.

He hoped the first shooter was still hiding back there.

The teakettle's ear-splitting screams traveled through the broken kitchen windows. How long would the water continue to feed steam through the spout?

Flint aimed the Glock and fired toward what he'd guessed to be the shooter's location.

Quickly, he ducked back for cover and listened for return fire.

His shots should have surprised the two shooters.

They probably hadn't expected him to leave the house.

Or at least, hadn't expected him to leave through the front door and meet them on their turf.

Their expectations were more than reasonable. It **had** been a risky move to leave the women unguarded.

But Greta seemed more than capable. All he could do now was trust that he'd made the right call.

Flint waited at least three full beats after his test fire.

Almost simultaneously the two shooters realized what he'd done. Both released a volley of rounds in his direction.

He fired again and this time they both fired back immediately.

Which was all good.

Now he knew exactly where they were.

One was behind the corner of the shed closest to Flint.

The other was on the far side of the backyard.

“One thing at a time,” Flint muttered under his breath.

He dropped and rolled, hoping to reach the old tractor he remembered was parked about halfway between his position and the shooter before the guy could duck out from around the corner to fire again.

# Chapter 54

When Flint reached the old tractor, he crouched on the right side, putting the engine between him and the first shooter. He was chilled to the bone now. His clothes were wet and clinging like an ice cube sticks to dry skin.

He'd made several tactical choices. Educated guesses, really. Based on training, experience, and thirty-four years of living by his wits.

If he guessed wrong, the outcome would be disastrous. But he had to move forward or sit and wait to die.

Which just wasn't his style.

Not even remotely.

He expected the enemy to be wearing his thermal vision equipment instead of mounting a scope on his weapons. Mostly because they were shooting with handguns and not rifles.

Which meant the thermal vision was at least partially covering their eyes and interfering with peripheral vision.

Which also meant the shooter had to come out some distance from his cover, turn his head, and scan for Flint's body heat amid the fog and the interference from farm equipment and other junk strewn about the backyard.

His body would be exposed. He might be wearing body armor to compensate. But body armor had its vulnerabilities, too.

Flint readied the shotgun and settled to wait.

He imagined the shooter listening hard and hearing no movement.

The shooter would want to take a look.

Human nature coupled with superior equipment, bone-chilling cold, and overwhelming forces would lure him out.

It was only a matter of time.

In the end, Flint didn't need to wait long.

The shooter turtled his head from behind the building. He scanned the yard as well as he could. The fog provided plenty of cover on its own, but the building and his equipment limited his sight lines as well.

Weapon ready, the shooter stepped forward and leaned his body a little farther from the corner of the shed. The teakettle invaded the quiet with its piercing screams.

He rotated his head, giving the infrared a sweeping arc to cover the area.

But the fog limited the distance the tech could distinguish human body heat, even if Flint were standing in the center of the open grass.

Which he wasn't.

The enemy grew a bit bolder.

Or maybe he thought Flint had given up and returned to the interior of the farmhouse.

He stepped wide of the shed to give himself a broader viewing range.

Which was when Flint adjusted his aim and fired.

From the relatively short distance, the shotgun blast was more than sufficient to knock the man down. The shotgun pellets spread out in a cone-shaped pattern, causing multiple wound channels to his body.

He screamed and went down. Blood flowed from several wounds on his torso, legs, and arms.

His heart was still pumping. He was suffering from internal bleeding, punctured organs, and broken bones.

But he wasn't dead.

Which meant he could still shoot.

Flint's instinct was to hurry toward the injured man to finish him off.

But almost instantly the second shooter fired from across the open space.

Flint was forced to adjust his position, moving around to the opposite side of the tractor.

He raised his pistol and returned fire, crouched low, and retreated to the safety of the farmhouse walls.

When he reached the building, he flattened his back against the cold stone, breathing heavily.

“One down. One to go,” he murmured.

The second shooter’s position was impossible to see from the northeast corner of the farmhouse. Fog covered the distance across the property with a heavy, wet cloud.

Flint couldn’t see the second man at all.

Whether he could see Flint was dependent upon the quality of his thermal vision equipment.

Smartest thing was to assume the enemy had top-of-the-line stuff. Even in the heavy fog, he could at least make out Flint's heat signature on open ground.

Which, to a marksman with the right weapons, would be good enough.

If the two shooters were amateurs, the second one might run to the first one's aid.

These guys were not amateurs.

The teakettle was winding down. The steam was failing. As a distraction, the kettle had served well, but its usefulness was over.

Flint reloaded the shotgun and checked the magazine on his pistol.

Where was the enemy's position?

He didn't know.

Somewhere on the south side of the property. Near the house, most likely, given the limitations of his equipment.

The shooter couldn't see the north side of the farmhouse. But could he see the other three sides?

Safer to assume so.

Which meant Flint was stuck here on the north side until he figured out a better plan.

Flint flipped around to hug the wall of the farmhouse with his belly. He extended his arm beyond the corner and fired a couple of rounds toward the south side of the open yard.

As soon as he'd fired, he turned and dashed toward the front of the house. He took the corner in two strides and ran toward the front door. He pushed it open, jumped inside, and closed the heavy door behind him.

When he looked into the room, Greta stood with the shotgun aimed straight at him, her finger on the trigger.

“Greta! It’s me. Flint,” he said, holding his hand palm out, just in case fear had blinded her.

She blinked as if returning from a trance. He held his breath until she relaxed her trigger finger and lowered the gun’s barrel.

He took long steps toward her and removed the gun from her grasp.

“Sorry,” she whispered in a daze. “I didn’t know it was you.”

"Right. No worries," he replied gently. "Where's Hanna?"

Greta gestured toward the corner where Hanna had been hiding when he left. She was still there. Crunched into herself. Knees up, arms around them. Eyes wide and face permanently frozen like a petrified child.

"I think she's in shock," Flint whispered. "Has she said anything at all?"

"I've been talking to her, but she doesn't say much," Greta replied, shaking her head. "How many are out there?"

"Two."

"Are you sure?" Greta asked.

"Let's get both of you into one of the bedrooms where it's warmer." Flint shivered in the cold breeze still moving across the house from the broken kitchen windows. He moved toward Hanna's hiding place.

The teakettle was silent now. He wondered how long it could sit on the hot burner without starting a fire in the house.

He didn't bother to try to persuade Hanna to leave her comfort zone. He shoved the sofa aside and swooped down to lift her. She weighed so little it was frightening.

"Lead the way," he said to Greta, who did as he asked.

She hurried along the dim corridor toward the bedroom, Flint following behind with Hanna in his arms.

# Chapter 55

When they reached the bedroom, Flint placed Hanna on the bed and covered her with the thick down comforter. Greta sat on the bed beside her, still holding the shotgun.

"Now what?" Greta asked.

"One of the shooters is dead," Flint said, as if he knew for sure that was true. "There's another one. I can't get eyes on him outside."

Greta's eyes widened when she realized what he planned to do. "You're gonna fight him in here? In our **home**?"

Flint understood her horror. But he didn't have a better plan. If he could lure the second shooter into the house, Flint could kill him. Outside, the shooter had every advantage.

“When I leave the room, you lock the door. Don't open it again until I tell you it's safe.” He gave her a steady stare. “No matter what happens. Okay?”

Greta nodded.

“You keep that shotgun ready. Anybody tries to come in here other than me, you blast first and ask questions later,” Flint said urgently, giving her hands a squeeze. “Okay? You understand?”

“I do. I don't like it. But okay,” Greta whispered.

"And if I don't come back, call the police." Flint turned to go.

"I can't call the police. You know why," Greta replied.

"Lock the door," he said on his way out.

He stood in the hallway listening until he heard the dead bolt move into place.

Flint double-checked the dead bolt on the front door and headed toward the acrid smoke from the teakettle.

He flipped all the lights on in the kitchen, illuminating the room brighter than a football field at a night game.

The second shooter should have noticed the lights come on. He'd be able to pinpoint Flint's body and know at least one person was inside the house.

It wasn't a foolproof plan.

The shooter could try shooting into the house again instead of coming inside. But he'd need to change his location first.

By the time he repositioned and had a clear shot, his target wouldn't be in the kitchen anymore.

Flint refilled the kettle and set it on the burner. The scorched kettle could never be used for making tea again, but the whistle should still function.

He moved about the kitchen opening cabinets and pulling food from the fridge as if he were setting up for a meal.

While waiting for the kettle to boil, he walked into the front room, leaving the kitchen empty and, he hoped, inviting. He turned all the lights on as he passed through.

"Level the playing field," he murmured. "Now I can see you, too. Your night vision and thermal imaging are useless."

The enemy would probably figure out Flint's ploy to lure him into the house. But Flint hoped the chance to kill all three of them was an offer too good for the enemy to refuse.

The alternative was for the shooter to spend hours in the miserable weather waiting for Flint to leave again, which might not happen for days.

“Or he could blow up the house,” Flint murmured, because he couldn’t help himself.

A well lobbed grenade or strategically placed C-4 would level the house and probably kill everyone in it. Not quietly but effectively enough.

It was the **probably** Flint was counting on.

The enemy had to be sure he’d killed Greta and Flint, too.

Which meant he’d have to hang around to find out.

And he'd have to try again later if he failed.

Not to mention that an explosion would bring down the full force of the UK government on Hedinger's head. Flint was betting that was not something Hedinger was all that keen to experience. Hedinger was an obscenely wealthy man, but corrupting the entire UK government was surely a goal well beyond his means.

Flint found a good position to wait inside the front room and made himself as comfortable as possible.

The shooter would come through the kitchen. He'd bring sufficient firepower and he'd have his worthless detection equipment.

Flint's position and the house lights were his strategic advantages. He was determined to make the most of them.

Half a minute later, the shooter cut the electric power to the house.

Everything went dark. The lights, the night lights, the digital clocks.

The teakettle began its incessant scream.

Even as the gas burner on the stove kept the ear-piercing squeal at full volume and the total darkness eliminated much of his strategic advantage, Flint smiled to himself.

The enemy had taken the bait.

He heard the back door open. The wind whipped it out of the intruder's hands and slammed the door back against the dining table. A blast of cold, wet air invaded the front room, casting an even more frigid chill through the space.

Flint waited, holding his fire and his patience, as he heard the man's footsteps cross the kitchen tile and step onto the carpet at the threshold of the great room.

Two more strides and the shooter had come far enough.

Flint reached over to the bookcase and flipped two switches.

Two battery-powered ultra-bright LED camping lanterns flooded the room with a three-hundred-sixty-degree glow of more than a thousand lumens each.

The shooter's thermal vision goggles were not only useless but a liability now.

Assuming he was wearing body armor along with the helmet, Flint raised his pistol and shot him twice in the leg. The shooter screamed and fired back as his bones cracked and he fell to the floor.

Flint shot him again in the side of his neck, above the body armor and below the helmet, and then again for insurance.

"Two down," Flint said aloud, although he couldn't hear his own words over the screaming teakettle.

Flint kicked the weapon aside.

He pulled the man's shirt up over his bloody head and tied it. There was already blood on the carpet, but nothing he could do about that.

He pulled the body outside through the back kitchen door and dumped him in the dirt. Quickly, he knelt to pat the body down, checking for ID and additional weapons. His breathing had almost returned to normal.

And then he heard the unmistakable crack of a rifle shot and hit the deck.

## 779 Ground Truth

The bullet whizzed past the spot where Flint's head had been a second before.

Flint furiously crabbed his way along the cold ground and inside the house.

He'd been wrong.

There were three shooters, not two.

And one was still alive.

## Chapter 56

In the kitchen, Flint closed the back door and locked it. He crouched below the level of the cabinetry to the stove and flipped off the burner under the infuriating teakettle.

He stayed low as he moved into the living room, where the blazing lights made him a clear target through the windows. He punched the buttons to turn the lights off, plunging the room into darkness again.

Flint was counting on the heavy walls and thick glass to weaken or eliminate his heat signature. Given the fog and the shooter's location, the odds were in Flint's favor. Small comfort.

He hurried down the hallway and knocked on the bedroom door. "Greta, I'm going outside."

As she opened the door, she said, "I heard the gunshots. Is he dead?"

"Two men down. One left. He's got a rifle and a thermal scope. Which means he can see your body heat in the dark if you come out of the bedroom."

She shuddered. "So we stay in here. How long?"

"Until I give you the all clear. Okay? Just wait for me to come back," Flint said.

Greta cocked her head and narrowed her eyes. Flint could tell she was wondering what she'd do if he didn't return.

"Is it Ernst Hedinger? Did he come to kill me himself this time?" Greta whispered.

Flint wondered how much Greta knew about Hedinger's involvement with her boating accident. Sounded like she had worked some of it out at some point.

"Look, Greta, you're a smart woman. You escaped Hedinger once before." She gulped but he kept talking. "You'll do it again. This will be the last time."

"How do you know?" she whispered.

“Because this time you’ve got me. Just stay in there and keep the door locked. Take care of Hanna. I’ll be back. I promise,” Flint said, even as he realized he was making promises he might not be alive to keep.

Greta stared at him a few moments more. Then she stepped back, closed the door softly, and threw the deadbolt.

Flint slumped against the wall. What the hell was he thinking, coming here without backup and bringing Hanna into this?

“Stupid question to be asking now, Flint,” he said.

On the way to collect his weapons, he gave himself a little pep talk. He tried to put some salt into the words, the way Scarlett would have done it if he'd had the good sense to bring her along.

"Hedinger followed you here. He'd have followed you here no matter when you came and whether you had backup or not. In fact, Greta's a lot better off with you here than she would have been otherwise. So stop the 'woe is me' and get the damned job done."

He collected the shotgun and the extra shells and checked his Glock and the extra magazine again.

"Yeah, yeah, yeah," he replied like a surly teenager. "Okay, Hedinger. It's gotta be you out there. You think no one can do the job as well as you can do it yourself. Let's just test that theory, shall we?"

Flint went out the front door and once again flattened his back against the stone walls behind the trees that lined the front gardens.

The fog hadn't lifted. Which was the good news. It meant Hedinger had to be not only within shooting distance but also close enough to see his targets.

Hedinger might have started out posted on that hill across the road and up in the trees.

Flint had noticed the spot on the drive in from Inverness and thought at the time that it would make a good place for a hunting stand. Hunting game. Not humans.

But Hedinger loved to hunt. He'd hunted big game around the world. He might have chosen that location initially. But circumstances had changed. He'd know exactly what to do under current conditions.

Flint was counting on it.

The rifle shot had come from the south side of the house. Close to where the man who had entered the kitchen was staked out earlier.

Which meant Hedinger had repositioned himself to be able to get a visual on Flint.

It was a good bet that they'd all made this plan together. With Hedinger having the final word.

Which was why he was the last of them still alive.

Hedinger was the kind of guy who sent good men to the cannons to preserve his own sorry ass.

Now Hedinger should simply pack up and go. He'd failed. He could withdraw and live to try again.

But of course Hedinger wouldn't retreat. He was no doubt enraged by now.

He must know it was Flint who had breached his impenetrable fortress, destroyed his organ-selling business, and now killed two of his top soldiers.

By now Hedinger might also know that Flint had stolen his precious Stradivarius.

Whether he knew or not didn't matter. Hedinger would stay to do the job himself. He'd need to be sure this time.

"Fine by me. Just means I won't have to hunt you down later," Flint mumbled.

The frigid air was thicker and heavier and even more chilling as the hours passed.

Flint ignored it all. His focus was on one thing only. Hedinger.

He made his way around the house to the southwest corner as silently as possible. Any small noise could alert the enemy.

Flint's vision adjusted to the darkness and the fog. He could see as far as it was possible to see.

Which wasn't far enough. He shrugged. Nothing he could do about that.

He stopped moving and listened to the disembodied night sounds of rural Scotland.

Someone nearby had chickens. Which meant coyotes and foxes. Which meant dogs to keep the coyotes and foxes away.

This was a farming community. There were probably all sorts of livestock. He could smell dung and hear the gentle lowing of cows in a pasture not too far along the road.

Where would Hedinger be?

Not close enough for Flint to engage him in close combat, for sure.

Hedinger wasn't that man. He didn't get his own hands dirty. Shooting was one thing. Wrestling in the mud was another.

But Hedinger was armed and dangerous and close enough to hear any small noise.

The crunch of twigs and leaves underfoot as Flint moved sounded exceptionally loud to his own ears. He smelled the damp earth and decaying vegetation.

Suddenly, a noise split the air.

Flint froze in place, all senses alert, listening hard because lives depended on it.

Hedinger.

Had to be.

Flint heard Hedinger moving as he changed his location. Footsteps crunching, he inched along the ground heading in Flint's direction.

Had he seen Flint through his scope? Or was Hedinger, too, operating on experience and instinct?

Suddenly, Flint heard Hedinger's sharp intake of breath way too close.

Had Hedinger spotted him?

Flint still couldn't see the son of a bitch.

He did the only thing he could do. He rushed obliquely forward toward the sounds. When he got close enough, Flint could see Hedinger. He began to scream like a banshee.

The noise surprised Hedinger. Maybe he hadn't spotted Flint before. He swung the rifle around quickly. But he'd hesitated a moment too long.

Flint lunged forward, grabbing the rifle. He knocked Hedinger flat on his back.

Hedinger refused to release the rifle. He pulled the trigger. The shot fired into the air.

Flint was younger and more fit than Hedinger, but the older man was surprisingly strong.

Hedinger swung the rifle and hit Flint's left biceps. The blow hurt like hell and must have damaged a nerve. His left arm went numb.

Hedinger used the brief pause to move the barrel of the gun to Flint's belly. His index finger had been wrenched aside. As soon as he could reach the trigger, Hedinger would fire.

Flint slammed Hedinger's chin with the butt of his hand, snapping Hedinger's head back and slamming it on the ground.

Hedinger was momentarily dazed. Long enough for Flint to wrest the rifle from his hands and stand up.

Flint held the rifle in his right hand and pointed it at Hedinger's snarling face. "Get up."

Hedinger didn't move.

"Get up," Flint demanded again.

Hedinger rolled over onto his side as if he might try to struggle to his feet. He didn't.

He brought his left leg around swiftly and delivered a strong kick to the side of Flint's right knee.

Flint's knee buckled. He went down, landing on his left knee on the soft earth.

Hedinger had managed to stand. He lowered his head and prepared to charge Flint like a bull in a pasture.

Still on one knee, Flint twisted his torso, aimed the rifle, and fired.

The first bullet fired close range put Hedinger on the ground.

Flint's left arm and right knee were throbbing. But he held his position.

If he had to shoot Hedinger again, he would.

Hedinger's eyes were still open, dazed but staring at Flint. He blinked. Twice.

Shortly after that, he stopped breathing.

Flint waited a good long time before he lowered the rifle and checked the man's carotid to confirm.

No pulse. No heartbeat.

Flint used the rifle like a walking stick to push himself off the ground. Haltingly, he limped back to the farmhouse.

# Chapter 57

### Houston

Scarlett had sent a text an hour ago asking Flint to meet them. He'd dressed in running clothes and jogged a couple of miles to the dog park.

The run should have been easy enough. Flat ground and good pavement all the way. But covering the distance seemed much harder than it should have been.

Not surprising, really. Even Olympic athletes trained every day and began to lose conditioning after four days of inactivity.

## 797 Ground Truth

His concussion had sidelined him too long. But the head injury had fully resolved according to his follow-up visit with the doctor yesterday, and he was determined to get back into fighting shape.

Scarlett was seated on a bench watching Maddy and Whiskers run around the track near the pond. Every now and then Whiskers would bark at another dog, which caused Maddy to clap her hands and squeal with laughter.

“Hey, lady. This seat taken?” he joked as he plopped down next to Scarlett on the bench.

Scarlett offered him a friendly smile. “How’s the running going?”

"Better and better," he said, which would eventually be true.

"I followed up with Greta Campbell. She and Hanna are okay. Things were a little touchy on the law enforcement side. But we helped out with that. They'll have questions to answer, but no charges should be filed against them."

"Sounds like they'll be okay. Drake will be grateful, too. He'll help them work out the rest of their issues." He tossed his chin toward Maddy. "You should forgive me for the puppy. Maddy really loves him."

"Sure she loves him. He's adorable. Everybody loves him." Scarlett gave him the side-eye. "But she's seven. Who takes care of him? Who walks him in the cold rain? Who makes sure he's fed? Who takes him to the groomer and pays the grooming bills? He's like having a second child."

"You love kids and you had too much time on your hands anyway." Flint laughed.

Scarlett balled her fist and punched him in the arm.

"Oh, come on. You don't have a man in your life, and you can't work all the time," he said seriously.

"Yeah? Well, let me know how you feel about this after you've spent two weeks taking care of Whiskers," Scarlett said, but she wasn't really angry.

"What? I thought you got a real dog sitter," Flint replied with mock horror.

"I did. Drake. And he's not up to the task yet."

"I saw him yesterday. He's up and moving. How hard can it be to deal with a ten-pound puppy?"

"Yeah, no." Scarlett's grin widened. "You're at bat, my friend. Two weeks. We'll be lounging by the pool in Orlando and dining with Mickey Mouse and you'll be cleaning up after Whiskers. Anything happens to him and Maddy will kill you."

They watched Maddy and Whiskers for a few minutes, both smiling at their antics on the grass. Now and then another puppy would approach and instantly Maddy made a couple of new friends.

Maddy was a great kid, but she spent too much time alone because her mother worked too much. Whiskers would force Scarlett to take it easier and take better care of herself, too, Flint hoped.

His recent health issue reminded him again that neither of them was invincible. The work they did made life a precarious proposition every day.

“So when are you leaving?” Flint asked.

“Tomorrow. I’ve got all of Whiskers’s stuff in the car. I’ll drop it off when we’re done here.”

Flint leaned back on the bench and crossed his ankles. “Okay. Is he house-trained at least?”

“Sometimes.” Scarlett smiled.

She cleared her throat and said in a more serious tone, “I checked those phone records for the call to the crematorium the day we went to check on Marilyn Baker.”

“And?”

“The call came from a burner, now untraceable,” Scarlett said. “And the caller didn’t come to collect Baker’s remains before they were sent off for burial in a mass grave.”

“Interesting,” Flint replied. “Who else would be interested in Marilyn Baker?”

"You think Baker had more than one kid?" Scarlett asked, eyebrows arched. "Maybe another relative of some sort?"

Flint shrugged. "Possibly. But the caller asked about me, specifically."

"So you're gonna follow up? Find out who the dude was? What he wants?"

Flint didn't reply because he didn't know the answers to her questions.

They sat with their thoughts, watching Maddy and Whiskers.

"Now that we have that settled, I need to confess something," Scarlett said, uncomfortably breaking the silence. "While you were busy on the Greta Campbell matter, I sent one of those bones you took from the box off for DNA testing."

Flint kept quiet.

"Your DNA is already on file," Scarlett said. "So they were able to compare the results."

On some level, he wasn't surprised. Scarlett always did whatever the hell she wanted, regardless of his stated preferences. Why should this situation be any different?

Because he'd asked her to respect his wishes, that's why.

If he'd wanted Marilyn Baker's DNA tested, he'd have done it himself. He'd made that perfectly clear.

And she just barreled through anyway.

Working with her was like participating in a constant game of Scarlett Knows Best.

To be fair, he'd done the same thing to her with Whiskers. Even though he felt, somehow, that giving Maddy a puppy wasn't on the same level as burdening Flint with a dead mother.

Scarlett waited a bit to let him absorb what she'd said. "Don't be pissed. You can live with your head buried in the sand of denial for another thirty-four years if you want. But it's not healthy. And you know it. It's time to move on. Long past time, actually."

Flint said nothing.

"Do you want to know the DNA results?"

He didn't need her to tell him what he already knew.

If the test had proven Marilyn Baker was not his mother, Scarlett would have simply said that and been done with it. He'd have been no worse off than before he'd stolen the bones.

Because she was asking the question at all, the DNA must have conclusively proven what Flint had already internalized.

Marilyn Baker was his mother.

Which meant he now had no choice but to find his mother's killer. He couldn't hide behind the ambiguity anymore.

"We'll be gone for two weeks. You can stew and brood and do whatever it is you do. But only for two weeks.

Not forever." Scarlett took a deep breath. "Take care of Drake and Whiskers. We'll see you when we get back."

Flint did not respond.

Scarlett stood up and called Maddy, who came running, laughing, bubbling over with joy. She scooped Whiskers up and held him squirming under one arm as she threw herself into Flint's lap.

"Hi! I love you so much!" Maddy said, kissing him on the cheek and then lifting the wriggling puppy to lick his face.

Flint laughed and squeezed them both and told Maddy he loved her, too.

What else could he possibly do?

## ABOUT THE AUTHOR

**Diane Capri** is an award-winning **New York Times**, **USA Today**, and worldwide bestselling author. She's a recovering lawyer and snowbird who divides her time between Florida and Michigan. An active member of Mystery Writers of America, Author's Guild, International Thriller Writers, Alliance of Independent Authors, Novelists, Inc., and Sisters in Crime, she loves to hear from readers. She is hard at work on her next novel.

Please connect with her online:

DianeCapri.com
Twitter.com/DianeCapri
Facebook.com/Diane.Capri1
Facebook.com/DianeCapriBooks

www.ingramcontent.com/pod-product-compliance
Lightning Source LLC
Chambersburg PA
CBHW020346310726
48979CB00015B/2518/J

* 9 7 8 1 9 6 2 7 6 9 3 2 7 *